On a receipt left in a suit pocket, a good wife
discovers the name and phone number of her husband's
French mistress—then later decides to contact her, in
Mary Rose Callaghan's "Windfalls."

Mary Dorcey's "The Orphan" thinly laces a debate by
lust and greed, and a woman's sudden liberation from a
childhood of abuse and a lifetime of guilt.

In Liz McManus's "Dwelling below the Skies," a woman
finds herself alone in the middle of a party
among drunken friends contemplating her
mother's past, conflicting family allegiances, and her
own middle-aged existence.

It's a last, ironic good-bye for a long-separated couple in

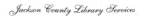

IN SUNSHINE OR IN SHADOW

Edited by
Kate Cruise O'Brien
and Mary Maher

Delta
Trade Paperbacks

A Delta Book
Published by
Dell Publishing
a division of
Random House, Inc.
1540 Broadway
New York, New York 10036

This book was first published in Ireland by Poolbeg Press Ltd.

Book design by Susan Maksuta

ISBN: 0-385-33335-8

Reprinted by arrangement with Delacorte Press

Manufactured in the United States of America

February 1999

10 9 8 7 6 5 4 3 2 1

BVG

Foreword

This book marks the introduction of divorce in Ireland. We have no wish to either celebrate that event or lament it; but the very fact that the debates of the '80s and early '90s roused so much passion, that the constitutional amendment was finally carried only by the narrowest margin in the State's history, is testimony to the depth of our feeling about love, marriage and the family.

In the struggle to reach this point, all sides have learned. We know more about marital breakdown. We understand that however necessary legislation may be, the interests of the men, women and children involved are better served through counseling and mediation. Women are far more likely than men to suffer economically when marriages end, women are also far more likely to seek an end to unhappiness.

With both points in mind, we invited nineteen Irish women writers to address the themes of love and marriage in short stories. The response, from the most successful and acclaimed writers to the relatively unknown, was immediate and enthusiastic. The results are an anthology that is a first of its kind. These voices include, as they should, the accents

Foreword

of New York and London as well as Dublin and rural Ireland, and present a broad and varied perspective on modern Ireland and the contemporary world.

Kate Cruise O'Brien
Mary Maher

Contents

IN SUNSHINE

OR IN

SHADOW

What Big Teeth

∾

Ivy Bannister

"Forty is the beginning of death," Aunty Sonia says.

Uncle Brian looks up and laughs, his lovely, throaty laugh that makes me think of Father Christmas, even though it's hot here, hotter than it ever gets in Dublin. We are sitting in front of our rented villa, in a resort near Fréjus, in the south of France. Uncle is reading yesterday's *Irish Times,* which he's just bought at the local *magasin de journaux,* and Adam is playing inventively with his toy engines.

"And don't call me Aunty," Aunty Sonia says. "Call me Sonia instead."

I nod. Sonia. The very name is music to me. Thanks to Sonia, I'm here minding Adam, when by rights I should be up to my armpits in school socks and uniform, with my nose stuck in a copy of *Much Ado About Nothing.*

Mum was against my coming, and not because I'd be missing school. The fact is that Mum doesn't really approve of her sister, because before Uncle, Sonia made a terrible mess of her life. She was having a relationship with a man who was married to somebody else. But when Sonia married Uncle, Mum was all smiles. "A happy ending," Mum said, and it was, especially after little Adam came along.

Anyway, as I said to Mum, I had to come on this holiday, on account of its being good for my French.

∾

The pool at the resort is huge and luxurious, but the acres of flesh—and especially the bare breasts—make me nervous. So I occupy myself with Adam, blowing up his water wings, and rubbing sunblock into his shoulders. Then something weird happens. It's a shadow that hits me first. I look up, and there's this man towering over us. His chin is stubbled, and his skin is almost black. But it's his way of looking that gets to me. His eyes creep and crawl over me, lingering on every part. Half embarrassed, half angry, I pull Adam toward the water, sending the bottle of sunblock skittering across the tiles.

The man laughs, more a bark than a laugh; then he leaps on powerful legs up into the lifeguard's chair.

Adam splashes in the pool. My reflection trembles in the azure water: I see a stick-legged freak, an alien in shapeless togs, an unsophisticated Irish girl. I dive in, shattering the picture, relieved as the water swallows me up.

At night we eat on the terrace in front of the restaurant. Sonia and Uncle and Adam and myself. The breeze whispers through the trees, and the distant sea glitters. As far as I can tell, we are the only people here who speak to one another in English, although Sonia's French is fluent, and I know bits from school. Adam slurps a Diabolo menthe, a French mineral which turns his lips green.

When Sonia laughs, her parrot-shaped earrings soar through the air like gorgeous birds. Then she picks up a bottle and splashes wine into my glass.

"You needn't drink it unless you want to," Uncle Brian says.

But I want to. The cool bowl of the glass nestles in my palms. Mum would be furious.

There are gold streaks in Sonia's hair, and gold bangles jingle on her wrists. I know her wardrobe inside out. My plan is to grow older like Sonia, and not like Mum, who is getting thick about her middle and developing a regrettable interest in sensible shoes.

Uncle's arm trails across the back of Sonia's chair. When he smiles, his face goes all crinkly. He is older than she is, a lot older, with two grown-up sons by his first wife who died of cancer. He is wearing a French fisherman's jersey, the largest that Sonia could find, but it's still too tight across his barrel chest. Uncle reminds me of my favorite teddy, the one that I'll never part with. The fact is, that with Uncle around, I feel that nothing can go wrong.

I taste the wine cautiously. It's red with a tinge of violet. The smell tickles my nose. Through the rim of my glass, the world looks quite unlike itself.

Then I see him, through the glass, on the far side of the terrace. The lifeguard, his sun-darkened body now dressed all in white. White trousers and white shirt, open to the breast. A white that shines in the growing shadows.

"Arnaud," someone calls. He turns his head and bares his teeth.

Arnaud. Even the name sounds alarming. His teeth look sharp and pointed. I take more wine, letting it swirl in my mouth. What big teeth you have, Arnaud.

"Tell us, Katy," Sonia says. "Will the boyfriend miss you?" She tilts her head attentively.

I know who she means, of course. I picture his boyish face, his pale grin. I watch him recede in a crowd of schoolboys, who nudge one another like heifers, slapping with their book bags. He seems to be very far away.

"I don't have a boyfriend," I say rather treacherously, then I drink some more.

Insects whirr in the pines around us.

"Cicadas," Uncle explains. "They're cicadas." Uncle knows a lot, the names of things and places, even the dates when events occurred.

The wine flows through my body. I feel it purpling my insides, staining them like Adam's Diabolo menthe.

It's almost dark. Adam snuggles against me. I stroke his little head, the fine hair like silk beneath my fingertips. I love the way he smells, all sweaty and sticky and childlike.

I long to have a man who looks at me the way that Uncle looks at Sonia—kindly and protectively and indulgently. I want to have a child like Adam. I want to grow up and get married, and to live happily ever after. And I want to take holidays, exactly like this one, in France.

❧

In the morning Sonia takes my black togs off the clothesline and drops them into the bin. "You can't wear those," she says. "They make you look like a spider."

I'm not sorry that she's thrown them out.

"You are coming with me, Mademoiselle, to get something decent."

She takes me in Uncle Brian's Mercedes to a boutique along the sea front. The shop smells of perfume, and there's a thick white carpet underfoot. Sonia rummages through the racks. "This," she says at last. She holds out a gleaming swimsuit. It's yellow and blue, as blue as the kingfisher in my biology book.

I look at the tag that flutters from it. I cannot believe how much it costs.

Sonia snaps open her handbag. Inside there's a wodge of bank notes. They're hundred-franc notes. She counts out five.

She sees me looking.

"Brian's good with money," she says. "He's the only person I know who prefers work to everything else."

The swimsuit is lovely. I hold it against my cheek, its fabric like a new baby's skin.

Later, when I study myself in the mirror, I see that my own skin has darkened to a ripe amber. I pull on the swimsuit. I hardly recognize myself. My breasts are shaped and my hips have new curves. Would my schoolmates know this stranger that I've become?

My eyes sink to my thighs, where the suit's legs are cut high. A few wiry hairs squiggle like black worms. They spoil the picture, those hairs. They are dirty, secretive and dark.

Catching them between thumb and forefinger, I pluck them out, one by one. Then I jut out a hip and pose for an imaginary photographer. Click, click.

I wonder, would he stare at me now?

"Arnaud." I say his name out loud, stretching my mouth to the foreign syllables.

How old is he anyway? Twenty-two? Twenty-three? Old, I think. Impossibly old. And I know that Mum wouldn't care for him, not one little bit.

❦

Adam drags me toward the pool, anxious to dive. He stretches his arms over his head and topples forward. His hair floats up like a golden mane.

Suddenly I feel the hot breath against my neck. He has crept up behind; he has stalked me. His paw swipes at my shoulder, shifting the strap of my new swimsuit ever so slightly. There's black grime rimming his fingernails. Is it earth from the forest floor?

"Comme il est beau," he whispers. "Comme il est beau, ton enfant."

"Ton enfant." Laboriously I translate. Your child? Is that what the lifeguard has said? Can he possibly believe that I am Adam's mother?

How dare he think such a thing? "No," I reply icily. "*Non*. He is my cousin. I am his au pair. Au pair!" My awkward mix of French and English is ridiculous. But my anger is clear.

He backs away. The hair curls thickly on his chest. His loose shorts flap in the breeze. A packet of Gauloise is tucked in the waistband. He slips a cigarette into his mouth, letting it droop from his lower lip.

I am glad when he's gone, but his image remains fixed in my head.

∾

At night I dream. I do not dream my familiar dreams of home and family. Instead my dreams are a chaos of purples and reds. Disembodied images tumble. Jowls and steely eyes. A burnished pelt. And somewhere in the recesses of my sleeping mind, there is a violent kissing, rough stubble scraping my skin.

I am dreaming of him. I am certain of it.

And then, wide awake, in the middle of the day when the poolside is deserted, I creep up to his chair, the lifeguard's chair; and I stroke the cushion which still bears the imprint of his muscular hindquarters.

∾

Most nights we eat seafood. It is Sonia's idea. She says that it's madness to come from an island—a port, in fact—and never to eat seafood. So the waiter with the bristling moustache brings us great platters of exotic-looking seafood. I eat with enthusiasm, strange creatures with heads and tails still intact.

Sonia watches with interest. "You're looking very well. Are you sure that you're not in love?"

I shake my head.

"Don't embarrass the girl." Uncle Brian pokes disconsolately at a great orange claw. "What I like best in a holiday," he says, "is doing exactly what I do at home."

"Which means eating spaghetti bolognese?" Sonia asks. "Here, try this." Sonia hands me an oyster.

I know that if the oyster is not quite alive, it hasn't been dead for long either. I tilt the shell against my lips. It slithers down my throat. The empty shell seems lined with pearl.

Fruits of the sea. That's what they call these great platters of seafood. *Les fruits de la mer.*

I eat and eat. My tummy stretches. And if it bursts, I wonder, what strange creature will emerge from underneath?

∾

I wake before dawn. I slip out into the dark. I wander through the dreamland of sleeping villas. I pass the shuttered restaurant, the deserted terrace, the echoing tennis courts. No one stirs, only me in this strange, tropical world. My feet wander toward the boundaries of the resort, toward the wall beyond the olive grove, where I know I will find his caravan.

Its creamy sides gleam in the dark. Clothes flutter on a line: his loose shorts, a white shirt, the wispy pouch of his briefs.

Heart thumping, I press my cheek against the flimsy caravan wall. I listen. I hear his measured breathing, I am sure of it. In and out, in and out, like the rhythm of a sleepy melody.

Above my head, a window beckons. I swing up on the branch of a tree and peep in.

I inhale sharply.

Why, he looks so different! The light and shadow of his

torso rises from the loose folds of sheet. His features are chiseled, his skin translucent.

He has a dimple that I never noticed before.

He looks soft; he looks vulnerable. How I long to pull that sheet right up to his chin, just as I would Adam's. Surely this calm creature is the real Arnaud.

I could watch him forever.

But when his lidded eyes flicker, I drop to the ground, land on cat's feet and escape.

"Arnaud," the trees whisper as I run away. "Arnaud."

❧

The moon glows, and the air smells of lavender. We sip wine on the steps of our villa, myself and Sonia and Uncle. Adam is fast asleep inside. The sounds of a late night tennis game filter toward us on the breeze, and I am bursting with happiness.

But Sonia flicks a pebble against a tree. "I am bored," she murmurs. "I am so terribly bored."

"Then why not take Katy dancing?" Brian says. "I'll mind the fort."

"Let's go!" She jumps up, brushes her fingertips down Uncle's sturdy neck. The gold of her sandals sparkles in the dark.

In the Mercedes she slips off her wedding ring and drops it into her handbag. "It pinches," she says. "Poor Brian," she says. "He can't bear to wee in foreign lavatories."

She takes me to a bistro on the waterfront which is packed with tiny circular tables and hazy with smoke. A sea

of faces envelops us. I focus on the mouths, mouths shouting with riotous pleasure. I down my wine in a gulp.

"Fun?" Sonia roars, her body alive to the music.

"Brilliant!" But there is barely room to move, and nobody
dances.

A waiter plonks a carafe in front of us.

"Burgundy, Bordeaux, champagne!" The words spill from
my lips. It's the only French I can think of, but nobody
hears me, because Sonia has disappeared. I slosh more wine
in the direction of my mouth and close my eyes. "Burgundy,
Bordeaux, champagne."

When my eyes open again, Sonia has returned. But not
alone. A sinewy body is crammed into the third chair at our
table, three bodies pressing toward the center point of a
circle.

"Arnaud," I yell.

"Arnaud." He nods, acknowledging the name as his own.
The cigarette juts from his mouth. I feel his knee hard
against my own, all bone, blood and muscle. I search for his
eyes, but when I find them, they are shining at Sonia. He
grabs her glass and drains it, licking the splash of purple
from his muzzle.

"Beast!" Sonia cries, but she is laughing. She says something else in French, but her words whirl away in the smoky
air.

Then Arnaud pushes back his chair and snarls. Grinding
out his cigarette, he slinks back into the crush.

Sonia's eyes narrow. "Pig-face!" she says. "He is drunk."

"Drunk!" It's a wonderful word. It sounds most amusing.
Stealthily, I slip his cigarette end into my pocket. My hair

flops over my face. Could it be that I am drunk myself? With difficulty, I focus upon my aunt, gorgeous in a creamy sarong with orange blossom that twines over the one shoulder. Her bare shoulder is smooth and honey-colored; her upper arms are trim.

She is so beautiful. "I love you!" I roar. "I love you!"

She holds out a ringless hand. "Steady," she says. "Come on. We should be getting you home."

∾

It is still dark when I wake up. My mouth is parched. My head aches. With a shaky hand, I drink some water. I think of him, Arnaud, the two-faced Arnaud. The beast in the bistro, the sleeping prince. I know which face I prefer. I tuck the end of his cigarette into my mouth, and out I float, past the fountain and the sleeping villas, down the winding lane. My feet know the way. Will I wake my sleeping prince with a kiss?

But something is wrong. I hear it before I even see the caravan. It's a throbbing kaleidoscope of sound. Pain, pleasure and urgency, all at once, and it's a sound that gets louder and louder.

Suddenly I'm frightened. The cigarette drops in the dust beneath my feet. I long to go back: back to the villa; back to Ireland; back to the child that I was. But I swing up onto the branch that overlooks the window. I see a picture that I never wanted to see. The white cleft of his thrusting buttocks, a crumpled sarong, her hair on the pillow, the gold bracelets jingling.

❧

I've hidden myself in the greenery. Branches snag at my hair and slap my ankles. I am lying in wait for her, for my aunt who's slept with the lifeguard.

And she called him beast and pig-face!

Now she is coming, strolling up the lane, the golden sandals in her hand, the lovely sarong baring both thigh and shoulder.

I step out in front of her, threatening.

"And where did you come from, Pet?"

Pet? How dare she call me Pet?

"I saw you." My words crash between us. "I saw you with Arnaud."

She stops. She studies me. Her smile fades. She touches my hand. "I see," she says softly. "You are in love with someone after all."

"I am not in love!"

A bird shrieks. The first pale rays of the sun dance upon her shoulder.

I hate her. I want to punish her. "I am going to tell Uncle," I say.

"Tell away." She shrugs. "Poor Brian. I should never have married him, not when I loved someone else."

I step back, silenced. Then I see it in her eyes, a cavernous sadness which sucks me in. With a great shudder my tears begin, tears that will never stop, for if that's what marriage is, then I want no part of it. I sob and sob, until her warm embrace comforts me.

Ellie's Ring

∾

Sheila Barrett

My first memory of my aunt Ellie is a pair of ankles rising out of long, narrow feet in high-heeled shoes, steep shins in straight-seamed hose; a neat wool skirt, silky blouse, a necklace of pearly, crumpled-looking beads, a pair of very blue eyes, face a perfect oval, and white, white hair.

It was after the war, when my parents had moved back to Dallas. She stooped down beside me where I was playing on the footpath in front of my grandmother's house. She had gathered long, brittle shards of bark shed by the two great sycamore trees that arched over our heads, and she showed me how to make little square houses out of them, houses like log cabins without windows or doors, only long, spindly gaps between shards. "We'll make card houses, too," she said. "And tonight I'll tell you a story. I'm a storyteller, did you know that?"

Ellie's stories began as little threads in my life. They were innocent, neutral stories you could find in books—stories about how the bluebonnets and the Indian paintbrush got their colors and how the Spanish came looking for the Seven Cities of Cibola and got lost. At some point the skein thickened and our family became part of these stories, probably when I unearthed the old photograph album. Then Ellie told me about our ancestors with their tender, sepia faces and old-fashioned clothes.

> *Billy became engaged to a beautiful Catholic girl in New Orleans when he was only nineteen, but after he came back to Texas to tell his mother about her, he fell into a decline for seven years. He never married, but women always loved him. . . .*
>
> *When your great-grandmother Mamie was a girl she was courted by an unsuitable man. He went away to Arkansas to work, and they intercepted his letters to her. On the day she married your great-grandfather, poor thing, they told her what they'd done, expecting to be thanked. But even though her old beau had become governor of Arkansas (proof of his low character), she was furious. . . .*

These stories had meanings for me that I couldn't trace, no more than I could see the blood in my veins. It wasn't until I was preparing to elope that I realized that the most romantic story of all in our family, and the most relevant, had not been told. Ellie had eloped on the night of her high school graduation in 1926. She was seventeen years old. I hardly know where even these meager scraps of information came from, because nobody ever talked about it. All I had ever heard from Ellie was "Always remember this, Jane Anne: don't marry too young." Calling me "Jane Anne" meant she was serious. Usually she called me "Pet" or "Pudding."

Ellie was divorced years before I was born. By the time I knew her, she had gone back to her own name and her own life: she lived with her parents again, and we spoke of them that way, Mary-Pop-and-Ellie. They lived together in their mellow bungalow on a street near the university where Ellie worked as a counselor.

I'm not sure how she found out about the latest trend in our school. Later I reckoned that she must have heard about it from a counselor there, a wraithlike woman who could materialize from nowhere, who had once sent Travis and me to the principal for "familiarity" because she saw me scratch an itchy place on his back. When four of the seniors eloped the autumn that Travis and I were sixteen, this lady panicked, weaving into every nook and cranny of the school like ectoplasm, phoning parents at will. This only added to the excitement.

The seniors had discovered that practically anybody in Durant, Oklahoma, just over the Texas border, was entitled to perform a legal marriage ceremony for two people of any age, shape or size who were able to get themselves there and utter the responses. One girl had already been widowed; the marriage came to light when her husband, an older man of seventeen, was killed in a car crash. Two days later she was back in the lunch room at school, her friends in their best makeup like a covey of ladies-in-waiting. She looked the same, though thinner and sad. She was beautiful: the girls who eloped were invariably beautiful. Their husbands tended to be on the football team.

Clandestine marriage had everything—secrecy, sex—all the attractions of sin without its sordid side, and a total dearth of dishwashing. Add volatile, consuming passion—and we all thought about that, whether or not we actually felt it—and the prospect was enthralling.

Ellie got me into the back bedroom at Mary-Pop-and-Ellie's for a chat after the Sunday dinner. "I don't think I ever showed you my engagement ring," she remarked.

I knew that Mama would be fretting in the sitting room, wanting to go home and have a drink, but I was riveted. "You mean you kept it?"

"Well—it was mine! I thought I'd give it to you some-day."

"Your engagement ring? Gosh." I hadn't thought Ellie had time to be engaged.

She eyed me for a moment. Then she opened the big cedar chest that stood under the window in her room. Everything in it, like Mamie's old quilts and lace-trimmed handkerchief cases, smelled like cedar. Ellie reached deep into the chest, moving aside tissue-wrapped lengths of silk and a damask tablecloth her foreign students had given her. Finally she produced a small silver-colored cardboard box that I had never seen before. She opened it in an offhand, impatient sort of way, as if it held fuses or washers. There was a nest of cotton inside and within that, a ring. She put it into my hand. It was the kind that has a parting in the band on the underside so that it will fit any finger. It was a nasty hot brassy color where the tin wasn't showing through.

"Well, how do you like my diamond?" Ellie said. A green-ish bit of glass winked meanly from the band.

I swallowed. Tears came into my eyes. "It's so romantic! Oh God—Ellie!"

"Try it on?"

I held it in my palm. It was so light I could hardly feel it. I shook my head. Ellie produced one of her boxes of colored Kleenexes and put the ring away again.

"Where's your wedding ring?"

Her blue eyes sparkled.

"Did you give it back to him?"

"I dropped it off the Viaduct, Pudding. Into the Trinity River."

This was worthy of Ellie. She would have had to walk way out along the Viaduct to do it—she never learned to drive.

"What about him?" I asked her, cautious.

She gave me a sad, impatient look. "It was all over, Jane Anne," she said. "You just remember one thing, Pet. Don't marry too young."

∾

I went home soon after that, driving carefully past the police station in the next block as if they could sniff my plans from inside the building, though what Travis and I had in mind was legal in Texas as long as it was done in Oklahoma. That old man in the trailer beside the gas station in Durant could make us man and wife. Travis, a "man"! We were pretending to plan a picnic at the lake on Saturday. Instead we would drive straight up the Central Expressway and just keep going until I was Jane Anne Henderson and he was my husband. In a few days, when we were over the shock, he'd tell Drew, his best friend, and I'd tell Karen. In a year or so we'd tell our parents.

I felt uncomfortable about Ellie, with her advice and her suffering, so I brought Travis to meet her. We waited for her Tuesday evening outside the Student Center where she worked. She paused for a moment on the top step when she recognized me in Travis's convertible, then came down the steps in a jaggedy way, as if her knees were stiff. Good Lord, I thought, she looks old. Travis got out of the car and walked around to meet her.

"This is Travis," I said. "And this is my aunt Ellie."

"Well, how do you do, Travis. I've heard such a lot about you. Is this your car? My!" Travis began to discuss horsepower and roof-raising mechanisms with her at once. People always talked to Ellie. She asked all sorts of questions: she quite liked to hear about cars, as a substitute for driving. By the time Travis drove the few blocks to Mary-Pop-and-Ellie's, they were delighted with one another.

Travis gallantly stepped around the front of the car to open the door for her. His hair, still streaked from summer, shone like bronze in the autumn afternoon sunlight. He was six foot two inches tall and he moved like a big cat. He had a roundish, peaceful-looking face and sleepy hazel eyes. He was first-string guard on the football team, and in our last game he had knocked an enormous Cleburne player named Big Elroy Turner straight up in the air.

In the parking lot after the game, Travis opened his shirt to let me stroke a big bruise on his chest. "Oh," he breathed, "this'll get even better, Jane Anne." The car was sweet with the smells of his Old Spice aftershave and the starch on his shirt. I snuggled against his chest, which was warm and smooth and very wide, kissed his bruise and felt safe.

I braced myself with this memory after he brought me home from Ellie's that afternoon, because somehow her showing me that ring had thrown a shadow across my certainty. I wondered for the first time why Ellie, who was so forthcoming about everything, said so little about her marriage and why she had chosen that moment to open up more than ever before.

That night the phone rang about the time Travis usually called, but it was Ellie looking for my father. My mother, who was having one of her bad spells, threw up her eyes and muttered something. She didn't like Mary-Pop-and-Ellie butting in. More muttering, and a sooty look into space. The Chopin record was playing, always a bad sign.

After a while my father drifted back into the sitting room. He looked confused and a little rebellious. I was reminded that he was Ellie's younger brother.

Mama exhaled a long plume of smoke. "What do they want?"

"Just saying hello," my father said. "That all right?"

Mama shrugged.

"Would you like a Coke?" he asked me.

"I'd like a martini," Mama said.

"Yes, ma'am," said my father.

I trailed after him into the kitchen. "Don't get it for her!"

"Oh?" He raised his eyebrows. He got ice out of the refrigerator, and a Coke. Then two stemmed glasses, Vermouth, gin, the jar of olives. I sighed. Travis was a Baptist. Hallelujah.

"You've got a day off from school tomorrow, is that right?"

"Yeah," I said, cautious. Travis and I had considered that day for our elopement, but his father wanted him to mow the grass in the morning and the coach had commandeered the afternoon. Travis was most wary of the coach. If his father found out about the marriage, he'd just throw him out of the house; the coach would throw him off the team.

"Come have lunch with me around twelve?" my father said. "Thought we'd get old Boyle and go to the City Club. Maybe old Briggs would meet us, too." He put down the bottle of Coke. "Is something the matter, hon?"

"No," I said. It was hardly the time to be ungracious to Daddy.

The next morning he phoned from the office. "If you'll get mobilized, we can drop over to Alamo Title and Guaranty before lunch, if that's all right with you."

Dad had never mentioned Alamo Title before. We went up to the fifth floor in a wheezing elevator. "Who're you meeting here?" I asked, looking around at the glum decor. The small lobby had cracked vinyl seats and cheap framed prints of cattle drives on the walls. There was a brass spittoon in the corner that looked like it saw more business than anything else in the place.

The door opposite us opened and a young woman hurried toward us. "Mr. McKay? Mr. Rudebaker'll be right with you." She smiled pleasantly and sat down at a brown metal desk in the corner and began typing with impressive speed. Her dark cotton dress was worn but very neat, like her brown hair, pulled back in a French twist. She wore a gray Orlon cardigan that didn't quite go with the dress but had the soft texture that comes from careful hand washing.

"That's some typing," my father said. "Watch out someone doesn't come rustle you away from Mr. Rudebaker."

The girl laughed. "I'm sticking here till that man of mine's through college. Then I'm staying home!"

"Anybody tries to rustle this gal will be in awful bad trouble with me," said a nasal voice from the door. "How are you, Mack?"

The man who spoke seemed to fill the little lobby. He was about Travis's height but he must have weighed twice as much. He made me think of a kindly turnip with his pale face, bald head and wide, light-gray eyes. His tan suit made him look even bigger, and I wondered if it quite met over his stomach, which was like a big clean pillow sticking out.

"This is my daughter Jane Anne, Charlie."

"Jane Anne! Well, I swan. Good Lord. Time sure flies. Well! How's your sister?"

"She's doing fine."

"Tell her I was asking about her. And thanks for this business, Mackie," he went on, accepting the large manila envelope my father held out to him. "Believe you're going on to lunch."

"That's right. Why don't you come along?"

Mr. Rudebaker looked alarmed. "I, ah. Much obliged. But I'm pretty tied up today." He laughed inconsequentially. He had big beige teeth. "Give me a rain check?" He held out his large, grayish hand to my father, then to me.

"Why do you suppose Mr. Rudebaker wouldn't come to

lunch?" I asked when we were on our way back down in the elevator.

"Why, hon, did you want him to?"

"Well—no. He just seemed kind of—scared." I shrugged. Something about the whole transaction was so fishy that I wondered if Mr. Rudebaker was a bookie taking bets on the Cotton Bowl.

I hadn't much appetite for lunch. Impending marriage quashed hunger. When we finished, my father gave me a claim check for the garage and said, "Hon, will you just hop over to Mary-Pop-and-Ellie's on your way home? Your grandmother's fixing to clear out the hall closet and they need you to reach up on that shelf."

I bid my farewells, grinning and fuming. So much for my plan to shop for a lacy nightgown. On the way past Turtle Creek, my mood lightened. Travis and I had spent happy afternoons there, throwing leftover bits of our nasty school hamburgers to the ducks. I felt shivery with longing, thinking of how it was all about to change—how close we'd be, and forever. For some reason the girl in Mr. Rudebaker's office swam back into my mind. Something my father said once about the girls in his own office came back to me: ". . . fine bunch of young women. Bringing up those kids on their own after putting those boys all the way through school."

∾

Mary, my grandmother, stood in the hall while I got a box of old photographs down for her. We sat together at the breakfast room table, examining them. There was Mamie, a pleasant-faced old woman with bright, shrewd eyes, who hadn't married the governor of Arkansas. *When they finally got to their land at Abbot there was only an old shack and a rotten haystack. Mamie got out of the wagon, took one look around, threw herself on the haystack and cried.* I looked at her closely.

Mary persuaded me to have a Coke after she had left the box on her ottoman where Ellie, who appeared to be the one who wanted it, could look at it later.

"Well, did you and Brother have a nice lunch?"

I explained that we had, and mentioned that we were a little late because of stopping by some Mr. Rudebaker's office.

Mary's gentle face darkened. "Mr. Rudebaker?" she cried, her hand fluttering to her breast. "Mr. Charles Rudebaker? A great big man?"

"Well, yes," I said, unaccountably thinking of Travis.

"Oh, my land," my grandmother said. I had only seen her that rattled when the bird bath fell on the spaniel puppy. "Oh, my."

"Mary, is he some criminal? Is Daddy in trouble?"

"Brother, in trouble? Brother would not be in trouble."

"I don't understand," I said flatly.

"Didn't Ellie ever tell you about—well—Mr. Rudebaker?"

I shook my head.

"There wouldn't be any reason," my grandmother said slowly. "We never think about him. We really don't."

An extraordinary idea was uncoiling in my mind.

"You're kidding," I said.

"We never. Ever. Think. About that man."

"That's Ellie's husband? Ex-husband? Mary, I figured El-lie's husband was dead or something! Nobody ever said he—"

"Well, yes . . . he's always . . . There was nothing really wrong with him," she said sadly. "They were too young. I can't forgive him for getting Ellie to run away with him, but he was so infatuated. . . ." She sighed. "Ellie didn't find him interesting. Just right away, she . . ."

My back prickled. It was eloping she'd found interesting.

"She never liked cooking," my grandmother went on. I thought of Ellie saying, "I'm fiery."

The front door slammed. "Oh, my," my grandmother said, struggling up. "And I haven't put on the coffee."

"I'm back," Ellie's voice called.

"I've got to go."

"But Ellie's just here," said my grandmother. "Don't you want . . . ?"

"I've loads of homework, Mary, sorry. Hi, Ellie!"

"Well, hello, Puddin'!" She put down her purse. She was wearing a dark wool jersey dress with a high collar and gored skirt and around her neck, her big silver Manx cross on a chain. With her white hair and blue eyes and black eyelashes and brows, she looked like some senior priestess of love. I thought of her and Mr. Rudebaker kissing.

"What's the matter, Pet?" But I was out the door, blow-ing kisses vaguely in her direction.

That night, Travis and I ate dinner in his house, a severe test of our nerve. Travis's family seemed well insulated against the romance that haunted ours. I felt their peaceful plainness as both a disappointment and a reproach. Their home was a haven of order and good sense. I'm not sure why it seemed gloomy to me as well; my own home offered plenty of genuine gloom. The Hendersons simply lacked volatility. Yet wasn't that exactly what drew me to Travis? The only time his face darkened was when it flushed with passion for me or football. I knew exactly where I was with him.

"I believe your aunt works up at the university," Mrs. Henderson said when we first met. She had got Travis to ask me to dinner right away.

"Yes, she's student adviser there."

"Oh," Mrs. Henderson said, with a gracious smile. "Mrs. McKay, is that her name?"

"Miss McKay. She isn't married."

Mrs. Henderson's narrow eyebrows went up at an almost pleading angle. Mr. Henderson cleared his throat. "Have some more peas, won't you, Jane Anne?"

"No thank you, Mr. Henderson."

"Now why did I think she was married?" said Mrs. Henderson.

"Oh, she was," I said.

"But . . ."

"She took back her own name."

"Oh I see," said Mrs. Henderson.

"I'd like some peas," said Travis. He gave his mother a look that was not dirty or disrespectful but that did say, "Curiosity killed the cat." I hoped they couldn't see me blushing. The blush seemed to come up from my toes, released by Travis's protectiveness.

Travis apologized between kisses in the Coliseum parking lot. "Mom kind of wants to know everything."

"She just loves you," I said, anxious to be charitable amid such goodness.

"She loves me," Travis said, "but she's nosy."

We never had a serious quarrel. It was almost impossible to quarrel with Travis, and sometimes I felt that there was a side of me that was not finding an expression in our love. The sharpness I undoubtedly shared with Mamie, Ellie and Mama dangled vestigial like an appendix that could go bad. As I curled up in my bed on that Wednesday night before our elopement, thinking of Travis's warm mouth and huge, slightly callused hands, I found myself wondering about Ellie and Mr. Rudebaker. Mr. Rudebaker seemed an innocuous kind of man. If he had been cruel to Ellie, my father would have hated him.

Had he been a bore? Was it—sex? To be honest, I could scarcely consider the romance part, as I thought of it. That was probably because of Mr. Rudebaker's teeth and Ellie's white hair. That had always made her seem old to me; it had made the divorce, never mind the elopement, seem too long ago to matter. When I was little I wondered about her hair, why it was even whiter than my grandmother's. She let me brush it with her silver brush, and it was springy and soft.

"My hair went white when I was twenty-three, Pudding."

"Why?"

"Well, I don't know—it just did."

Her hair was beautiful. But twenty-three? It had a familiar ring. As if that was the year of the divorce itself, the final step. As I drifted off to sleep I thought again of Travis, of lying naked in his strong arms and being his. Had Ellie kept a single picture of Mr. Rudebaker when he was young?

∾

The next evening I drove to Mary-Pop-and-Ellie's. "I've made cupcakes," I said. "Thought y'all might like some." Ellie's eyebrows shot up in amazement, but she almost pulled me inside the door. My grandfather, who was reading the paper, gave me one of his soft looks. Mary was already in bed. "She's tired today, Jane Anne," Ellie said, with a side-ways look. Almost as if it were my fault.

I accepted a Coke and a seat in the breakfast room, then went on the offensive. "I felt pretty stupid I didn't even know who Mr. Rudebaker was."

Ellie's mouth fell open in surprise. Then she recovered. "And why would you need to know that?"

"Politeness."

"Politeness!"

"Yeah. Yeah! Trust!"

Ellie looked puzzled.

"All those romantic stories about you eloping—"

"Did I tell those stories?" Her blue eyes glittered.

I thought. "No," I said at last. "Mary did."

"And what did she say exactly, Jane Anne?"

"That you eloped! That you ran off on your graduation night. Then you got a divorce."

Ellie never took her eyes off me. "Well, does your mama know every single thing about every single thing you do?"

"Well, no. Of course not—"

"And do I? Know about every single thing you do?"

"Well, why should you? Why should Mama?"

"Jane Anne, what do you want?"

I was so stung by the way she said this, I didn't reply.

"Well?"

"I want to know why the hell you ran off with Mr. Rudebaker!" I said loudly.

Ellie put her hand on her hip. I had never seen her do that. "I guess you thought Mr. Rudebaker wasn't much to write home about," she said softly. "You just come with me, Jane Anne McKay."

This time she said nothing while she opened the pine chest and extracted the silks and damasks. She handed me a candy box—Whitman's Sampler—and gestured for me to open it.

The first picture was of her, not Mr. Rudebaker. Her hair was brown like I'd never seen it in my lifetime, wavy and soft like a cloud around her face. She was sitting in a car, one of those open old cars, with some other kids, and she looked wild, as wild as the wind.

The next picture was of Mr. Rudebaker. I scrutinized it closely. It was a snapshot, a little faded. He was leaning toward the camera, a lock of thick dark hair starting to fall over his forehead, and he was laughing. The background was overexposed; all you could see was a bit of an old live oak tree and a split-rail fence. Ellie must have taken it. She loved taking pictures. He was leaning toward her, crazy about her—that was obvious—and do you know, he was really good-looking.

Ellie cleared her throat. "He was very, very hurt, Jane Anne."

28

"Thanks, Ellie." I handed the box back to her.

"Is that all you can say?"

"Yup."

"Well, you just beat the band! After wanting to know my secrets." But she gave me the strangest smile, and I smiled back at her. On my way home, I reckoned it was a real woman-to-woman smile.

In the end I'm not sure why I told Travis I couldn't do it, though the look on his face—devastation followed by sudden sheer relief—proved it was the right decision. It might have been the ring. Not the "engagement" ring that I saw, but the wedding ring that I didn't. I wasn't ready to go through that hoop into a world of forever.

Relieved or not, Travis was bitterly disappointed. That weekend he tried to remove my pants in the Coliseum parking lot. With one hand. Sideways. After I thrashed against the horn and the police, who were always lurking nearby, idled up to inquire how we were, Travis drove me home. He came around to open my door when we got there. I guess his mother would have been proud of that part of the evening, at least.

"How's Travis?" Ellie asked after Sunday dinner.

"Oh, fine," I said. "You got any more of your history there in the chest?"

"I think you've seen about all there is to see."

"Can I look at the pictures again?"

Ellie hesitated. "All right," she said.

I gazed at the photo of her, wild and dark-haired, drenched in winter sunlight. And that was the picture she let me keep.

Taximen
Are Invisible

❧

Maeve Binchy

A lot of the lads on the rank went to Italy during the World Cup.

But not Eddie. He couldn't be out of the house. Who would get the early morning tea for Phyllis, help her out of the bed to the shower, dry her back and sit her down at the knitting machine where she worked all day, with the kettle and little grill near to hand?

The children would have come in, of course, if Eddie had put it to them that he hadn't taken a holiday in twenty-two years.

But every day for three weeks?

And Phyllis would not have liked her sons or their wives dragging her poor body into a shower and out. And anyway, it would have been so selfish to spend all that money just drinking and laughing with the lads. Eddie only considered it for five minutes before putting it out of his mind.

He'd go to the pub and watch it there. A lot of people said that would be just as good, same crack as being there without all the money and the foreign food.

On June 21, 1990, when Ireland played Holland and drew one-all, Eddie met the couple for the first time. He was just about to knock off and go down to Flynn's when he saw the couple running toward the rank where he was the only car. All the other taximen were either abroad or already installed in good positions in Flynn's.

They were in their forties—the man might even have been as much as fifty—well dressed. They had come out of one of the redbrick houses with the gardens in the road that led down to the rank.

He could see them looking at each other with huge relief to have found a taxi—as they ran across to him.

"I'm afraid. . . ." he began.

And he saw the woman's eyes fill with tears.

"Oh, please don't say you can't take us, the car won't start and we're late already, we're going to see the match in my in-laws' house, please take us." She mentioned where it was, a good fare, but half an hour there and half an hour back.

"Look, I know you were going to see the match, but there'll be no traffic on the road and I'll give you twice what's on the meter."

The man was nice, too, he wasn't patronizing, just doing a deal.

It would be a good few quid extra. Eddie thought he might take Phyllis shopping tomorrow in the wheelchair, she'd like that.

"Get in," he said, opening the door.

They had little to worry about, this couple. A big solid house where the roof wasn't a permanent anxiety. They had the use of their limbs, both of them. The woman didn't have to bend over a knitting machine and the man didn't have to work long hours in a taxi that he shared with another fellow.

Eddie wasn't normally envious of the passengers that traveled in the back of his cab, but there was something about this pair that got to him. They seemed relaxed with their money and good clothes and ability to get a taxi and cross Dublin to go to a big party in a house where no one would ever have supported soccer a few months back. They didn't nag each other about the car that hadn't started, about one making the other late.

He called her Lorraine. Eddie wondered about names. No one in his street was called Lorraine or Felicity or Alicia. They were Mary or Orla or Phyllis.

Lorraine; it suited her somehow. Gentle, calm—and she seemed happy too.

They spoke with the easy confidence of good friends. He wondered how long they were married. Maybe twenty-three years like he and Phyllis were. It would have been a different kind of wedding.

They gave him the extra money with an easy grace, and they left him with huge wishes and hopes for Ireland's victory.

Eddie tuned in the car radio. They would be just in time for the match, he would be twenty minutes late in Flynn's.

Taximen Are Invisible

∾

It was only a few days later, on Monday, June 25, 1990, the day that Ireland played Rumania and won on a penalty shoot-out, that Lorraine's husband met a girl with big dark eyes. A lot of them had gone from work straight to a bar and there had been great excitement. The girl had come in from her office nearby and somehow they had all got together in the celebration, and then, of course, nothing would do but they all had to have a meal. They could get taxis home afterward, nobody had brought a car.

Eddie had cheered the match to the echo in Flynn's, but he had been drinking red lemonade. He could get in a great couple of hours on a night like this. The other fellow who shared the taxi wouldn't want to be driving even though it was officially his night. Eddie might take in thirty quid if he got a few good fares. Half of Dublin seemed to be wandering around the street looking for taxis.

He recognized the man and assumed that the other woman was Lorraine. He was about to say wasn't it a small world, but he stopped himself.

"First we want to go to . . ." The man was checking with the girl.

There was a lot of giggling and then whispering, and the man said, "Actually, that's all, we'll both get out here," and then there was the sound of nuzzling and kissing. The man looked Eddie straight in the eye as he paid the fare. He didn't recognize him.

Taximen are invisible.

∾

Lorraine came to the rank next morning. She recognized Eddie.

"You're the man who drove us when the car broke down," she said.

She had nice eyes, trusting eyes.

"And did it break down again?" Eddie asked.

"No, but Ronan's office was celebrating the match and they obviously all got pissed so they decided to stay in a hotel, the lot of them," she said. "So I need the car to go up to the school and I'm going to pick it up from outside his office."

Eddie grunted.

It was as if he had sent a signal of disapproval.

Lorraine sounded defensive. "Much better to have done that than drive home drunk," she said.

"Much," said Eddie.

"And there wasn't a taxi to be found on the street," Lorraine said.

"Never is when you need one," said Eddie.

∾

Dublin is small, no matter what people say. There's over three quarters of a million people in it, but it is very small.

Eddie picked up the girl with the big dark eyes at Heuston Station.

She was with her mother, who was coming to Dublin for an operation.

The older woman was nervous and bad-tempered.

"Most other women of your age, Maggie, would have a car of their own instead of throwing away money on taxis," she grumbled.

"Mam, don't I live in walking distance of work and isn't it healthier to walk?" Maggie said. She was about thirty, Eddie decided, long dark curly hair.

"If you had a car you could come home for weekends."

"I come home every month on the train," Maggie said.

"Any other woman of thirty-five would have three children of her own and a house where I could stay instead of a one-room flat."

"You're sleeping in the bed, Mam, I'm sleeping on the sofa."

"That's as may be. But it still doesn't mean that you shouldn't settle down."

"I will, one day," Maggie sighed.

"Oh, yes," her mother said.

∾

Ronan got Eddie's taxi from the rank when he was going to the airport. Eddie saw Lorraine waving from the garden.

A boy and a girl were also waving, they looked about fifteen and sixteen.

"Nice to have children," Eddie said as they pulled out into the traffic.

"Yeah," Ronan said absently. "Of course they're not children anymore, lives of their own, they don't really care about home at that age."

"They might, you know, without showing it," Eddie said.

Ronan didn't answer, he was rooting in his briefcase. He

was a man who didn't want to chat all the way to the airport.

When they pulled up to the curb at Departures, Eddie got out to take the case from the trunk of the car.

He turned in time to see Maggie running into Ronan's arms. Ronan took the case and they went hand in hand into Check-In.

∾

Eddie always worked Christmas Eve. He drove Maggie and Ronan to Heuston station. Maggie was crying. "I can't bear it, four days," she kept saying.

"Shush shush shush, you'll soon be back."

"But they're such special days, I want to be with you," she wept.

"Sweetheart, they're just days. They'll pass."

"All that Christmassy lovey-dovey stuff," she wailed.

"You *know* there's no lovey-dovey stuff," Ronan said.

He went into the station to put Maggie on the train, then he asked Eddie to drive him to a florist and a supermarket. In both places he had orders ready, a huge flower arrangement in one, a hamper from the other.

Then he went home. The door of the big redbrick house opened and from his car Eddie saw Lorraine and the children running to greet him. In the cold night he heard Ronan calling out "Happy Christmas!"

∾

Ireland lost to Italy and the dream was over. But life went on.

After Christmas Phyllis had to stop working the knitting machine because her hands got too misshapen.

There were two new grandchildren that spring and the babies were often brought around for Phyllis and Eddie to mind while the parents had a night out or day off. They sat there and looked into the two prams.

"Life didn't quite turn out as we thought it would," Phyllis said one evening.

"It doesn't for anyone, Phylly," said Eddie. "Let me tell you that from experience of the world."

That day he had taken four suitcases from the redbrick house and a box of papers and books. He had driven them with Ronan to the block of flats where Maggie lived. It was a different flat, a bigger one, one that would have room for them both.

∾

Ronan had left the car behind him at the redbrick house.

He was in walking distance of work; he was now a member of the serious taxi-taking community. So it was only natural that in the month that followed, Eddie should meet him from time to time.

As on the day when Eddie transported the suitcases, he never entered into the man's life. Ronan didn't invite it, and although always courteous and pleasant with small talk, he gave no evidence of ever having seen Eddie before.

Also, Eddie wanted to punch him hard in the chest for having left that nice woman with the kind eyes.

Eddie looked up at her house often. The garden had become neglected, a fence was falling down. The paint was peeling slightly off the hall door.

In his own house Eddie had done a few improvements. His sons had helped him repair the roof. They came up every Saturday until it was done. Then they put a coat of paint on the place. He bought them a lot of pints in Flynn's to thank them for their work.

Over the months he saw his own property improve while Lorraine's house went downward. He was interested in her life because he had seen her so happy before it all fell apart. He wondered whether the children were a help to her. He knew that they went out with their father on Saturdays. Eddie saw them getting the bus. Their mother would wave from the house, but it wasn't a jaunty wave.

He knew that's where they were going because once the bus had been full and they had taken his taxi instead.

They had talked at the back of the cab.

"Please God he won't bring Lady Margaret again this time," the girl said.

"She's okay, just a bag of nerves, and she always says the wrong thing." The boy was more tolerant.

"She can't keep her hands off him. She's always stroking his sleeves and things, it would make you throw up," the girl said.

"Well, she has to do something, he won't let her smoke in front of us, because it's a bad example," said Ronan's son.

"He's quite mad in a lot of ways, isn't he?" Ronan's daughter said in a conversational and casual tone.

❧

Eddie watched the next World Cup not in Florida but in Flynn's.

Most of the fellows on the rank were deep in debt when it was all over. Some of them got sunburned, and had red scaly heads as well. From time to time Eddie thought of the sunny day he had driven Lorraine and Ronan across Dublin, before Maggie had come into their lives and changed them forever.

Eddie still worked long hours. It had become a habit with him. He couldn't stop. He was tired and depressed on the cold February evening in 1995 when the hooligan element that came to Dublin for the Ireland–England match wrecked Lansdowne Road. There seemed no point in a game when a minority of thugs could take it over. He sat glumly by the fire.

Phyllis asked Eddie not to work so hard.

"You're only doing it for me, and honestly we have enough. We got the roof mended way back, the house can't fall down. The kids have all got jobs. What I'd really love is if you spent a bit more time at home, and maybe we could go out to the new cinema complex once a week and maybe for a pint afterwards. I had someone check it out, and it's all on the level, no steps anywhere, wouldn't it be a great outing?"

Eddie thought how true it was that life doesn't turn out as you think. Five years back he would have thought there was nothing good ahead of them, now they had fine times. They were luckier than a lot of people.

∾

He saw Ronan and Maggie from time to time. They were like man and wife. Even more so when their baby was born. A little girl who was baptized Elizabeth. Eddie had driven Maggie's mother and sister from the christening.

Maggie's mother had not improved in temper.

"Well, I'd say the Blessed Virgin is delighted to have that scrap called after her own first cousin."

"Aw, Mam, will you stop, didn't they have it christened to please you, isn't that good enough?"

"It is *not* good enough," Maggie's mother said. "All this talk of partners and union and everything, with everyone in the church knowing that he's a married man and that Maggie deliberately set out to have a child out of wedlock."

"Shush Mam, the taxi driver will hear you."

"Hasn't he his eyes and mind on the road, or he *should* have," she said, and closed her mouth with a snap. Just in case.

Lorraine didn't seem to mind Ronan calling to his former family home.

Eddie took him back from there to the flat where he lived with baby Elizabeth. It was all very difficult. Eddie could tell that Ronan found the old house restful.

His children were not always free on a Saturday nowadays, there was a match or a project or a date.

They said that Daddy shouldn't be so doctrinaire, even if he lived at home he wouldn't be seeing them on a Saturday, nobody's parents saw people on a Saturday.

So Ronan did a few of those little jobs around the house, propped up the fence, painted the window frames and the hall door.

Eddie thought he seemed loath to go when the time was up.

The flat was festooned with baby clothes, he didn't get all that much sleep, probably.

Eddie didn't believe they would get back together, but things were definitely less hard for Lorraine with the kind eyes than they had been in the days and weeks when Ronan had first left the nest.

Eddie drove Maggie and the baby one day.

It was on a trip to examine a new baby-minding facility, apparently the first two had not been satisfactory.

Maggie lit up a cigarette.

"Don't tell me it's a no-smoking taxi or I'll jump into the Liffey," she said. Her big dark eyes were anxious.

"I don't mind, but is it good for the baby?" Eddie said.

"Of course it's not good for the baby," Maggie snapped at him. "Any more than living in a flat in the center of the city is, or the belching fumes of diesel or her mother having to go out to work every day."

"So what does your husband think about it all, is he a smoker?"

"No, you must be psychic, he hates it, and he says I'm damaging her little lungs at one remove, and that it's a bad example, and I'm not allowed to smoke in front of his two great louts of children. Not that he cares about her little lungs when she's bawling with them at three o'clock in the morning, he even sleeps in a different room because *he* has to work. There's nothing about *me* having to work."

"Well, could you give up work?" Eddie was interested and caring.

"No, because he's not my husband, he's my partner, and when you live with a partner you go out to work. It's the wife who sits at home and collects the money. That's reality. That's the way things are."

Her face was angry and upset. Was it five long years since he had seen her first?

He had been annoyed with her then, home wrecker, selfish. Yet here she was a forty-year-old with a baby, and very little security.

"Roll on November," she said, and inhaled her cigarette down to her toes.

"November?" asked Eddie.

"The referendum, the divorce referendum, twenty-sixth of November," she said and looked out at the traffic.

∽

In Eddie's house there was a bit of aggravation about which way to vote.

Phyllis was voting Yes. She wanted people to have the right to start again if they made a mistake. She didn't want to punish them.

Eddie wasn't so sure. If you made things too easy, fellows upped and went. He was going to vote No.

"Women could up and go just as soon as men," Phyllis said with spirit. Phyllis, who would never get up and go from her wheelchair and would never want to be a day without Eddie.

"I've seen a lot of unhappiness as a result of divorce and people leaving their homes," Eddie said, shaking his head.

"Well, if you have, you haven't seen it in Ireland because

there isn't any divorce here yet." Phyllis spoke with authority.

They debated not going out to vote at all, since one
would cancel out the other, but neither of them wanted
that.

"My side needs it more than yours," Phyllis said.

"I'm not totally convinced that you're right," Eddie said.
He had been listening a lot in his taxi and thought that a No
vote was much less than certain.

∾

On the day of the referendum he had Phyllis neatly tucked
in the front of the taxi.

They saw a woman with long hair struggling with a baby.

She hailed them and seemed very disappointed when she
saw it was engaged.

"I know where she's going, I think I'll stop for her,"
Eddie said.

Maggie and young Elizabeth fell gratefully into the back
of the cab.

Phyllis talked to everyone that she met, and Maggie was
no exception. By the time they got to the apartment block
she had discovered more about Maggie's life than Eddie
would have discovered in a decade—that Maggie's mother
had her heart scalded, that her boss was getting very cross
about time off to mind the baby, that she had hardly any
friends left these days and had just voted Yes, and that if the
referendum passed, her life would change.

"Good luck to you," Phyllis said. "That man's marriage is

well dead by now and he can start again properly instead of just messing about."

"Yes, that's what I say. I suppose it will take a year or so, but then the world will settle down."

"I expect the two of you are planning it already?" Phyllis said eagerly.

"He hasn't said anything, but I expect he's thinking about it." Maggie was biting her lip.

"Well, of course he is," Phyllis said. "Of course, what kind of a man wouldn't want to look after you and the little girl properly?"

Maggie's face was troubled.

Eddie suddenly agreed. "Ah yes, of course he'll marry you, what else would he be living with you for and having a child with you, if he weren't going to marry you?"

Phyllis looked at him with surprise. You never knew what way Eddie would turn.

"And why isn't he voting with you?" Eddie asked.

"He has to see his big dreary children," said Maggie. "He won't be home until late tonight."

From his vantage point at the rank Eddie saw Ronan going into Lorraine's house. He had a tray of winter pansies. She brought him out a mug of something as he worked. They laughed together as old friends. There were no signs of the big dreary children that he was meant to be visiting. Eddie smiled to himself.

He would work late tonight. Phyllis would watch endless television discussion on the referendum, and then as far as tomorrow was concerned he would be glued to the results nonstop.

He thought about Maggie alone in her flat.

He thought about how life never turns out like you think it will.

❧

On November 27, Eddie saw Ronan coming out of his office.

By now Ronan sort of recognized Eddie and would say, "There you are again," to show that he was aware they had met.

"It's going to be close," Eddie said.

"Too damn close," Ronan said.

Eddie looked puzzled. "Well," Ronan went on, "it would be better if the whole country was one way or the other, this way it's divisive."

"That's true. Anyway I expect even if it does pass, most people won't bother getting divorces at all, most people have their own arrangements made by now, perfectly adequate arrangements." Eddie could sense Ronan eager to agree.

"It's interesting that you should say that, it's my own view precisely. If it ain't broke why fix it, that's what I say, or am going to say if the matter is brought up."

Eddie paused for a moment to think. What he said now could be quite important. It might even make a difference. He could come down in favor of fair play for the wife or the partner, but not both.

He nodded sagely. "Of course, if you're in a proper relationship it doesn't need bits of paper, and registry office marriages and amendments to the Constitution. Any reasonable woman would understand that."

Ronan leaned forward.

"Could you say that again? I'm going to have a bit of an ear-bending tonight."

Eddie said it again and added more.

∾

There was a lot of celebration in the kitchen, Phyllis and her friends were raising a glass to the New Ireland.

But Eddie wasn't thinking about it, he was thinking of the people who traveled in his car.

He knew that he must not be foolish about all this. Ronan would not return to the redbrick house where he had planted the winter pansies, but he would visit it often and easily.

And Lorraine, the woman with the kind eyes, would not have her husband back to live. But there would surely be a little unworthy feeling of satisfaction that there was no second wedding day, no second wife, even though the law of the land had changed to say that there could be.

And Eddie smiled to himself, thinking of the small but not insignificant part he had played in bringing more peace to the troubled gray eyes of Lorraine.

He decided not to think at all about the dark, anxious eyes of Maggie. He wasn't God, he couldn't solve everything.

Windfalls

❧

Mary Rose Callaghan

My story is banal. It couldn't be more so. There were even clues left around. I'd been doing my morning chores: picking up my husband's socks and underwear, hanging up yesterday's rumpled pin-striped suit when I saw it needed cleaning. As a good wife I checked the pockets. My husband had a habit of leaving credit cards there, keys, medical notes. But there was only an envelope—with *Desirée* and a phone number scrawled on it. The number was Rathmines. A patient, I told myself. My darling's a shrink, an expert on the aberrant behavior of others.

But there was a second clue.

Our local cleaners have a two-for-one offer, so I looked for another suit of equal type—that's one with a waistcoat. My husband wears them, having come to the age of unreason—fifty. The charcoal gray was nearest to hand. The Mothercare pram receipt was in that pocket—with the same number on it and the same name. One clue was bad, but two downright careless.

I sat in the conservatory, staring out at the garden.

Who was Desirée? The name was out of a novel from my distant past. And the pram was a puzzle. It couldn't be for anyone in our family. Our two grown sons had produced nothing yet to my knowledge. James, the elder, probably would. But Ruairi, the younger and, although I shouldn't say it, my favorite, was gay, both literally and metaphorically. "I'm queer as a kipper, Ma. I'll never make you a grandma," he'd announced cheerfully at fifteen. A fact I accepted, but something my husband, being a pillar of society, couldn't.

Finally I got the courage to dial Desirée's number.

It rang and rang.

Then a voice said, "Yeah?" It was young, perky.

I tried to sound official. "This is eh—Kathleen—from Mothercare, Stephen's Green Shopping Centre. There's been a mix-up in our delivery department. I'm checking that you got the right pram."

"Oh, yeah. It came last week." The accent was French.

I cleared my throat. "You paid by cash? Or was it by credit card? I need to know for our records."

"Dr. O'Reilly pay by credit card."

"I see. Thank you very much—eh, you're Mrs. O'Reilly?"

"No. I'm Desirée du Pont." A baby cried in the background. "Just a sec."

I came out in a sweat. When she came back I said casually, "Yes, I remember Dr. O'Reilly now. Dr. Thomas O'Reilly. He wanted the big pram and you wanted the smaller one."

She was naturally puzzled by this.

"He's your doctor?" I probed hopefully.

"No, he my fiancé. He getting divorced soon. He want our baby to have a father."

I almost dropped the receiver. "Well, thank you, Miss du Pont."

She sounded bats, but it explained the pram receipt. My husband was Desirée's fiancé? It was like a Christmas cracker riddle.

I stared numbly at the coppery beech hedge. It needed to be cut again. Tom left the garden to me. He left everything to me, weeding, shopping, cooking, laundry. He had to be accessible to his patients. I admired his concern, but often he didn't get home till late at night. But what were we to do now? You collect so much baggage in life.

Tom and I met on my first day in UCD. He was second med and I was starting law. We were introduced on the main steps of Earlsfort Terrace and have never looked back. We did the usual: held hands in the cinema, went to insufferable dress dances, got engaged when he qualified. We got married after his intern year and spent five years specializing in Chicago, where Tom became an expert on unhappiness. Oh, he called it depression or "serotonin deficiency," but it was still unhappiness. We were average two-point-fivers: two children and one miscarriage, and two and a half homes. Our first had been a Victorian redbrick in Rathmines, our second this rambling Killiney mansion with its chandeliers and stripped-pine doors. The "point five" was our holiday home in Kerry. We had never been to the Continent together. Tom had always promised we'd go to Greece, but there'd never been time.

I poured myself a cold coffee. Then flicked the radio on and off—there was yet another crisis in the government.

Had Tom gone completely crackers? His name was in the hat for a Trinity professorship. He had published a book, dozens of articles, and had an enormous private practice. How could he be marrying someone with such a young voice? Lately he'd been drinking more. But I'd put it down to middle-aged angst. He'd been okay at breakfast. It was the usual silent affair. Although he liked a fry, he'd eaten cornflakes without complaining, given me the usual kiss on the cheek and gone to work. I'd always thought we were happy. But he was a husband of certain years.

The phone rang.

I picked it up. It was our daily lady. "Sorry, Mrs. O'Reilly, but Jimmy's chest's at him again."

I said I was sorry, too. Her grandson was a bad asthmatic.

"He'll be better by Friday," Joan went on. "Remember the doctor's havin' his Vincent de Paul evenin' then."

They came early to discuss plans for helping people cope with Christmas. I'd forgotten, but Joan doted on "the doctor." She was more of a liability than anything. When I wasn't collecting her, I was driving her home. Now she was probably hung over. I knew from the depleted state of our gin. But she was company, a cheerful voice in the house.

❧

When number one son came into the kitchen, after lunch, I still hadn't dressed. James was the clever one. A florid-faced lawyer with his father's ears. He was dressed in an expensive dark suit with an expensively impeccable shirt. Although living in a Temple Bar apartment, he still brought laundry home.

He dumped a black plastic bag on the floor. "How are things, Ma?"

"Pretty awful." I went into the utilities room off the kitchen.

He followed, handing me a shirt. "Joan's drunk again? She didn't iron this properly last time."

I shook my head. "No. Closer to home. It's your dad."

His eyebrows arched. "Dad's developed a drink problem?"

I loaded the washing machine. "No, not yet."

"Trouble at the hospital?"

"He's divorcing me."

He gave me a lawyer-like pat on the back. "Everyone has rows."

I put in soap and conditioner. "Yes, but there's another woman. With a little one."

He paled. "A *what*?"

"You have an infant sibling. Sorry, I don't know what sex."

My son caught his breath. "It can't be?"

I nodded wearily.

He wagged a legal finger. "Look. She could be chancing her arm."

"You mean, your father shouldn't accept responsibility?"

His eyes bulged. "Why should he?"

"But if he's the father?"

"She says he's the father! Christ, he could be paying college fees at seventy!"

"They've been abolished."

But James was distracted. "Ma, this could be awkward."

I agreed, examining last week's shirt. "I'll run an iron over this."

"Thanks, Ma. There's no hurry."

He pecked my cheek and went back to his office.

It had been a windy night. I checked the birdseed, then roamed the garden in my dressing gown, deadheading. A TV garden program had advised it to keep chaos at bay. We had a man to cut the hedges, but it took all his time. There'd be windfalls in the apple orchard. We'd even get some from the next garden. It was important to get them before the worms did. A priest had once told me that God was the next person who needed you, but nature was my religion. All around me there was mellowness. The leaves had turned, littering the grass, the year was dying. Except it would come back, whereas my hair would stay gray. My veins would always bulge, my body sag. What could you do about gravity?

I stared into the kitchen mirror. Motherhood had meant everything to me, even those cumbersome months of pregnancy. I'd loved being needed, the years of school runs, of fetching and carrying. Now I was a laundress, going gray. Lately our love life had staggered to a stop. Losing was an art, I'd heard in a poem on *Poetry Please*. But I couldn't just sit there, cursing the dark. I made a hair appointment at Peter Mark's in Dun Laugher Shopping Centre.

When Tom came home that night, I pretended to be asleep. I groaned when he kissed me good night. When he was snoring, I got up to read but couldn't concentrate.

Windfalls

Looking back there were hints of an affair: missed dinners, guilty hugs, strange late night phone calls which disconnected when I answered. But I'm not Sherlock Holmes, I didn't keep a notebook.

∿

The next morning at the hairdresser's people chatted happily around me. My hair was washed then highlighted and expertly wrapped in little bits of paper. Feeling oddly detached, I sipped coffee. An ancient Egyptian warrior stared back at me from the mirror. I had a double chin. Was that why things had tamed in the passion department? Or did it happen in every marriage? People never talked about it. I'd read about cures—an explosives patch which the man wore, but which gave headaches to both. A contraption which you popped on at the vital moment. But I'd been afraid to mention them. When I suggested professional help, Tom had snapped, "I am a professional!" You never met a cobbler with a decent pair of shoes.

My hair was rinsed again and cut in a bob. It came out lighter, also considerably shorter.

"It's not too blond?" I asked hesitantly.

Janet, my stylist, held up a small mirror to show the back. "Okay, hon?"

Tears came. Although a child, she had a habit of calling me "hon." It sounded weird in a Derry accent.

"But, hon, what is it?"

"Nothing!" I blew my nose hard.

She touched my shoulder. "Your hair's lovely, hon. Promise. Your hubby'll love it."

I smiled back. Tom wouldn't notice. That night he came home earlier, but poured a Scotch and slumped tiredly in front of the TV.

∾

By Friday I still hadn't talked to him. But I'd collected some windfalls for apple jelly. The Vincent de Paul were coming that evening and Joan hadn't shown up. So I moved mechanically through the morning, boiling eggs for rolls. I laid out whiskey glasses for the men, teacups for the ladies. Tom was an active society member. Every summer he went to Lourdes with the Dublin diocese and joined a yearly pilgrimage to Lough Derg. Over the years he'd sent jokey penitential postcards to me and the boys. Had he met Desirée there? The irony was that Tom hadn't voted for divorce. While he stood firmly on the far side of the fence, I'd gone doorstepping for change. Too many young people were in limbo. Now I was in it myself. But I had only myself to blame. They all told us, all those anti-divorce, anti-referendum types. They told us it'd be a case of "Hello, divorce, good-bye Daddy." Their ad was in every damn DART station. Daddies would pack bits of cheese into hankies and go to seek their fortunes.

Mammies and children would wave them off at the gates. Those ads damaged our cause, but we won.

Or did we? I have trouble with people being right.

Dublin was a tangle of traffic. I got the bridge rolls and Mr. Kipling's Lemon Slices in Quinnsworth of Baggot Street. Then Ruairi, number two son, buzzed me into his

Mount Street studio. In an untidy room at the top of the stairs, he slashed a wide red mouth on a big white canvas.

I looked on admiringly.

Ruairi's into Bad Art and a follower of some American who founded the movement but whose name I can't remember. Crudeness was the important thing. Their manifesto: Why paint beauty, when life is so awful? I didn't argue the point.

My boy was white-faced himself with an eerie beauty, even if I say so. He's slight and has an intensity, quite the opposite to his burly brother. He finished painting and gave me his usual hug. "Your hair's great, Ma."

"Thanks—I was going as gray as a badger. How's Ken?"

"Great." Then his expression changed. "What is it?"

That's Ruairi—sensitive.

Holding back tears, I threw down my handbag and coat. "Well, having supported divorce, I'm being dumped."

He looked mildly curious. "Dad's found someone else?"

"Someone called Desirée. She's had your father's baby."

He picked up a brush and painted silently.

I felt desperate.

He wiped a hand on paint-splattered jeans. "Hope it's a girl. I always wanted a sister."

"Is that all you can say?"

He made me a cup of tea. "We have to accept that it's happened, Ma. Have you talked to Dad?"

That was my boy, loving, kind. Yet he didn't come home now, because his father wouldn't accept his partner. "I cured a boy the other day," Tom had once declared sadly, as if it were a matter of popping a pill. Our son, needless to say, didn't see himself in that role.

The truth was, Ruairi might've had a sister. But at forty I'd miscarried. I was devastated, but Tom had seemed relieved. Men didn't want sleepless nights, nappies, mess. But now Tom was starting all over again. He was a good man, but never a hands-on father. What did he want? What did I? It was a changing world, but people still needed love more than anything. And you only valued something when you were about to lose it. How could I win against Desirée? I decided to confront my husband on neutral ground.

Tom shares consulting rooms in Merrion Square with two other doctors. As it was Friday, he'd be seeing his private patients from two o'clock on.

I found parking in front of the house. Mary, his secretary, opened the huge Georgian door to me. "Mrs. O'Reilly, what a surprise. I haven't seen you for ages!"

She was pretty with lovely legs. A tactful Florence Nightingale in a white coat.

"Is my husband back from lunch?"

"I'll tell him you're here," she whispered. "He's with someone now."

"Desirée?" I suggested.

Mary looked alarmed. "Oh, no, Mrs. O'Reilly. It's a patient."

So Desirée hadn't been one. That was a relief. But she'd been here. Why was the wife always the last to know?

The waiting room was sprinkled with people silently

reading magazines in large comfortable leather chairs. I found a place and flicked through *Hello!* magazine. There was an article on Princess Di. Another *Hello!* had an article on Fergie. At least we were fashionable.

After about ten minutes, Tom opened the door. "Kay?"

He's a big man with large cauliflower ears and wild hair. No oil painting, but solid and comfortable to hold on to.

In the hall, I said matter-of-factly, "You've invited the Vincent de Paul tonight."

He banged his head. "Forgot!"

"I thought you had. By the way, I know about Desirée."

He deflated instantly. "Oh . . ."

I followed him into his consulting room.

Tom sat behind his desk, looking at me anxiously over his half-moon glasses.

I sat down and passed the pram receipt. "Last Monday I found this in your pocket. I wasn't spying. Just putting your suits in the cleaners."

He raked his wild hair. "The strain has been terrible."

I felt sorry for him. "Why didn't you tell me?"

He shrugged helplessly. "How could I?"

Typical. I wanted to ask the dreaded question—how many times? But didn't. "How did you meet her?"

He looked miserable. "She's an au pair."

I was puzzled. "Whose au pair?"

"A family in Dalkey. I gave her a lift during the bus strike."

As we sat in silence, I felt very tired. *The Psychiatrist and the Au Pair Girl* sounded like a Mills and Boon title. "What do you want to do now?"

He groaned. "Oh, Kay, I love you."

"That's funny, Desirée thinks you're marrying her."

"She keeps pushing me." His head was in his hands. "She said she was on the pill. Please forgive me, Kay."

"You've never forgiven Ruairi."

He looked up sadly. "Can we call a truce on that?"

I phoned Desirée that night, this time admitting who I was. She was surprised, told me firmly again that my husband was marrying her as soon as divorce was passed. But we agreed to meet in the Westbury the next afternoon.

I got there first and found a free table near the marble stairs. All around me the impression was pink. There were pink lamp shades and discreet pairs of pink brocade armchairs placed around tables. Behind me a dinner-jacketed pianist played, "Smile, though your heart is aching. . . ." From her wall portrait, an eighteenth-century maiden stared saucily. I wondered who she was. Why did everyone suddenly look so young and desirable? Even the portraits on the wall?

At five past four a young woman with round dark glasses and a baby at her front came up the stairs and looked around the lounge. She had stringy shoulder-length blond hair and wore a long black coat, black leggings and big black boots. It was Desirée, I knew immediately. Tom was marrying someone younger than his sons. But not especially pretty.

I stood up.

She didn't seem nervous. "Hi, I'm Desirée."

I pointed to the couch. "Kay O'Reilly."

She put the baby carefully down and sat beside it.

Steeling myself, I stared down at the bundle. I couldn't see anything of Tom there. It was just a baby. But there was nothing dysfunctional about it. Things were obviously working.

"How old is it?"

"A month."

"It's very small. Is it a girl or a boy?"

"Girl. We call her Lucy."

Flinching at the *we*, I hailed a waitress. "I'll order afternoon tea. Tea or coffee?"

Desirée smiled cheerfully. "Herb tea."

When our order was taken, Desirée breast-fed the baby.

I was fascinated. Although a mother of two, the size of newborns always intrigued me. "In my day breast-feeding wasn't the thing. They're all for it now."

She nodded, looking down at the baby. "Better for baby."

I watched her. "You're probably on your own a lot? Tom, eh—my husband—is very busy. He's not practical."

She looked over. "His ivory head's in the tower?"

I had to laugh. "That's a good way of putting it. For instance, he's in the Vincent de Paul. Yesterday he invited them out and completely forgot."

The girl stared at me. "Vincent Who?"

"Never mind." Then I went on suddenly, "Why don't you come out to Killincy?"

Her big eyes widened behind the glasses. "I go Killiney?"

"Yes. Now."

She was puzzled.

"You'll need to know how things work. There's lots to learn. Now, holidays, for instance—Tom goes to Lourdes and Lough Derg. They have dry toast there and no milk in their tea."

The baby whimpered, so she moved it to the other breast. "Tom no tell me this. Eh—you not upset about me?"

"Of course not!"

She looked shocked.

"I'm off to Greece. Think of all the freedom I'll have! No more cooking. Don't worry, I'll show you how everything works—the washing machine's quirky. There's a bit of laundry, by the way. Our elder son leaves in his mending too. And ironing. He'll keep you busy. You'll be there on your own a lot. But the birds are company. And there's the daily lady to look after—that's when she shows up. You drive? No? Oh, dear, that could be a problem. Tom doesn't get home early. Oh, the dogs need to be walked. And fed twice a day. And the cats once. They have a problem with fleas. . . ." I looked around for the waitress. "They seem to have forgotten us. I'll see what happened to our tea."

When I came back, Desirée was gone.

Would she have been desired so long as she remained a mistress? I don't know. Perhaps the baby gave her too many needs.

But my story didn't end there. We couldn't leave a young French girl alone in Dublin with a baby.

Desirée moved into our gate lodge, so we've become an extended family. James objected at first but even he came round. Coincidentally, Desirée's keen on gardening and helps me when not looking after Lucy. She's walking now, and Desirée has found a boyfriend her own age. I've become a sort of grandmother to my husband's daughter, which is another Christmas cracker riddle. Tom is more and more dedicated to others. Except now he's a bit careful about giving lifts.

But there have been other windfalls. Ruairi comes home now. He and Ken are good with children.

Breaking

~

Kate Cruise O'Brien

At half past two on a Saturday morning Constance O'Leary
walked out through her patio doors into the instant glare of
her security lights. She stepped daintily, Constance did, in
her high, high heels though she was carrying, as far as I
could see, an entire dinner service on a tray. Plates, piles of
them, and soup bowls, pudding bowls, even finger bowls.
There was also a soup tureen, which I coveted in a slightly
contemptuous way. She stood in the middle of the patio
wiggling her little bottom. Jiggle, jiggle. Well, it's not easy
for a small woman to balance a large tray. My own back
ached in sympathy as I watched her. And then she lifted her
pointed, pixie face to the sky and made a noise like a dog
growling, howling. Somewhere between the two. Her narrow arms strained against her tight sleeves as she raised the
tray and hurled it up, up, up and away from her.

I screamed as the china shattered. No one answered. The
husbands were not at home tonight.

It had started a long time ago. A long time ago in human

terms, that is. Or woman terms. Or adolescent terms. My brother used to sing a song when we went traveling as a family for holidays in a small, hot car in the fifties. Tin box, really. That bored his great gangling body. "Time goes by so slow-ely," he would warble from the crowded backseat as we burned up the dreary miles between Dublin and Galway, "and time can mean so much." Time for women at home in houses seems to go by at much the same pace as adolescent time in crowded cars with siblings. Slow-ely. Men at work always wonder about how time flies. Women at work do that too. Oh rush, rush and isn't it strange that Christmas is almost upon us again? Not at all strange, I think, considering all the time that has gone between.

What happens in between is that women wait for men.

Just think about how much of a woman's time is spent waiting. Get up and make the breakfast and wait for him to get up. Wait for child to get up. Bang on doors. Will they, won't they, make it to office/school on time? Sob in bathroom when they snarl at you. Was that what you were reared for? To *nag*. Yes, well, you tell yourself as you wipe your poor tired red face with toilet paper in the loo, that's what you *were* reared for. You're meant to wait and make things work. Tense stomach, mind racing. Shave, shower, dress. Are these sybarites who have to pamper their lily-white bodies? Do you think they could ever skip breakfast or not fuss about which scarf and what coat and I'll really have to listen to the weather forecast—why didn't *you*, Mother dear? And then the door opening again, startling and slamming because of the things, the briefcase, the book, that you'd forgotten to remind them about.

My tirade, not Constance's, not at the beginning anyway. Constance, when I knew her first, was not waiting. She was getting there on time. She was working, not scratching her face with coarse toilet paper in miserable moments in the loo.

We moved into this gentle Victorian terrace house, quietly situated between inner-city Dublin and the suburbs, in the days before crime. Well, of course, crime happened then, but the Gardai told us when our house was burgled that it was probably the itinerants. Not endemic, you know, because itinerants came and went. Not part of society, as it were. To my eternal shame I believed the slow-speaking, pipe-smoking Garda Inspector who sat in my grandmother's faded brocade button-backed chair and told me the problem was temporary. The itinerants wouldn't go *on* stealing my television.

I'd watch the itinerants, traveling people, just people who lived over the wall, as they built three bonfires a day, chop, chop, chop of wood splitting, and I'd see little girls pushing babies around the rutted building site in prams. Family life. I liked it really. Why did I have to think that what the inspector said was true? There was the day when a dirty disposable nappy arrived over our wall and Damien, who had been waiting for trouble ever since he watched the herd of caravans enter the building site behind our back wall, climbed up on a ladder and yelled.

"Don't throw this in our garden! Not ever again!" said he, shaking the dirty nappy at them. Well, you could see that an endless stream of airborne dirty nappies was going to interfere, seriously, with our happy family life.

Breaking

"Sorry mister," said the polite little dark-haired girl, wheeling the pram backward so she could see this voice through the ivy. "I didn't know there was a house over that wall."

I used to envy those families as I watched from my upstairs window. Their time of wood and prams and family fires made more sense than mine did.

I thought you could buy time with a house, on the never-never. I wanted a house for the rest of my life. Damien wanted to get out of the freezing flat we were sharing with a college pal. Very amusing it was, with a grill pan made of tinfoil, dripping walls and a bathroom one flight down. Ceiling plaster in the bath and a wire coat-hanger for a lavatory chain. When we left the priest who owned it said we'd made "improvements." That was because I'd cleaned it, painted it and torn the musty carpets from the floor and put them in a shed in the back garden. After the carpets had gone the flat got even colder. Cleaner and colder. The floorboards glistened with black gloss and dirty little breezes blew between the gaps. Damien, I think, was in despair. He didn't really want a house but he didn't want that flat either.

I fell in love with our house because it had a "through" room, stretching from front to back with French windows opening into an overgrown garden. They shouldn't really let little girls read fairy tales. As soon as I saw my house I knew I'd seen it somewhere before. Roses and thorns in November, tapping the stained glass in the upper windows. Windows and wood everywhere.

"How many people do you think have died here?" asked Damien, looking at the little piles of crutches in the corner of a front bedroom. There were broken beds in a demented row. There was a great torn, shredding hole in the ceiling. Light streamed and glimmered through the dust. When Damien heard that the house agent had accepted our offer he went pale. He leaned against the dripping wall in our cold flat.

"I thought they'd never accept our offer," he said. "We can't live in that house."

"And where else will we live now, Damien dear," I said spitefully because I was spiteful in those dreary days. "On the side of the road?"

Damien said nothing.

I was, I admit now, a bitch, but I went to work. I wasn't a lazy bitch. When I was a little girl I had wanted to grow up and have a baby. In a pram, preferably. Now that I was an adult I wanted a house to put the pram and the baby in. Damien was the father in this scenario. Father of the house, the baby and the pram. True, Damien showed no very great enthusiasm for this role, but I had provided the baby and now I was going to provide the house. I painted and cleaned and scraped late into the night, early into the morning, and Damien wondered why we had to live in an atmosphere of paraffin oil and paint fumes. There was no heating in my dream house.

"Couldn't we just go back to the flat?" he asked.

"No," I said.

Constance's arrival was very different. She reminded me of the itinerants, curiously enough, with their chop, chop, chop and three fires a day. Constance planned things. She had system and rhythm.

Breaking

"The builders have moved in next door," I told Damien. "But I haven't seen any people yet."

"Aren't builders people?" asked Damien.

When the builders had gone, the painters arrived and then the garden experts, patio layers (if that's what you call them), the security firm with their lights and their alarms. Cleaners came and carpets and curtains.

"Pelmets!" I marveled to Damien. "She has pelmets!"

"How do you know it's a she?" asked Damien. "The only person I've seen around that house who isn't a painter or a workman of some sort is that guy with the pink shirt, the baby and the beard."

"I didn't see any guy with a pink shirt, a baby and a beard," I said indignantly. It's the indifference that maddens. I'd been chattering about pelmets when Damien had seen the very first persona in this drama.

"You might have mentioned."

"Well, I thought of telling you but you were looking out the front window at the vans with the carpets and I was in the bathroom looking out at the patio and there was this guy out there with a baby in a sort of sling, small baby it was, tugging at his beard."

"It can't have been all that small a baby if it was tugging at his beard," said I, fascinated at this glimpse of a solitary Damien in a bathroom peeping at a patio.

"I don't know what size of a baby it was," said Damien. "It was quite small. The beard was sort of cradling it and patting its head and giving out to the guy who was doing the patio at the same time. I didn't like him."

"The man with the beard?" I asked.

"Yeah, the man with the beard," said Damien, who had taken up the paper and opened it to the TV pages. He'd wasted enough time on trivial gossip. Now was the moment for a serious man to watch television.

"But why didn't you like him?" I asked. Damien has strong likes and dislikes. He states them but doesn't describe them. He would shudder if you told him that these likes, dislikes are purely instinctive, but they are. He thinks he's logical because logic, he believes, is as far away from sentimentality as you can get. Damien hates sentimentality.

"I didn't like the way he shouted at the man spreading the concrete in the patio, if that's what it was—patio, it looked more like a mini car-park to me," said Damien, curling up the newspaper in his big hands. "And I didn't like the way he was with that baby. There was something wrong about it. Possessive, like a woman."

Constance was not possessive. When I paid a welcoming visit—pure curiosity really—Albert answered the door. Albert was the man with the beard but the baby was absent and the pink shirt turned out to be some sort of ethnic smock. He showed me into a white, white kitchen. I disliked it on sight. All the interesting bits and pieces, the pots and pans and cheerful packets that I use as kitchen furniture, were hidden behind closed white doors. This was an executive kitchen.

Constance was sitting at a white kitchen table with a notebook in front of her.

"How nice," she said, accepting my bouquet of whatever was blooming in my garden that morning. "Flowers from your garden." She handed them to Albert with a gesture that reminded me of the queen (their dear queen) giving the children's birthday daffodils to the lady-in-waiting. "Very nice," she always seems to say. "But don't you think I can afford my own flowers?"

Albert put them in water. He cut them and bound them and tidied them until the exuberant bunch was as neat and tidy and boring as the kitchen. I watched his fussy movements with fascination. Stalks in white garbage can before flowers in water. A few dropped, dusty leaves meant cleaning an entire working surface with a sponge. Blue, alas.

Constance sat in her pink floral Laura Ashley dress looking as if none of this domestic activity had anything to do with her. I wasn't offered coffee or a drink or even a seat. Constance chattered away, making a note in her notebook from time to time, as if we'd just met, by accident, in somebody else's house.

"Just a small playschool—not a crèche you know. It's why we bought this house. The large rooms, particularly the one with French windows giving on to the patio. Albert's away a lot and I don't want to let my training go to waste. I'll start with five children and engage them myself." Nod, nod, her little blond head let me know that I'd better not ask what *engage* was.

"Constance is very fond of children," said Albert.

"We've had two more bathrooms put in," agreed Constance. "Would you like to see the house?"

"I'll have to hurry back, I just came to say welcome," I lied. I do like seeing other people's houses but this one was, disturbingly, the mirror image of my own. All the wrong way round. I was disconcerted and repelled by that kitchen and I didn't feel as if I could face the inevitable master bedroom with en suite bathroom behind louvered doors, the mirrored wardrobes, the brass bed with patchwork quilt. A house for people who don't care to live in houses. I wondered what the local residents' association would have to say about a playschool as I scurried away.

Albert and Constance had nothing to fear. They were quiet and no one in our road could care less if you stripped naked in the middle of the street as long as you did it silently.

Children began to stagger around the patio and Constance was joined by a Constance look-alike, fair, pale, and dressed in Laura Ashley pink with buttons and bows. I rarely saw Albert on the road. Albert was, as Constance had said, away a lot and he always took the car. He also always did the shopping.

"She doesn't even have her milk delivered," complained a neighbor. "Not very friendly is she?" Community life starts on the street, and if you don't go shopping with your cart or your plastic bag, if you're not out there to put out your bottles or to take them in, no one can get to know you. Constance, it was decided, was snooty. Albert was forgiven because he had "such a way" with his son. That is, he carried the boy out to the car, strapped him in the baby seat in the back and took him shopping on those few days a month when he was at home.

I wondered how Constance survived. Mothers came and went with toddlers and baby bags and bottles, but the summer evenings were long and empty and it seemed almost frightening to me, who loved the street and the casual chats with the neighbors about the weather, that Constance was shut away all day and all night.

"Surely she must need milk at least sometimes. You can't freeze milk can you?" I asked Damien.

"LongLife," said Damien. "Maybe she's agoraphobic."

Could an agoraphobic run a playschool? Surely not. I reminded myself to look up *agoraphobia* in the library sometime, but, as usual, I forgot. But the thought of Constance, lonely and silent in the evenings, distressed me in a small but persistent way. The patio doors were often open in the evening, but I never heard the sound of a radio or a TV. After the toddlers and the look-alike had gone the house was quiet save for the odd gurgle of a water pipe or the flushing of the loo. I didn't even hear her son babbling or crying. Just a sort of breathing silence.

Then one Wednesday evening after the playschool had closed, Constance arrived on my front doorstep. She was even thinner than before and the Laura Ashley number, blue this time, was crushed and crumpled.

"I feel dreadful," she said when I asked her in. "I haven't been very neighborly, I know, and now I've come to ask you a favor I wouldn't even ask a friend for." She was staring around our astonishingly formal dining room, which no one ever used. We sit in the kitchen but the dining room is our parlor for the entertainment of guests who don't happen to be friends. "Lovely room. I didn't mean you're not a friend," added Constance teetering from foot to foot in her silly little high-heeled sandals. She had painted her toenails red, I noticed. "It's just that I'm embarrassed."

"Ask," I said. I'm not usually so abrupt, but I was annoyed. Constance had ignored me since the flowers episode and she'd made me feel foolish then, as if she knew it was nosiness and not neighborliness that had prompted the gesture. "Ask," I said more gently, remembering those long, silent evenings and the absence of milk bottles on her doorstep. "Ask and it shall be given."

"Seek and ye shall find?" replied Constance, grinning. "It's just that I, well, I need money. I mean, I wonder if I could borrow some money. Ten pounds, something like that. It's very foolish of me but I usually keep a reserve, and some of the parents haven't paid for ages, and Albert's away and there are some things I need and you seemed so kind the time you dropped in and so I wondered if you'd mind?"

I didn't mind. I wondered. But I didn't mind. I thought that most people had bank accounts and checkbooks and credit cards. This was slightly before the ubiquity of ATMs but there *were* such things and people like Constance, organized, businesslike people, used them. I never did because I was afraid of the buttons and a machine that was sure to swallow my card and say no. I kept cash in an old tobacco tin under the mattress, but I wasn't efficient and I *did* have a checkbook. Still.

"Of course," I said. I was almost as embarrassed as Constance by this stage. "Of course. I'll just be a minute." When I came back with twenty pounds, Constance was still twitching from foot to foot, almost in tears. "Look," I said, "I don't have less than twenty, keep it in a tobacco tin you know, twenties are handier, you see. You take this and pay it back when you can."

On Friday an envelope containing a new twenty-pound

note came through the letter box. *I can't thank you enough* was scrawled on a card that read *Constance and Albert O'Leary, At Home. Albert,* and *At Home,* had been slashed out with a heavy ballpoint. I didn't show the note to Damien or tell him about the visit or the money. Albert came back and was visibly AT HOME. He shopped furiously all one Saturday morning. I watched bags and boxes of bottles being carried into the house and listened to the clitter-clatter of polite chatter from the patio that evening.

Constance and Albert were At Home. But not to us.

I was more puzzled than cross. Parties bore me. I didn't like Albert. I did, for some reason, like Constance. I liked her grin and the bit about "Seek and ye shall find." I suspected that underneath the fear, for it *was* fear of some sort, and the brittle efficiency was someone who could be a friend if she'd let me. If Albert would let me.

The playschool closed for August. I thought that Constance and Albert and baby would take off for Provence or Greece or Jamaica. Somewhere stylish. But Albert drove off on his own as usual and left Constance and the house quiet. The patio doors shut with a squeak—"needs oiling," said Damien—every night at eleven and I began to listen again for the phantom sounds next door.

Then Constance appeared on my doorstep again. "I'm *sorry*," she said. "It's the same thing . . . I've come to ask you . . . Oh I'm so ashamed."

"Money?" I asked, leading her into the dining room again. "Well, you paid me back last time. . . ."

But she hadn't really paid me back, of course. You can just about ask friends and relations for urgent loans of cash without offering explanations, but if you drag rejected neighbors into the peripheries of your private problems by demanding solutions for them, well then you've got an obligation to pay for their curiosity. Not friendly, perhaps, but then I wasn't a friend of Constance's and she'd chosen it that way. I don't know whether Constance understood all that from my unfriendly face or whether she'd been longing to confide in someone all along but she sat down on what had become the Garda Inspector's chair and said,

"I suppose I owe you an explanation."

I said nothing. I felt that she *did* owe me an explanation for my worry about the breathing, brooding silence next door as much as for the money. But I wasn't Constance's mother. I couldn't say, "Darling I've been so worried about you," or tell her that worry had kept me awake at night, which it had. I was slightly ashamed of my worry, anyway. Twenty pounds doesn't give you the right to worry about somebody else and I'd worried before the money. We're all supposed to be involved in mankind, in this case womankind, but when you do get involved, when you hear the sound of the bell before it tolls, you feel nosy and guilty, prurient almost. I was thinking about all this, about all the cases you hear of people saying "I wish I'd known" and "Why didn't she ask for help," all the squalid, domestic disasters that occasionally percolate through the calm surface of Irish family life, when I realized that Constance had begun to talk in a rapid, wheezy voice.

To this day I cannot remember exactly what she said at the beginning of that conversation or how she said it. I remember the end of it all right, when we spoke with different voices. But when she was telling her story her words became my words. It was as if she was telling me about a life that could have been my life, would have been my life, but for a decent husband, better parents and a moment of rage that still resonates. Guilt, Constance talked about guilt. She went right back to the beginning of her marriage to explain how guilty she was, she went further back and further. Her mother (widowed) had always found her "difficult and ambitious." Selfish, terribly selfish. Constance had got a scholarship to college and insisted on taking it instead of supporting Mother. Mother died of a heart attack after threatening to do so for most of Constance's young life. And then Constance met Albert and wanted, of all unforgivable things, to marry him. Albert was reluctant.

"He was very insecure," said Constance. That is one of the few things I remember her saying then, perhaps because she said it so often. "Albert was very insecure." At the time when Constance sat down in the Garda Inspector's chair, I'd just read an article about wife battering which explained that men hit women because they can't tell women how much they need them and depend on them. They love. Therefore they hit. When the little woman walks out the door, typical wife-battering male doesn't say, "Come back—I need you!" He hits her instead *because* he needs her. I'd laughed, albeit uneasily, when I read that article, but I didn't laugh when Constance told me that Albert was "very insecure."

Albert overcame his insecurity and married Constance though it was difficult for him because Constance's impecunious mother had left her, oddly enough, a lot of money. Constance didn't bother to explain why Mother had needed support when she had had over fifty thousand pounds in the building society. Constance didn't really explain why the money went to buy the house next door and why the house was in Albert's name alone—not Constance's. She did tell me, her wheezing voice ascending to a whine, that because Albert felt so very insecure, because she'd asked him to marry her and not the other way around, because of all these things Albert couldn't, really couldn't, bear for her to have a bank account, a checkbook, credit cards or cash. Constance was allowed to keep the money she earned from the play-school, but she had to pay the look-alike in cash. She had to pay for the school materials. If the milk ran out—Damien was right, it was LongLife—or if she needed Tampax, which Albert couldn't be expected to buy during his monthly assaults on the supermarket, then Constance went short.

I remember half listening to all this and thinking about guilt and gratitude. Which comes first, the oak or the acorn? Are women born feeling guilty or is it men and marriage that make them that way? Why was I being so cold about this? Why couldn't I just hug Constance and tell her that something like that had happened to me?

Nearly happened to me. The fact is that as I sat there asking unspoken questions—Why is Albert so insecure? Why didn't you put the house in your joint names? What about all that compulsive housecleaning of Albert's?—I began to feel a little smug. The house was in both our names. We had a joint bank account. I'd even taken back my maiden name, thereby exchanging one man's surname for another, but it *was* on our joint checkbook. And then Constance said something about hiding broken crockery. She was clumsy and had got more so because Albert, sweet Albert, made her pay for the damages out of her playschool money. The worst part of this litany of Albert's petty tyrannies was the matter-of-fact way in which Constance spoke about them as if of *course* Albert had to punish Constance for being so naughty as to break her own crockery and of *course* he couldn't trust her to clean the house without a major mishap when he was around and of *course* he had to mind the baby when he was at home—though what Albert thought would happen when Constance was alone with home and baby and no careful Albert to mind them was not explained. Perhaps they had no reality for him when he wasn't there as head of the household.

But the bit about hiding the broken crockery—why not throw it out?—took me back. When you feel guilty you don't throw things out, you hide them. I didn't break crockery. I wrecked clothes. I tore them, got paint on them, burned holes in them and then I hid them. I can still see them now, those guilty little bundles under the two single beds which had been pushed together to make one and were never moved, not even to dust. I hid jewelry there too, rings that lost stones or beads that spontaneously exploded around my unlucky neck.

"You have to stop feeling guilty," I said to Constance.

"How?" said Constance.

It was a facer. I didn't quite know how. I'd never altogether managed it myself. But Constance was gallant and could grin. She ran a playschool.

"Stop speaking to him. Behave as if he'd done something

wrong—and he has, he has—but don't tell him what it is. Then think about what he's done wrong and . . . no?"

"No," said Constance firmly. "I've thought about all that. When we were living in a flat I had a friend," Constance spoke as if friends were an endangered species, "and she talked to me the way you do. She told me to stand up for myself. She was very kind and definite but it was no use. It just made me feel worse. I'd try to use her voice and think like she did but it didn't change me or make me braver. It made me resent Albert. Do you know, I think confiding in people, women confiding in women, is very dangerous. I mean I have to live in that house with Albert. I don't mean to be rude but, well, you *don't*. You wouldn't be there when I was acting on your advice. And you don't love Albert and I do. I'm a different sort of woman when I'm with Albert than I am with you or with women friends. You have to live alone in a marriage—don't you find that? You can't really bring your friends along as well. They distort things."

"Have I distorted things?" I asked.

"Me talking to you has distorted things," said Constance, standing up. "Not so much what you said but what I said. It wasn't fair to Albert. I haven't really given him a chance, I moan behind his back but I don't tell him how I feel."

"Because you're frightened?" I asked.

"Because, well, because I don't want to know the end of the story and what would happen if I did tell him. You know when you tell off a little bully, the way his face gets red and he tries not to cry? The bullies are hard to tell off because they're so vulnerable." With these enigmatic words

Constance tried to depart but I insisted that she wait while I raided the tobacco tin again.

"And you'll ask me if you ever need money again?" I pleaded.

"Probably not," said Constance. "But thank you anyway."

Oh, why do the guilty make the guilty feel so guilty? It wasn't my fault that Constance had confided in me, but the silence from next door was more threatening than brooding in the next few days. I felt, ridiculously, as if we'd both taken bits of each other's skin off. I yelped and shouted out loud as I cleaned around the house and then I sat down on my bed and tried to remember everything Constance had said to me and everything I had said to Constance. Nothing there to feel guilty about, but I went on yelping and shouting, a little more quietly it is true. And I wondered how therapists and counselors stayed sane when, if you listen to somebody else's problem, you end up thinking about your own.

Damien woke me at dawn—well, the sun had just about come up and the birds were twittering—about a week later.

"There's the most terrible row going on next door," he said. "I don't know how you could sleep through it." He looked exhausted, bruises under his eyes and his skin dry and stretched. "They've been at it for hours. He's leaving her and she's leaving him and they're shouting and yelling and the baby's crying and I can't stand it." He was shivering.

"Constance and Albert?" I asked, though I knew already. "Never mind, Damien, you get back into bed."

"I can't!" He sat there, hunched over at the side of our bed in his thin pajamas. "You didn't hear them. It was horrible. They said the most terrible things to each other . . . and I could hear him crying, Albert I mean. I could never understand why you wouldn't agree to have the house soundproofed. You can hear everything, *everything*, through these walls."

I could have told Damien that it wasn't the walls that counted, not even our extraordinary, sound-conducting walls, but the people behind them. Damien suffers from selective amnesia. He doesn't remember the times when people had to listen to us through the walls. The times he shouted about my middle-class self-indulgence, my sloppiness, my extravagance, and the times I screamed back, "If that's the way you feel you can leave me! You sanctimonious puritan you!"

"People do have rows, Damien," I said. "We did."

"Not like this." He smiled at me. "We always knew we'd stay together and have more rows. I went out in the garden, you know, to listen to them because I could hear the row but I couldn't make much sense of what they were saying. They were downstairs and the patio doors were open and Albert, well, he was sobbing. You know the angry way that kids cry when they've been found out?"

I thought of Constance's vulnerable, red-faced bullies and nodded.

"I know," I said.

"He was crying like that and protesting at the same time and then he said, shouted really, that he didn't need to stay here to be insulted. Can you imagine that, to be insulted? He had another wife, a real wife, in Cork."

"Do you think that's true?" I asked. I was shocked, horrified, fascinated but not really surprised.

"It doesn't much matter what I think," said Damien. "Constance thought it was true."

A few hours later Albert loaded up his car and disappeared down the road for the last time. Before he left he took the baby seat from the backseat of the car and left it on their front doorstep. No babies, perhaps, with the "real wife" in Cork. Constance came out once that day to take in the baby chair, but the house stayed quiet and the patio doors closed. I didn't even think of going next door. Guilt, guilt, I'd done enough. Damien slept all day and then got up and said that he was sick of the house and the street and would I like to come out to see a rather sad French film about the Spanish Inquisition? We were both exhausted, better apart, so I told him to go on his own and not to come back early.

"You're going to sit by your window and hold a vigil?" asked Damien.

And that is what I did do. I sat by my window and thought of Constance and the baby and the "real wife" in Cork and of Albert and his insecurities and his job. A neighbor had told me he was a "traveling salesman." Did he drive around Ireland, with a wife here and a wife there? Did he control these wives, polish the furniture, punish them for breakages and then drive on leaving them weltering in guilt? But as night wore on into early morning, the vigil became what a vigil should be. If I could have prayed for Constance then, I would have, but I just sat there in my window, thinking of her.

And then at half past two on a Saturday morning Constance O'Leary walked out through her patio doors into the instant glare of her security lights. . . .

Do the Decent Thing

∾

Ita Daly

The room is far too warm and inside the double-glazed window the air is stagnant. Rosa wonders why nobody seems to mind or notice, why every other member of her family sees nothing wrong in a five-hour lunch; how, at the end of that time, they still find things to talk about and giggle over.

She tries to catch her husband's eye but Jerry is engrossed in whatever story Maeve is telling him. Rosa notes how well her husband and sister seem to get along; in fact, how well everyone seems to get along with everyone else in this three-tiered family circle.

Except for her, playing her usual role of spoilsport.

That's what Jerry will say if she forces him to leave before the others. But if she stays much longer she will start screaming at people, such is the level of her irritability.

Her mother has made yet more tea and backs her way into the room now with a laden tray. Her father dislodges his granddaughter from his knee and, courteous as ever, rises to place the tray on the coffee table. As he bends with his burden Rosa glimpses pink skin peeping through the silver hair. At last then, signs of decay and vulnerability. At last, he is beginning to get old.

Her heart is clutched by sudden panic but she ignores it and snaps her fingers toward Jerry. "It's time we were off, love. Megan's exhausted."

Maeve tells her to relax, for heaven's sake, and have a cup of tea.

Her mother laughing, points toward her father. "What are you talking about, Rosa? Just look at the pair of them."

Her father has resumed his seat by the flaming gas fire. He sits with his legs stretched out in front of him, offering a hand to two-year-old Megan who is balancing herself on his ankles. She is looking up at her grandfather, chattering away at him.

Rosa's mother nods her head. "Reminds me of you, Rosa, at that age. Daddy's little girl."

Rosa roots in her bag and takes out a packet of cigarettes. "I'm going for a smoke."

Nobody stops her. All of them, all three generations, disapprove of her smoking and are quite happy to see her retreat to the dank garden to indulge her filthy habit.

Rosa lights up, drags on a jacket, bangs the kitchen door after her. Daddy's little girl. The phrase has hurled her backward and she is spinning down a dark tunnel until she emerges in sunshine in the summer of her twelfth year.

It is July and school is out. Nothing moves in the streets of the little town as the white afternoon light settles over every house and shopfront. In the square the red sandstone of the Northern Bank is bleached by the intensity of the light so that the building seems to lose its solidity as it simmers uncertainly.

But inside all is darkness and calm. Rosa lies on her bed looking down at the deserted street, eating Mikado biscuits from a brown paper bag. She is alone in this part of the building as her mother has taken Tom to have his hair cut and Maeve is away for the whole month of July, waitressing, her first summer job, in Bundoran.

Rosa is glad that Maeve is not coming home, for Maeve is a bossyboots who tries to lord it over her younger sister, just because she is seventeen and away at boarding school. Tom is older than Rosa too, but only by a year. Poor Tom, his mother calls him, suffering as he does from a precocious younger sister who outshines him in every sphere and who will be entering sixth class with him in September.

Tom loves Rosa, follows her everywhere. Rosa loves Tom too but in an absentminded sort of way, for Rosa has many calls on her affections. Sometimes she does feel sorry for him, particularly when Daddy ignores him. Daddy likes clever, glittering people like himself, and Rosa glitters and performs much more successfully than her brother.

Daddy is the manager of the Northern Bank. This confers a certain status upon him and his family, but Daddy has taught her to despise this nonsense. "The day job" is how he refers to his duties in the bank. He is really a poet and he writes his poetry with a gold-plated Parker fountain pen in a long notebook with a blue leather cover.

For his fortieth birthday on the seventeenth of May, Rosa wrote him a poem, which he had read with tears in his eyes, calling her his petal, his angel-child, his own little darling.

Because they are both poets, Daddy says that they are not only father and daughter but kindred spirits. He explains how important that is for him, living as he does, surrounded by coarse, simpleminded country folk. Although Rosa can be willful and naughty where her mother is concerned, she is careful not to displease Daddy. She feels she can never be lonely with a father who is a kindred spirit, a soul mate.

Rosa finishes the last biscuit, licks her fingers and heaves herself off the bed. It is past three and the big double doors of the bank will be already shut, the staff departed and Daddy all by himself downstairs. He often lingers after everyone else has gone home. He has told Rosa that he likes the feel of those empty rooms, the silence and the peace after the commerce of the day.

The children are not really allowed into the bank, but Rosa now decides that she will go down the back staircase, the one Daddy uses, and wait for him on the bottom step, outside his office. She moves quietly down the narrow stairs, feeling her way in the half-light. The door to Daddy's office is closed and she is about to sit down on the bottom step and wait when she hears a sort of snorting noise coming from behind the door, followed by a squeaking sound, as if something is being pushed across the linoleum.

Robbers: she and Tom have been waiting for this moment, knowing that it was bound to happen. She turns to run back upstairs, then changes her mind. Daddy's life may be in danger. If she can hoist herself up to the window between his office and the staff toilet she may be able to throw something at the robber or distract him in some way.

It is easy enough to get up to the small window by climbing onto a chair and from there to the edge of the big old-fashioned handbasin. Rosa pushes at the window, which opens inward, and pokes her head in after. Down below, her father's office is lit like a stage set. In the middle of the floor, away from its usual position behind the desk, is her father's big leather armchair. Lying with her legs spread wide and her skirt hitched up, Miss Lacey, the junior clerk, possesses the chair, while on top, his trousers down around his ankles, Daddy rides up and down, his white bottom quivering like a birthday jelly.

Before she can withdraw her head, Miss Lacey has seen her.

"Sweet Jesus," she cries out, and Rosa, grazing her ear on the frame of the window, pulls back, jumps down and runs for the stairs.

She waits in her bedroom for her father. He does not come upstairs until long after her mother and Tom have returned. When he does come she can hear the heavy deliberation of his footsteps. They pause outside her bedroom. Then there is a knock.

Rosa has not dwelt on what she saw in her father's office. This is the moment she has been waiting for in dread.

"Come in, come in," she whispers, unable to find her proper voice.

He doesn't look angry but infinitely sad. When he speaks his voice is gentle.

"My heart is broken," he says. "You've broken my heart today, Rosa."

Rosa can say nothing. She feels she may never speak again.

"I really didn't think that you, of all my children, would betray me. I didn't think that you would spy on me in such an appalling manner. In your sneaking around and your underhandedness I really cannot recognize the child whom I have loved so dearly. I do not see you anymore, Rosa. I cannot see you."

And he withdraws from the room, gently closing the door.

When, years later, Rosa told this story to Jerry, he had made light of it. He was fond of his father-in-law and he thought his wife was being melodramatic, dredging up all this old stuff. "For God's sake, look at what you read about in the papers all the time. At least he didn't abuse you."

But Rosa called it abuse, the sudden withdrawal of her father's love. At first she had thought that he would forgive her, that she could make it up to him and they would be as they had been before. She spent the rest of the summer trying to please him, to regain his love. But by now he had taken up with Tom, had started to bring him on fishing trips and to the golf course. There was no time left over for Rosa.

When he was at home her father treated her with a distant politeness that nobody but she seemed to notice. Skillfully he deflected her advances, keeping the distance between them, his coldness cloaked by a convincing briskness so that her mother noticed nothing except that her husband was spending more time with his son.

Rosa grew depressed and then angry. The anger remained with her and fueled her adolescent years until she ended up despising a man who would betray his daughter to save face, manipulating her so that she became the wrongdoer in her own eyes.

And Rosa has never recovered from this betrayal. Witness the man she has chosen to marry: good, decent, likeable, but deliberately chosen because she knows she will never fall in love with him. Love, Rosa knows, leads to betrayal.

In the chilly garden Rosa takes a final drag on her cigarette, then flicks the butt in among the withered stalks of the herbaceous border. She turns to stare in the window where her family are shown in sharp relief, lit by the many lamps which her mother has placed around the room.

He is getting old. She sees him raise a hand and run his fingers through Megan's dark curls. The skin on the hand is splattered with dark age marks, the veins are raised and knotted.

She looks at him dispassionately, thinking that he may well die soon. She hopes that she will be able to forgive him before that day arrives but she knows that there is no guarantee.

She goes up to the window and tells him the paradox which she knows he cannot hear. "It would be all so much easier if I didn't love you so much, Daddy. For years and years I tried to stop loving you, I thought my hate would kill my love but they just went on growing side by side. And now it's the love that won't allow forgiveness."

Inside the window her father throws back his head and laughs at something that Megan has said. Rosa recognizes the movement. Wasn't it only yesterday that she made him laugh like that?

She bangs a fist against the window but nobody turns to

look. "You just go on living, you bugger," she says. "Don't you dare die before I can forgive you. At least do the decent thing as your final act."

And when she walks away back toward the kitchen, Rosa finds herself smiling for the first time that day.

A Girl Like You

❧

Margaret Dolan

I stand on my balcony. The lightning is streaking the Manhattan skyline. Night cackling in static as gut-roaring thunder rolls over me, the alien. Resident alien.

I stand on my balcony, drenched under the wacky clock, numbers askew. The city spreads before me twinkling with myriad jewels like a flashy brooch. A breeze ripples the brooch, showering the night with gems. Lightning flashing my jewelry. Neck, wrists, ears, all sparkling. Fingers cluttered with diamonds and precious stones. Some are quite vulgar. Others exquisite.

I've put it all on. The whole caboodle. All the real thing. The Nanny haul. The jewels Nanny brought out of Austria in her knickers in 1939.

One long lightning thread picks up the dazzle on my small white hands. Every finger adorned with one or two rings except the little finger on the right. It has a ring of its own. A perfect circle of pearly white.

❧

"Mickey Mouse has only four fingers," Henry said to me, making even my dress shiver. But he wasn't going to cut off my finger. Of course he wasn't. He's a surgeon, for God's sake.

And he had chosen me for my hands. He passed them through his, weighing them. Weighing me up. It was my neck that attracted him first, he said. A swan's neck.

I met him at a staff party at the hospital. I was as usual compressing myself into invisibility. Neck crunched into my shoulders, hiding behind my pall of lank black hair, when Pamela said, "Look at your man ogling you."

"Who?"

"The big fella. Openly lusting after you. Real 'across the crowded room' stuff."

"Don't be ridiculous." My neck springing to its full length in surprise.

He was definitely looking, or leering or something. Nobody had ever ogled me. Noticed, yes. As in, great long streak of misery with a neck like a drake. Even my own mother so described me. I telescoped my neck into my shoulders and shuddered like a tuning fork as he larded across the room toward me.

"Your neck," he said.

"What's it to you?" I said belligerently.

"It's so beautiful. So elegant."

I was about to tell him to sod off when I saw he was being serious.

A big, cuddly bear of a fellow, fine eyes with a frieze of

woolly curls across his forehead, dancing as he spoke. And dimples. And great fat trousers pulled up under his armpits. I am going to enjoy this night, I thought. And I did.

"You beautiful swan," he said.

I loved him for that. Calling me a swan.

"A neck to hang jewels on," he said later. And he did. The finest. The most exquisite. Eventually all the Nanny haul was encrusted on my fingers or hanging on some part of me. I was deliriously happy. I stopped scrunching my shoulders. He was forty-nine, ten years older than I was. A surgeon by trade.

∾

"Ursula is particular," my mother used to say to her sisters at the weddings of my much younger cousins, her sour mouth prickling with disappointment.

"An answer to prayer, a godsend. All those novenas," my mother said when Henry appeared on the scene. Before Henry there weren't any mister rights or wrongs. Not even an indecent proposal.

"A doctor in the house. A surgeon no less. A miracle." Her voice ascending into heaven.

She insisted on introducing Henry as Doctor. Even to her sisters. Especially to her sisters. Henry, I'd say. His name is Henry. Henry the Eighth.

"It's well you have something of mine," she said, referring to my hands, when I showed her my rare pink diamond engagement ring. My mother is small and neat. Even her wrinkles are in perfect symmetry. She was once considered cute. Lisps at men as if she still was.

I was radiant that day in my antique lace wedding dress, gratitude and surprise blazing out of every pore. Henry dressed as Henry the Eighth. His dimples holing his chubby cheeks. "Off with her head" jokes bandied about.

"Fine feathers make a fine bird," my mother sniffed but boasted to her sisters. Telling the cost.

ॐ

This morning I had a sort of déjà vu which made my insides puddle. We were coming off night duty when Cherry tugged at me.

"You're in luck sweetie, Ken fancies you," she said.

"What?"

"Ken. You know, the big guy. A real sweetheart. And he can surgically enhance you if you want." She laughed.

"The plastic surgeon?"

I remembered him looking at me intently in the canteen. Rusty eyebrows banking twinkling blue eyes. More than likely thinking, I could do a lot with her. Make her over, give her a decent nose, cheekbones, lift that mouth.

"He's cute, cuddly," Cherry said.

"Yeah," I said, thinking, so was Henry.

"Free too. Newly divorced. This guy is genuine and he might do a cut-price job on me for introducing you." Her smile a fluorescent plea.

"Sorry."

"Give me a break, I could do with sucking out."

A girl like me should be grateful, Cherry was thinking.

"Aren't you even a teeny bit interested?"

"No."

I wanted to say, been there, done that, got the scars. If I told her she'd trade it with someone else for other juicy bits of gossip. Cherry is desperate for a husband. Twice divorced. Lately all her affairs have collapsed like hollow meringues.

"We used to mate like ally cats," Cherry was saying. "Then one day Rick is wearing an earring and Calvin Klein jeans. Into rap. Got himself a new woman with a tangle on her tongue."

"An impediment?"

"Naw, a red-hot rapper. Good at wordsmithing."

"Jesus wept."

"Yeah. I went to bed that night and woke up like Rip Van Wrinkle."

"Winkle."

"Same difference. I need ironing out. Look," she said.

I looked. Her nose is pert but wrong for her face. It sort of jumps out from between her collagen-enhanced cheeks. Her skin is like fine seersucker. Definitely in need of ironing.

"You look all right to me," I said.

"I'm going down to Barnes later, want to come?" Cheered by my lie.

Cherry has forsaken Hogs and Heifers, a singles bar in the meat-packing district, to browse and stalk the browsers in Barnes and Noble bookshop on the corner of Broadway and 82nd. A "lit. hit," she calls it.

"Meet your soul mate between the covers of a good book. Right?"

"Yeah. The chattiest ones I find are in psychology."

"Keep out of the serial killer section."

"Ah come on. Just a couple of hours."

"Next time," I said. "I'm going to skate around the Village."

"I don't know how you can live there. The residents look like extras from *Mad Max*."

"I know, that's its charm."

∾

Every night in my dreams a giant Henry chases me with a scalpel as I run with the loot around the wacky clock across rooftops. I hide in corners. Bracelets clinking giving me away. Wake. Muscles strung tight. I count my fingers. Feel my ribs.

∾

In the Village I strut my stuff, wear my shades and blades and plow through the thick air around St. Mark's. Curls of evaporated gas pinch my lungs. My mother wouldn't recognize me. The new me. Alien me. Tight blond hair with a squiggle at the back. I roll past a street market. You can root if you want to, I tell myself, so I skate back to the stalls. I buy a little '30s brooch, a silver swan. Making me feel really good.

Simmering in the heat outside Cafe Orlin I feel satisfied. I've arrived at the right place in the right time, in the land of my grandmother. Home, in the land of the skyscrapers. And I'm never going back to Lilliput.

This blissful moment has already passed in Ireland. Hours ago. It's nighttime there.

Henry tucked up in his bed. Jewels fretting his sleep. Mother shouting in her sleep, raging against her ungrateful daughter. Guilt surfaces and recedes. Followed by a delicious rush of power coursing through me. I feel I can handle anything. Anyone. Even Henry. The time has come to contact him. Tell him where I'm at. I'm ready. Come and get it, motherfucker. He'll come. For the Nanny haul. Have to. And pay the price. He'd have been on my trail ages ago if I hadn't given him a bum steer through my mother when I rang her from London en route here.

"Why are you doing this to me? Shaming me in front of my sisters, making me a laughingstock," Mother screamed down the line.

"Don't worry, Mum, I'm fine," I said.

Ignoring me, she screeched on. "How could you leave Henry like that? He made you. Transformed you."

"I'm grateful for that."

"And you show your gratitude by running away. A girl like you should be especially thankful."

"Thanks, Mum."

"Come back this instant, do you hear me?"

"I can't, I've got a job here in London."

"Henry's a generous, affable, warm human being. I'm sure he'll take you back."

"You don't understand."

"I understand you were forty in your stocking feet, a plain desperate woman, when Henry took pity on you."

"Thank you, Mother."

"A brilliant surgeon."

"But unhinged."

"Unhinged! He's not the unhinged one."

"He's obsessed with objects, possessions. Unnaturally obsessed."

"So what? I had to put up with your boring father and his boring books for thirty years."

"Dad was a saint to put up with you."

She clubbed me with my birth, ten and a half pounds, tearing her asunder.

I tell her I didn't ask to be born and put down the phone.

Philip Larkin was dead right about parents fucking up their children.

I got Henry on the rebound from his aunt. His beloved aunt Ellen. Henry never tired of telling the tale of the much-loved aunt. How a pretty little Irish girl inspired such passion in the jeweler. The jeweler to the Hapsburgs, who was crazy about his red-haired colleen. The plucky Irish Nanny leaving Austria in '39 with the jewels in her knickers. She was Henry's father's sister. Photogenic, unlike Henry's mother, a big soft-looking woman, slatternly, with dimples staring at the camera surrounded by a clatter of scrawny kids. A pudgy baby squashed against her balloon breast. Henry the eighth and last child. Handed over to the aunt. The aunt with money. Rescuing him, shielding him. Loving him. Leaving him everything. All the Nanny haul.

Giraffe neck, I was called at school. Knees permanently bent, crouching. At twelve, towering over my mother. At fourteen, over everyone. My gaucheness singling me out for the school play. The ugly sister along with another. We attacked, seething with hatred, not Cinders but each other. Our mirror image.

"I want to be small like Mum," I whined to Dad.

"You take after your American grandmother. Six foot tall. Thought she was in Lilliput when she arrived in Ireland."

"Did she mind?"

"At first. But she embraced life, even the Irish weather. Called herself a cockeyed optimist. You'd have liked her very much."

A pang of wistfulness for a mother like my grandmother seared through me.

"Everything about your mother is small. She is small-minded and her brain is a pea. Now you wouldn't want that, would you?"

But I did. I hated him for his genes, his plainness, his long, skinny body.

He faded away retreating further and further into books until one day he was gone. A shadow gone.

Mother whimpered. Pretending.

∾

"You can have everything you want except central heating," Henry said when he first showed me the house. Edwardian. Deliberately drab on the outside. Inside impeccable. Everything in period except a '50s record player and a collection of Elvis records.

"Central heating would buckle and twist my furniture. Light as many fires as you want. You may employ Babs Anderson seven days a week if you like."

Babs came every day except Sunday, lighting fires in the dining room, drawing room and bedrooms in the evenings. Her mother had cleaned for Henry's aunt and then Babs took over. She was the same age as Henry. Knew him as a child.

"He's exactly the same as when he was seven," she said one day.

"Is that good or bad?"

"Odd I'd say."

∾

"Give up your work and scout for me," Henry said a few months into our marriage.

"Give up nursing?"

"I'll pay you well."

He did. Very well indeed. Kitted me out with a wardrobe of fine clothes. And the jewels to go with them. I entered his world of antiques with a passion. Pinging like a trinket. Reading everything, attending lectures. Mesmerized. Even did a course in mending fine porcelain.

"Let us prey," Henry'd say, and we'd go on a spree. Passing through Dublin auction rooms, car trunk sales, flea markets, with the arrogance of the chosen. Gliding along as if on castors. Eyes flicking, checking everything. Sometimes bartering.

"You are such an asset," he'd say. "Worth your weight in gold."

I walked tall and began gesticulating with my nice hands.

When I wasn't out scouting I stayed in the kitchen warmed by my Aga cooker, mending the porcelain. Henry rushing home in the evenings. Enthusiastic, like a child. To see what I'd found. Mostly to watch me work. I didn't mind. I wasn't shy about it. Knew I was good.

"You have the gift. Dextrous," he said.

Folded over our coffee cups we'd pick a theme for dinner. Georgian his favorite, Art Deco mine.

A roaring fire, silver gleaming in the candlelit dining room, dressed up in period costumes, we'd dine. Just the two of us. The food unimportant. But the wines always good. After dinner we sometimes played silly games. Characters from fairy stories. Henry loved playing the giant. "Fee, fi, fo, fum, I smell the goods of an Irish man," he'd roar as he counted his jewels. It wasn't as daft as it seemed. Henry was doing an inventory.

"Invite your mother and her sisters. Show what a good catch I am. I'll even do my Elvis impersonation for them."

And he did, sending them home holding each other in gales of laughter with his "Jailhouse Rock." Mother was out of her tree with pride.

Giddy with happiness as well as wine, I banged against the table, wobbling the thin glasses. Reaching out to steady them, I knocked one, felling it. Splintering glass, bloodred wine splashing, seeping into the white linen tablecloth. Henry holding the stem of the broken glass, shaking like an aspen.

"Oh Henry, I'm so sorry," I said, aching into his arms. An animal growl ground in my ear as he folded me into him and squeezed. And squeezed. A grizzly bear hug. Flattening my lungs like paper bags. I heard my ribs crack. He walked away leaving me gasping for breath. Later he strapped me up. That hug dissolved the new me like a solvent. Back to my old image. Neck shrinking into my shoulders.

"Doesn't know his own strength. You're just skin and

bone," my mother said when I told her. I saw in her mean face a glint of a smirk. I saw what I never could admit, hatred. Hatred of me.

"You look a bit shook, missus," Babs said.

"I am."

"A row."

"Sort of. I broke a glass. Henry was upset."

"I bet he was. You're lucky he didn't pulverize you. Just after the aunt died I chipped an ugly Victorian joke mug and he went ballistics. I told him he was the same ruffian he was at seven when he beat me up for breaking his toy car. I could see he seriously wanted to hit me. And he could see I seriously wanted to head-butt him so he backed off, saying I was worth my weight in gold."

"Play it again, Sam," I said.

"I blame the aunt. Spoilt him rotten."

"What was she like?"

"A right little madam in every sense of the word. All her jewels didn't come from the jeweler if you get my meaning. Had admirers. Accepted gifts. Worshiped Henry. He was very good to her, I'll say that for him. Especially in her old age. Tender loving care wasn't in it."

∾

I replaced the glass. It wasn't rare, not even expensive. Days jittered along. Dread creeping up my back, paralyzing me when I heard his key in the door. Heavy footsteps. Henry smiling, bearing gifts.

"Don't know my own strength," he muttered.

Doesn't know his own strength, I said like a mantra, till I semi-believed it.

I was bought with a Jean Muir dress and a trip to Paris. Magic. Did the museums, galleries and the markets. Dined in wonderful little cafes where the menus were hand-written in mauve ink. Henry affectionate, caring. Brought home a tidy haul including Lalique. I settled back into the role I loved. The joy of picking up a little treasure in a car trunk sale or market was a real high. The bear hug forgotten. Well, almost. Whenever he took me in his arms I automatically poked my elbows into his chest.

❧

"To Aunt Ellen," he said, proposing a toast on her anniversary a few months later.

"Aunt Ellen."

"A wonderful woman. A saint," he said reverently.

I had gone along with this saccharine version of the noble Nanny but the wine had loosened my tongue and I went a word too far.

"That's stretching it. A great hustler more like."

"Sorry?"

"Get real. She was your man's mistress, for God's sake."

"Don't sully the good name of my aunt."

"All I'm saying is, she was his bit on the side. Not to mention the others."

As the words were leaving my lips he was leaving his chair. Color storming up his face. Eyes wild. His fist catching me in the stomach as I jumped up, causing a projectile vomit which landed on him. He froze as the slime rolled

down his face. Then raced for the bathroom. Queasy, my stomach feeling like a scraped grease bowl, I stumbled upstairs to my bedroom and locked the door. Glad of our separate rooms. I hardly slept that night. Expecting him to break down the door or something.

∾

"You look like a shit on a slate, missus."

"Thanks, Babs."

"What ails you?"

"A bug."

"Did Henry get it?"

"Yeah, right between the eyes. I threw up on top of him. A sort of gut reaction."

Hails of laughter beat the air. I joined in, holding my stomach.

I didn't feel as bad about that episode as I should have, on account of his own goal. He smelled for days. Kept washing his hair. Kept his distance, but I could smell him. Fee, fi, fo, fum, I smell the contents of Ursula's tum, ran through my head, twitching the muscles around my mouth in a snigger.

One day, with a huge chain around his neck, he crooned, "Put a chain around my neck and lead me anywhere. Just want to be your loving teddy bear." His voice a soothing current insinuating itself into me. Making me laugh. We began socializing and collecting again. Neither mentioning the Nanny.

∾

Our first wedding anniversary was marked with a lavish party to be followed by a cruise a week later. I bought him a Baccarat butterfly paperweight.

"It's incredibly beautiful," he said, filled with emotion.

And he gave me an exquisite little ring. A sapphire with tiny seed pearls.

"It's beautiful, Henry, but I'm afraid it won't fit. It's too small."

"It will fit your little finger."

"I don't think so."

"I bought it especially for your little finger." Agitated.

"We could have a piece set in."

His eyes fogged. His jowls flapped. "Cut it? Cut it?" he roared. "You don't hack perfection."

"It is perfect, but it's a child's ring."

"Try it," he said, savagely pushing it over my knuckle. "There, I knew it would fit."

"It's too tight."

"Rubbish."

All through the meal my finger throbbed and swelled as the ring became embedded in my flesh. Every time I went to the kitchen I ran my hand under the cold tap. By the time the visitors had left I was hysterical.

"Calm down, we'll get it off," he said, but even he could see my finger was too swollen.

He collected medical paraphernalia. "Don't worry. It will be quite painless. Least possible damage."

"But you might cut my finger. It's very swollen."

He looked bemused.

"No." I screamed, realizing we were talking cutting fingers, not cutting rings.

"Shut up, I'll give you an injection. You won't feel a thing."

"I'd rather go to the hospital." Really panicking.

"But sure there's a doctor in the house. A surgeon no less."

"Still, I'd rather . . ."

"Mickey Mouse has four fingers," he guffawed, jabbing me with a syringe.

∾

I awoke fuzzy. Lying in bed. The ring undamaged on the side table, winking at me. Hand bandaged, throbbing. "Mickey Mouse has four fingers" flitted through my mind, making me jump up and start counting.

"No damage done," Henry said. "Clean cut, fine stitches. A little bloodletting. Didn't have to cut the bone, slight bruising and discoloration for a while. Exercise it. We don't want it going stiff."

I lay there pain shooting out my fingertips. Fear and sadness attacking my body making me ill. If it had been a necklace, a torc, he probably would have slit my throat. He is stark raving mad.

∾

Babs confronted Henry with a look. Blaming without asking. His eyes cut past her. She mothered me. Made me chicken soup. Her kindness making me weep. Deliberately knocking against Henry as she swept in and out of the room.

"Stand up to the bugger," she said loud and clear.

Disorientated, webbed in diamonds, Henry fussing over me, we sailed around the Caribbean. Henry telling the Nanny stories to an intrigued audience. I sat mute. Bedecked in Nanny's finest. My misery infecting everyone. Women, their makeup finely tuned, their laughter ready to gush where a smile would do, were perplexed. How did this sullen lump land him? was in their eyes. I was chosen with great care. Chosen for my plainness and desperation, I wanted to tell them. Plain to show off the beauty of the jewelry. And desperate enough to make me both grateful and malleable.

My muteness was interrupting Henry's flow. I could see a hug in the offing. A grizzly one sending shivers shimmying up my body, triggering my mouth into issuing skimpy smiles. Panic expanding them. Even began prompting Henry into anecdotes. Smiles all round. The rest of the voyage a blue blur.

At home I faked my forgiveness well. Buying him bits and bobs. Nothing expensive. Nothing to make him suspicious while I trawled the "Situations Vacant" columns.

"You got it for nine pounds," he said, incredulous, holding a Webb glass dish embossed with fish. "What a clever girl you are." Delight causing a wobble under his chin. Light glistening through his foggy eyes. He loved a bargain.

With a nursing job in New York secured, I packed my bags. I had intended cutting the princess ring in six parts. One for every stitch. Instead I smashed it to smithereens with a lump hammer. Wrote Henry a Dear John letter from London. Thanking him for the jewelry he gave me. Saying I'd treasure it always. Bet that made him puke. And flew to New York.

A chuckle runs up the pipes. The lightning scurries over the rain-washed skyscrapers. I stand under the wacky clock denuded of jewels. All packed ready for Henry.

The sun is not yet itself, veiled in predawn lemony light.

The city is not yet itself, barely honking into being.

I am completely myself.

I start dialing.

The Orphan
❧
Mary Dorcey

Because of what I know I often look at other people and wonder. I see a woman, walking with a small child in the park, holding her by the hand, smiling and laughing, their faces pressed close together, or a woman in the supermarket, shopping at the weekend, loading up the cart with enough food for fifty. Or maybe, someone just standing at a bus stop talking to a friend on the way home from work, and I think how ordinary they look. And then I wonder if they are, or if they have secrets too, terrible secrets they could never tell anyone, like mine. And I wonder if this is the way everyone is. Is no one ordinary? Is everyone completely different on the inside from how they look on the outside?

For years I thought everything that happened was my fault. It's only now looking back that I can see it had nothing to do with me and everything to do with him. Even still I don't hate him. Hate would be giving him too much attention. I just wanted him out of my head and to never have to give him another thought.

And that's the way it was for years until I saw your program. That was the beginning of the change. Listening to all those people and the stories they told. Some of them said they had forgotten what was done. I never could. It happened too often and went on for too long for me to forget. But I didn't think about it. And I didn't feel very much. Even at the time. It was as though a great stone had been placed on my heart when I was a child. All these years I felt nothing but the weight of it.

My father used to call me "No one from nowhere." And that's what I was. And I suppose, because I was from nowhere it didn't matter what happened to me. I called him my father when I had to call him something. And still do. That was the word he used. But he wasn't my father. I didn't have one. Or a mother either. I was an orphan. Everyone for miles around knew that. I belonged to no one and so I belonged to everyone.

He would take me across the fields, my father, most days, over the stream and up the long hill to the corner of the half-acre and the broken gate that led to the crossroads. I remember how the water of the stream leaked into my shoes and how the wind chilled my hands in winter and the way sun scorched the back of my bare legs in summer.

We would stand behind a hedge and wait there until someone came. We never had long to wait. Sometimes, it would be a local man who might ask to see me several times in the one week and other times, it would be a stranger he'd met the night before in the pub. Neighbors or strangers, there was never any shortage anyhow.

The man would put some money in his hand and my

father would say "Don't take all day about it." And then he'd walk away and leave us to it. He never went far. To the other end of the field, only, where he could keep an eye on us. Then the man would climb down into the ditch and I'd follow him.

I did whatever they asked me to and let them do whatever they wanted without complaint. Whatever happened, I didn't speak. Not so much as one word to any of them. Night or day, friend or stranger. They called me the dummy. Some of them thought I was dumb. But it made no difference to them, one way or the other. If I'd been blind and deaf it wouldn't have mattered. Except to me. Maybe it would have been easier for me if I'd been born without sight or hearing.

I don't know if he got me in the first place because he wanted to make money with me or whether that only occurred to him later. He told me once that he'd meant to get a boy when he went to the orphanage but that when he got there I was all that was available and so he took me anyway.

It started with him. I don't remember a first time but there must have been one. At the beginning he used to take me out to the barn or the cowshed. He always did it outside. Never in the house. Even if it was at nighttime he brought me out first. I don't know if that was out of respect for the woman. Or because he didn't want her to hear. After a while, though, he didn't bother with me much himself. Only the occasional time. If he was drunk or angry.

At first when he stopped it frightened me. I thought it must be something I'd done wrong that he didn't want me. Or maybe that all the others being with me had put him off me. Whatever the reason, he gave up using me himself after a bit. And once I was sure he wouldn't punish me, I was glad of it.

He used to bring me with him when he went to the pub in the evening. Wait here till I tell you he used to say. And then he'd go inside to meet his friends. He would leave me standing outside, waiting at the door the way other men left their dogs. People went in and out. They walked past me but no one ever spoke to me. I was the orphan and they didn't see me. I waited in all weathers. If it was a bad night, from his point of view, I might be standing the whole evening before he came out again. But other times it would be busy and he'd come out every hour or so with a customer. They never exchanged money inside the pub. He considered himself a man of honor and he always let someone see me before they parted with any cash. Saves trouble later, he'd say. Not all of them wanted a child.

Although few enough ever refused. If the man was satisfied when he saw me, he would hand over a pound and my father would say, right so, take her round the back and don't be all night about it or you'll owe me another pound.

We always went to the same place. There was a deserted stone cottage behind the pub and that was where they always took me. There was no roof and the rain came in winter and summer. The chimney was still standing and there was a broken fireplace set into one wall. It always had the smell of urine and other waste left by the courting couples who came there after the pub closed. They only used it late at night and before that it was sure to be vacant.

I did whatever the men told me. Standing or lying or

kneeling on all fours like an animal. Most of the time I didn't have to take off any clothes. They just opened my coat and lifted my skirt. The thing I minded most was the cold of the ground that was always wet and the hard stones that cut into my hands and knees. It was better in summer because of the weather.

When the man was finished he would relieve himself into the fireplace and then walk ahead of me back to the pub. I would wait there for a while longer in case someone else was sent out. If not, I'd go back to stand at the door of the bar where there was some shelter from the elements and where my father would see me when he came out.

On the way home, if it had been a good night, he would bring me some sweets or chocolate. He'd toss them up in the air so that I had to catch them. More times they fell on the ground and I had to search for them in the dark. He would roar laughing watching me. There was never a female born who hadn't a sweet tooth, he'd say. When he drove home he would be whistling and singing. On those nights I was careful to do nothing to annoy him if I could help it. All the men who used me, knew not to get on the wrong side of him. Sometimes, for a bit of sport, he might cheat a newcomer out of more than was normally paid. But his temper was well known and no one risked crossing him.

He brought me round wherever he went. I followed behind him. He was neither proud of me nor embarrassed. He paid me no notice at all but he liked me to be with him, even when there was no business. Why keep a dog and bark yourself, he would say when people remarked on my being with him. And he would laugh when he said it and say that I had all the luck. If he had a good day with me at the cross-roads, he might go early to the pub and not bother to take me. I wouldn't hear him again until the small hours when he'd come in singing and then swearing when he fell over the step into the kitchen.

I was five when they bought me from the orphanage. It was in summer, I remember, because there were primroses and foxgloves growing in the hedgerows along the boreen as we drove up to the house. It was a whitewashed two-story house with a window on either side of the front door and trees growing behind it. I thought it looked like a house in a picture book and I thought to myself this is going to be a nice place, but I was wrong.

My father came on his own to collect me (they never went anywhere together). I was frightened of him from the moment I saw him, but any man I'd met before that frightened me, so I didn't think anything of it. I passed no remark about him and no one asked my opinion. He brought me home in the car that same day. I had nothing to bring with me so there was no reason for delay.

There was just himself and the woman. They lived on a hill farm on thirty acres of land. They had a herd of dry cattle, a few cows and grazing for sheep on the mountain.

From the day I came into the house they called me the orphan.

Sometimes "the girl" but nothing else. I was never called by my name until I left the country because in the orphanage we were known by our numbers only. When I grew up I had to choose a name because the one I had, Eileen, meant nothing to me. I called myself Jude. I saw it written on the front of a hairdresser's shop when I was leaving for the boat and I liked it.

I don't know why he brought me to the house. I never knew. They hardly spoke to me from the day I arrived. And they hardly spoke to one another. She would answer yes or no if he asked for something or gave her an order. I don't know if she resented him for bringing me home. I don't know if he had consulted her.

Anyway I don't think she had any desire for a child or any idea how to mind one. She put my food on the table and she washed my clothes and that was the extent of the care she gave me. I don't think she knew any better. She had no happiness in her life, that was one thing for certain. She seldom left the house and no one ever came to it. She wore the same clothes no matter what the weather and in all the time I was there I never heard her laugh. It was said she was from another parish, from a town land near the sea and that she missed her own people and had never got used to the ways of the mountain men. Her face was melancholy, pale and sharp, the eyes sunken in the sockets as if she were blind. Wherever I was in the house I heard the sound of her heavy sighing as she went about her work.

Though she was never a comfort, I can't say that she treated me badly. I had a room to myself in the back, over-looking the yard. I was let roam the fields. I had the two dogs for company and I worked in the house and helped with the cattle. For the first few years they let me go to the local school. I liked it because it made a change from the house and took me away from him. But the other children rarely talked to me except to taunt me and I had no reason to talk to them. So it was little hardship to me when I was taken away after a few years. The nuns in the convent said it would be more suitable for me to stay at home. I wasn't cut out for study, they said.

I don't know what the woman's opinion was. She never showed that she knew anything about what went on with him. But she must have. There was no way she could have been in ignorance. The whole parish knew. Or at least all the men of the parish. It was never said directly to my face. These things weren't spoken of at that time. But I knew how they talked behind my back.

But whatever she knew or guessed, I never heard her pass any comment on his affairs. She considered them no concern of hers. What he did with me and where he took me was no more pass remarkable to her than the price he got for a sheep or a cow at the market.

She had little enough to say about anything. "Himself" she called him. "Himself will be wanting his tea." "Himself will be fit to be tied if he finds the cows not milked." That was how she spoke. "Mind your own business and I'll mind mine" was the only thing I ever remember her telling me. I don't know if she hated me or only resented me. Maybe it was guilt she felt. She must have been glad, sometimes, because I took the burden off her. If he had used me that day he was less likely to be bothering her. I don't know if they had any normal relations. I never heard a sound of it anyhow though they slept in the same bed always. Maybe that was why he got me. They never had children, whatever the reason. Maybe she couldn't. Or maybe she didn't want them.

The Orphan

But I was better off than some, I know that now. I was well fed and clothed and housed. And not often beaten. That's more than many people can say, I know. Even at the time, I heard stories of what went on in other households. One of the neighbor's daughters got pregnant when she was only thirteen by her brother. She was put out of the house and had to fend for herself from that day on. No one ever saw her again. It was said she went to England. That's what happened to most. The brother went on living in the house and inherited the farm when his father died. He was a great man for sport and a very popular man always.

Anyhow, bad or good I knew no other way of life. There was no use in complaining. There was one thing I was fortunate in. Maybe because of the way I was treated, from an early age, I didn't mature as quickly as other girls. I was not a woman in the physical sense until I was nearly seventeen. And so I was spared the shame of pregnancy. I was terrified of it happening because I knew if I had a baby I would have to leave the farm. And bad and all as my life was there, I knew no one else and nowhere else to go.

When I did become pregnant I said nothing to anyone. Except to Peggy, who worked behind the bar in the pub and sometimes stopped to talk to me when she was coming in for the evening. She knew what went on with the men and she knew what to do about the consequences. She told me I would have to go to England. She told me where to go and she gave me some money.

I went on with my life as usual for the first few months. Either the men didn't notice or it didn't matter to them. I suppose some of them enjoyed it, with my body getting bigger every day so that I looked much older than I was.

I knew where he kept his savings, and the night before I left I took what I needed from the box inside the chimney and a bit more. Early the next morning, I walked into the town to get the first bus while he was still asleep. I left the place forever, with no more to carry out of it than I had brought in.

I got the train to Dublin and then took the boat to Liverpool, and I never saw either him or the woman again from that day to this. Nor anyone else who came from the place.

I got the address I needed when I arrived at Euston Station. It was a private clinic, neat and clean and efficient. It was like a small hospital that they tried to make seem a cozy guest house. It was full of foreigners, Spanish, Italian and Indian women who couldn't have the operation performed at home or not as cheaply. All of the Spanish women were crying because they were Catholic like the Irish and the sense of shame was terrible for them. The staff were English and very polite and helpful and did nothing to make us feel worse which was a blessing.

I felt guilty because I had no guilt. I had no religious beliefs of any kind left me. Still I was half afraid that some of it might come back on me because of all the stories I had heard about punishment and hellfire and the worst sin of all being the murder of an innocent. But as soon as the act was over I felt only relief. And a small bit of guilt at having suited myself and done what I thought was best without consulting anyone.

I made friends with one of the Spanish girls. Her name

was Maria Paloma. She told me the name Paloma meant dove and that she was in for the same thing as me. She was older than I was and had lived in London for several years. We left the clinic together and she said she'd like to take me to tea. She said we'd go somewhere special and she took me to Harrods. And that was the first completely nice thing that ever happened to me.

She became my friend after that. And still is. She was the best friend I ever had except for Peggy, who used to smile at me and give me money sometimes. Paloma said I could move in with her for a bit until I got myself fixed up. She had a flat in Camden near the High Street. She helped me find work as a night cleaner and eventually I moved into my own place in Kilburn with three other girls.

I went on with my life after that. Once the operation was over, I thought I could put it all behind me. The whole of my past had been sucked out of me along with that baby I never saw and never wanted to see. I made a promise to myself to leave everything that had happened back home behind me. The people and the place. I promised myself that no matter what situation I found myself in, in the future, no matter how bad things might be, I would never again let anyone buy the use of me with money. And I've abided by that ever since. It's the one thing in my life I'm proud of.

And the other thing I promised myself was never to breathe a word of what I did to another living soul as long as I lived. Not one syllable. I wouldn't stain myself again with words to describe it. If I said nothing, all the filth that was inside me couldn't escape. And it couldn't be seen. That was the only way to deal with it. To keep it in. To control it. To keep quiet. To go nowhere and say nothing. And keep to my routine of washing. I had a system that I worked out when I was still living on the farm and I kept to it ever since, no matter where I was or what else happened.

A few years later I got a job working in a hospital in the kitchens. I like hospitals because they are orderly and clean. And later on I got a job working for the health board visiting old people in their own homes and helping to bathe them. I loved doing that work. No matter how sick they were, no matter how frail, with their dry, flaking skin and their wrinkled flesh, I didn't mind. They were helpless and at everybody's mercy and I wanted to help them. Apart from my children it was the only time in my life I was able to touch another human being without fear.

After a few years working in the hospital I met Stephan. He was an orderly there and he came from Poland. He was reared in a small town in the provinces and he knew what it was to have grown up in another place. And to be forced to leave and to be a stranger in a new country.

Twelve months later we got married. We lived in Camden where there were lots of Irish but I didn't make friends with them. I was afraid to meet anyone who might have known me before. I was glad Stephan was a foreigner. I could never have lived with an Irishman. He was gentle and laughed often, even though he had sad eyes and I felt he understood some things about me. We lived in a nice house and after a few years we had children. Two boys. We called them Peter and John out of the Bible because I thought it might bring a blessing on them. It was the happiest thing I ever did to choose names for my children. I said their names every time I spoke to them to make up for never having heard my own name all those years.

And so, everything looked all right in my life and in some ways it was. People think that the kind of thing that happened to me would leave a mark on you forever. That you'd look different from other people. That there would be a way of knowing. But there isn't. I look just like anyone else. Ordinary. And people seeing me would think I look happy enough. Ordinary. And maybe I am. I go about my daily life. I cook and clean. I put food on the table. I go to my job. I bring the children to school. My children look like anyone else. And anyone seeing us together would think we were just like any other family. And maybe we are.

Except that I lived with the shame, day in, day out. A shame that was buried right inside me. It was like having a bad smell you can't get rid of. Or a sore that you have to keep hidden. I was always afraid that anyone who got close to me would find out. I was afraid to leave the house until I had washed myself so hard my skin was red. I used to cover myself up to the neck in all weathers. Even on the hottest day I wouldn't take off my sweater or my socks. I couldn't walk barefoot on the beach when we took the children for a picnic. That's how bad I was. Everyone used to laugh at me and tease me for being so modest but it was nothing to do with modesty. It was guilt that it was my fault. That I must be an evil person to have brought this upon myself. I was afraid it might show in my eyes, on my skin or my body, the things that had been done to me. I had the idea that there must be some kind of stain on me that my father could see that made him act the way he did. And if other people ever saw me without my clothes they'd recognize the same thing.

That's what I was frightened of. I was married four years and had two children before I could undress in front of anyone, even my own husband. And the worst part of it was I couldn't talk about it.

My husband suffered more than I did. Now that he's dead I can admit this. I told him, because I had to explain something about the way I was, that I'd been raped when I was a small child. And he always tried to understand. I went through the motions of a physical relationship with him because it was what he wanted. But I never felt anything I was supposed to feel. And though I could do it without any feeling because I'd learned that all my life, afterward I'd have this terrible anger. With the children and especially with him. That hurt him very badly and then I had to try to give an explanation.

Once when he said to me, I want to do this, to be close to you, to show you that I love you. I said to him if you knew what was going on in my head while you were doing it you'd never want to touch me again. And after that he almost never did. That was the saddest thing of all for me because it made him so sad.

I was glad it was boys I had. I don't think I would have been able for girls. I would have been too frightened for them. I wouldn't have been able to let them out of the house. And I wouldn't have known what to tell them. But with boys I didn't have to say anything. I left it to their father. And he was a good man and I knew it would be all right.

The Orphan

I didn't go back for twenty-five years. People used to say, "Do you never go back? You must miss it. It's such a beautiful country?" and I didn't say a word. Once I told Maria Paloma that I'd had problems there. I didn't say what they were but I said it was to do with something that happened to me when I was a child and I didn't want to see anyone I knew from the old days. And she said, if you just drove down no one would have to see you. You could stay in a guest house and go about quietly and have a look at the place and no one would need to see you. But she didn't know what these places are like. She didn't know that the moment a strange car comes into town everyone sees it and half an hour later the people on the furthest farm on the mountain are talking about it. And if the person driving the car is someone they know, even if it's forty years since they were last back, they're recognized and word goes around. And if you don't visit people, or call into the post office or the pub or go to see relations, the whole place would be whispering to know what you were so ashamed of that you couldn't get out of a car to speak to your own people.

But long after that (after I saw your program and decided to go for counseling) the doctor I went to said that sometimes it helped people to go back to the place it happened in. She said that maybe I'd get free of it and be able to move on in my life if I went back and faced them. And she said even if I went to the town and walked around it, it might make a difference. Wear a wig, she said, and dark glasses if you want, but go back.

And so I did. I didn't wear a wig. But I dyed my hair. It had gone gray anyway and I had color put in it. And so I went to Ireland, after twenty-five years, with blond hair and dark glasses and my coat collar turned up.

I flew to Shannon and hired a car. I had it all arranged. I wanted to be able to travel quickly, to sneak in and out unnoticed. A strange car and a strange face.

The first night I stayed in a guest house in a neighboring town. A place I hardly knew when I was living in the area. My father had said it was full of gombeen men and chancers and it wasn't worth setting foot in except on a fair day.

When I stopped the car at the top of the main street and saw the name of the place I came from on a signpost and the distance in kilometers my heart almost stopped beating. I was sick with fear. I wanted to turn back, there and then. If it wasn't that I had borrowed so much money to get there, I think, I wouldn't have found the determination to continue.

I was amazed by how different everything looked, the shops and the houses, all freshly painted and prosperous-looking. Almost every bungalow on the road in from the airport had a notice reading "Guest House—Bathrooms en suite." And seeing that sign gave me courage. It meant I could have somewhere private, where no one would disturb me. The house I chose was on the far side of the village with a Bord Fáilte sign on the door.

My hands were shaking as I rang the bell. A woman came to answer it. She looked friendly and well dressed. She was talkative but not curious and that surprised me as much as anything else. She showed me to my room and asked if I'd like some supper. The walls were covered in pale blue paper with a flower border and the curtains and bedspread were in a matching pink and blue. Every room had central heating, hot and cold water and its own bathroom. It was different from anything I remembered. So modern and comfortable. It was like another country.

I ate some sandwiches downstairs and watched the news on television. There was a program about the divorce referendum. The woman of the house came in with the tea tray. She paid no attention to the discussion on television as if she had heard it all before. When she saw I was watching she asked if I was a stranger and I said yes. And she said, Well it's a nice time of year to be visiting, and that the country was at its best. She asked where I wanted to go and I mentioned a few local places, all but the name of the area where I grew up. And then she said that it would be a pity if I didn't get to see a little village at the foot of the mountain because it was very scenic and not to be missed if I had the time. When she said the name I felt the blood drain from my face and sweat start out on the palms of my hands but I said nothing.

I didn't sleep that night. The next morning I got up early to wash and then went down for some breakfast. I made myself eat though I didn't want to. There were only three other guests in the dining room, an elderly couple and a commercial traveler. They were talking about all the changes in the country and they started to talk about the referendum. The commercial traveler said that it would ruin family life and lead to bitter feuds over land. But the elderly woman said that it was only facing up to facts. Acknowledging the world the way it was.

The man of the house came in and he started to clear my table. When he heard what they were talking about he joined in. He said so long as it didn't spoil the tourist trade he'd be happy. And then he said that the people who'd be worst hit would be the farmers' wives who'd be left with nothing if their men decided to go off with someone else. And the children, of course, no one would suffer as much as the children. He looked at me and said, "As a woman, wouldn't you agree with me?"

I didn't mean to answer him. I didn't mean to draw attention to myself. And I couldn't trust my voice to sound normal when I said anything about parents or children. But I spoke before I could stop myself. I said to him there were worse things could happen to a child than to have its father walk out. I was sorry the second I said it. My face must have looked strange because he seemed embarrassed and said, of course, people had different ideas in other countries. And then his wife came in. She must have heard what I said. She smiled at me as if she felt sorry for me and wanted to cheer me and she said: "Don't mind him—he's like the rest of the men—only terrified that if the women were given the chance we might all find better things to do." She lifted her eyes to heaven and gave him a little swipe on the arm with a napkin as he walked out of the room. "And who knows after all," she said, "he could be right!"

When I drove there it was raining. I saw the name on a signpost again as I drew near the town and once more I thought of turning back because the dread that flooded through me was so strong it wiped out every other feeling.

I had intended to walk about and call into some of the shops and maybe talk to a few people. But when I found myself in the town square looking up at the doors of the

church where I'd gone with my father on Sundays and remembered what happened every one of those mornings on
the way home and that no one spoke a word of protest, even
when they were coming from hearing a sermon, not even the
priests, who must have known what went on, I was so angry
I couldn't bring myself to get out of the car. I sat for a while
with my eyes closed and waited for my heart to calm.

So I drove to the pub outside the town where he used to
bring me in the evenings. I stopped the car at the top of the
boreen leading down to the beach. There was a row of fancy
new bungalows built at the top of the road and at first I
wasn't sure I was in the same place. I got out of the car and
walked. And then just near the pub I saw the house—the
ruined cottage where I used to be brought. The old stone
cottage, with the thistles growing at the door and the fireplace in the back wall where they used to relieve themselves
when they were finished with me.

I went close and stood outside it. I don't know how I
made myself because I was so terrified I could hardly see the
road in front of me. The place still smelled the same, of
urine and cow dung. And the nettles that used to sting my
hands when I fell against them in the dark still grew against
the gable wall. I stood there and the rain poured down on
me and ran down the back of my neck. And the wind blew
through the empty windows and howled in the chimney
exactly as I remembered.

I saw a magpie standing on a branch of a fir tree that grew
out over the broken timbers of the roof. I thought of the
rhyme they used to say long ago: "One for sorrow, two for
joy, three for a girl, four for a boy." And how when I was

young I hardly ever saw more than one at a time and I used to think to myself it was what brought such bad luck to me.

I remembered Peggy then and I wondered was she still working behind the bar. And I remembered that she said to me once, you should look after yourself, you're worth more than this. And that hurt me in a way nothing else that had happened to me did. And it made me cry for the first time because I knew she meant to be kind to me and that was worse than anything else.

I remembered other things then as well: the things all my life I'd wanted to forget but never could, even though I never gave them a moment's thought.

I remembered the way the stones of the ground used to cut into my knees. And the smell of stout from the men's breath and the smell of their cigarette smoke blowing into my face. They would come out of the pub holding a burning cigarette in their hand and they were too expensive to waste in those days. They would keep it between their lips all the time they were using me. I would be sick and choking with it blowing in my eyes and nose. I was only a child and maybe noticed them more. But from that time on I can't abide the smell of cigarettes. And I never smoked one in my life.

I remembered then, too, the names they used to call me when they were finished. They were always angry afterward. "You little whoore," they'd say. "Where did you learn to act like this? You should be ashamed of yourself but sure you're nothing but a little bastard anyhow!"

I went to the fireplace and I stood in front of it, letting myself remember all those things. And I made myself repeat in my head the words I'd been told to say that would make me feel better. I spoke to the child I was then and I said, "I'm sorry for you. I wish I could have protected you but I couldn't. You were only a small child with nowhere to go and no one to help you. But now you're an adult. You can make choices. You can choose where you go and who you go with. No one can make you do what you don't want to do anymore. They can't hurt you that way again. It belongs to the past. Now I live in the present and I can walk away from this place the moment I want to."

I heard voices then coming up the road and I was afraid suddenly. It would have looked demented to be standing there for no reason in the rain. And they would want to know who I was and what I was doing. I might be recognized.

I got into the car and drove without stopping back into town and out the other side again onto the Shannon road. I was crying all the way and I could hardly see where I was going.

I went back to the guest house and I went straight to my room and the bathroom en suite. I went into the shower and began my routine. Have I talked about this yet? The routine I've kept to all these years? No one outside the family knows that I do it. I couldn't tell anyone else. They wouldn't understand. They'd think I was mad. But it's the one thing that's kept me sane all this time. The only way I had of keeping everything in control. And of keeping myself safe and separate from all that happened.

I wash myself in the morning as soon as I get up. I get up an hour before anyone else to give myself time. I have a shower first. Then I begin on my hands. It takes me twenty minutes to scrub my hands clean. Next I put on rubber gloves. They have to be new every day. I lather myself with soap and scrub my hands and arms with a nailbrush. I pay particular attention to my fingers and the space between each finger. The backs of the nails, the cuticle. Then I scrub my arms. I have to work very carefully on the creases of the elbow. It can take ten minutes to clean my elbow properly. Sometimes I use a toothbrush for the really close work. I wash my shoulders and my back and every part of me. Then I do my legs, my thighs, and my knees and the soles of my feet. I spend even longer on my toes than I do on my fingers. I soap and scrub and rinse the soles of my feet and the backs of my ankles twenty-five times. I count. I count aloud all the time I'm washing. It's important that I keep to the same routine every day or I'd be completely lost. As it is, I never want to stop. I never feel I have done sufficient or tried hard enough. But at least if I keep to my numbers I have some sense of control. It doesn't matter, of course, I know that, how thorough I am because I can never get clean. I will never be clean again.

When I got home to England people asked me if I had a good holiday in Ireland. It's such a peaceful place, they said. It must be lovely. And they asked if I saw all my family again. Were they very changed? And they said how excited everyone must have been to see me again after all those years.

And I said yes.

And they asked if I did anything special and I said no, nothing out of the ordinary. But when Maria Paloma asked me the same thing I told her that yes, in fact, I had done one very unusual thing.

I didn't tell her about the pub and going back to the old house and what I said there because I've never told her anything about all that except to say that something bad happened when I was a child (I've kept my promise and never spoken to a soul all these years, only when I went to the doctor who was recommended for counseling) but I did tell her that what I did was different from anything else in my life.

I told her that when I was driving away from the town, I had seen a poster on a telegraph pole with a slogan written on it that had an extraordinary effect on me. I had seen something like it several times before on the way down. The other ones had been billboards; big black-and-white photographs, of a man and woman and a small child, and written underneath the same words: "Hello Divorce, Good-bye Daddy."

She gave me a puzzled look and so I had to explain to her about the government campaign to bring in divorce and how the country was in uproar, with the other side going around putting up posters like this, all over the place to frighten people. And how I had heard people saying that children were very upset by them and others saying that they'd have a lot more to be upset about if divorce came in.

I told Maria that the one I saw near the town wasn't a photograph, just a white cardboard poster wrapped around the telegraph pole with the same slogan. But that for some strange reason, when my eyes fell on those words, written in big black print, exhibited for all to see, a weird emotion flooded through me. Something I'd never felt before. Something like rage. Or excitement.

I knew it was wrong. I knew I would be breaking the law. But the moment I saw those words, I knew I had to do it. Maybe it was knowing I was leaving the place, and would never be back again, as long as I lived. Maybe it was that gave me the courage. And that made it so important.

I stopped the car at the side of the road and got out. The wind was blowing in fiercely from the sea and I was afraid of falling because I was never strong, but it was the only way to manage it. I stood up on the hood and reached up high with both hands and pulled the poster down from the post.

Then I jumped back into the car, clutching it to me, slammed the door and drove like mad to get out of the place. I was terrified that someone might have seen me because someone always sees everything except what they don't want to. I was frightened to death just having it in the car. I felt like I had a bomb ticking on the backseat all the way to the airport.

When I arrived at Shannon I put it at the bottom of my suitcase and checked in my luggage. All the way through the flight I kept looking over my shoulder, in case someone had come after me.

It's the only illegal thing I've ever done, I told Maria. I didn't know I was crying until I felt tears running down my cheek. And when she asked me why I said I didn't know.

She stared at me for a few minutes and I saw how worried she was. But why on earth did you do it? she asked me. She said it was totally unlike me.

And it was. I knew that. But I couldn't explain it because

The Orphan

I hardly understood it myself. I had never done anything like it in my life. I had never broken the rules. Whatever was done to me, I'd kept silent and I'd kept my place. And I had never before taken anything that didn't belong to me.

I looked at her face and into the big dark eyes that were fixed on me with a look of such sorrow. I knew then that was why I was crying. Because of the sympathy I saw. I wanted to tell her not to worry about me. I wanted to say that it was the best thing that ever happened to me. When I tore that poster down and the stiff cardboard came away in my hands, I felt something I'd never let myself feel before. Something that might be like power. The power to decide something and to carry it out. And something else I'd never felt. Completely alive.

I knew I couldn't explain this to Maria Paloma. Not unless I told her the whole story from the beginning. And when I saw the anxiety in her eyes, I knew that one day I would.

And on that day I'd tell her the end of the story. The strangest part of it.

When I got home, at last, after that journey, to my own house in Camden, I took the poster from under the newspaper in the suitcase where I had hidden it going through customs. Then I went into the bathroom. I had already decided what I wanted to do with it. I had thought it all out on the way back, when I was sitting in the plane, flying above the gray clouds that covered from sight the country I was leaving forever.

I put it up beside the mirror above the washbasin in the bathroom. And for a long time, I stood just staring at it.

Reading those words over and over again. At last, a great sense of peace came over my heart.

All my life I'd thought everything that happened was my fault. But at that moment, I saw that it had nothing to do with me. And everything to do with him.

I had called him father when I had to call him something. But he wasn't my father. I had no father. And no mother either. I was an orphan. Everyone knew that. I belonged to no one, and so I belonged to everyone. That's what he used to say.

But now when I see my face reflected in the bathroom mirror and read those words written in black letters beside it: "Hello Divorce, Good-bye Daddy," I know he was wrong. I belong to someone.

I have my house. I have my children. And I belong to myself.

Bishop's House

❧

Mary Gordon

The Morriseys bought their house in County Clare in the early sixties, before the crush of others—Germans mostly—had considered Irish property. It had been a bishop's residence, a bishop of the Church of Ireland, a Protestant, but it had fallen into decay. Repairs had to be done piecemeal. The Morriseys were both editors at a scholarly press, and they had three children who needed to be educated; it was twenty years before the house was really comfortable for guests.

The house looked out over a valley whose expanse could only be understood as therapeutic. So it was natural, given the enormous number of bedrooms and the green prospect, like a finger on the bruised or wounded heart, that the Morriseys' friends who were in trouble, or getting over trouble, ended up in the house. Sometimes these visits were more indefinite than Helen would have liked. But she and Richard must have known, buying such a house, that this outcome was inevitable. And it soon began to seem inevitable that friends from three continents—North America, Australia, where their son had lived, and Europe, where they had numerous connections—were always showing up, particularly now that the Morriseys had retired and were spending May to October of every year at Bishop's House.

∾

Lavinia Willis ran into Rachel, Helen and Richard's daughter, on the 72nd Street subway platform. Lavinia was crying, or rather she was sitting on a bench trying not to cry, but tears kept appearing under the lenses of her sunglasses. She was crying because she'd just broken up a fifteen-year-old love affair, and although she hadn't seen Rachel in three years, Rachel was the perfect person to run into if you were crying behind your sunglasses. You'd be able to believe she hadn't noticed since it was perfectly possible that she hadn't. Rachel was an oboist and she often seemed not to have too much truck with the ordinary world.

∾

She and Lavinia had been roommates at Berkeley during the troubled sixties, but had both avoided politics. Not that they were reactionary or opposed to what the demonstrations stood for. In Lavinia's case, it was that she had a horror of anything that she might understand as performance. In Rachel's case, it was simply that her devotion to her instrument, a mixture of passion and ambition, cut her off from quite a lot.

Lavinia's parents had divorced and remarried, both unsuccessfully, and had divorced and remarried again. When

Lavinia was at Berkeley, they were on their third partners. This made the decision of where to go on holidays a nightmare; even Rachel could see this. For all her musicianly abstraction, she had inherited something of her mother's thin skin for people in distress. She invited Lavinia to come home with her for Christmas of their freshman year.

Lavinia slept on a cot in the living room of the Morriseys' lightless, book-encrusted railroad apartment on the corner of 119th Street and Amsterdam Avenue. But she only did it once; in her sophomore year she left Berkeley to get married. Everyone understood why she'd done it, or at least they understood that it had something to do with the extreme disorder of her parents' lives. Those who thought the marriage was a good thing were happy that Lavinia would have a comfortable and stable home, for clearly Bradford Willis was the essence of stability. Those who thought Lavinia was rushing into something feared she had inherited her parents' heedlessness, a shaky understanding of marriage learned at her parents' joined or separated knees.

But it surprised everyone when, two years into the marriage, when Lavinia was only twenty-one and not finished with her degree at NYU, she became pregnant. Before that, her professors hadn't known quite what to do with her. She was studying history, focusing on the Dutch renaissance; a period she liked because of its subtlety and attention to detail. They could see she was an outstanding student but, since she was married, they were reluctant to suggest graduate school. So it was something of a relief to them when she got pregnant; they no longer had to consider her.

Brad was in a management program at Chase Manhattan,

and his parents were happy to help them with their rent. They lived on 81st Street between Lexington and Third, but moved three blocks north, a year and a half later when, surprising everyone again, Lavinia became pregnant a second time.

In those years, Helen Morrisey was more help to Lavinia than she would have guessed. She'd drop by once a month with a pot of jam and a book for Lavinia to read, something Lavinia in her fatigue had to work hard to concentrate on. But the mental effort reassured her, and she was strengthened by Helen's belief that she was still capable of abstract thought.

Helen would come on a Friday morning—she worked a four-day week—and talk to Lavinia about politics. She was a draft counselor and encouraged Lavinia to get involved but Lavinia said she was in an awkward position generationally; she'd feel uneasy advising men not much younger than herself. She was sure they'd see her as an East Side matron with two children, and it would make her feel finished, done-up. Helen absolutely understood. She left Lavinia the address of congressmen and senators to write to, and Lavinia did, regularly, following Helen's instructions, changing the text of her letters slightly each time in case that would mean something.

She loved Helen because Helen had a way of asking you for things that were a bit difficult for you, but not impossible. You felt enlarged doing the thing she asked you for, and never hopeless. She would do things for you, but she always made you believe they were things she wanted to do, and if she found them too onerous, she'd stop doing them. She made you feel that her life was full but not overcrowded. She and Richard always seemed to have room for people, partly because they worked as a tag team. More than Richard, Helen would suddenly need to be alone, and would wander off sometimes when someone was in the middle of a sentence, leaving Richard to say, to the bewildered speaker, "Yes, yes I know exactly what you mean." They seemed to swim through people, lifting their heads occasionally to offer a meal, a blanket, a magazine. If you were in trouble, they conveyed their belief that your situation was only temporary. They knew you had it in you to overcome whatever was, at that moment, in your way.

They managed to convey that to their own children because the three of them prospered quietly, unspectacularly. Rachel moved back to New York where she taught at the Manhattan School of Music and played in various chamber orchestras. Neal was working in ecological waste management in Melbourne. Clara was the only one who had made money. She and her girlfriend ran a catering business in San Francisco which had, for some reason they didn't understand, become fashionable. When Helen talked about her children she said she felt they all worked too hard. Only Neal had children, two sets, by his two marriages (his first wife had died in a train wreck), but they were in Australia. So Helen had room, in her grandmotherly imagination, for Lavinia's boys. She liked boys increasingly as she aged and grew more boyishly valorous herself, more romantic about the untrammeled, the ramshackle, the hand-to-mouth.

∾

When the boys were ten and eleven, Lavinia went to Teachers College at Columbia for a master's. She got a job teaching history at the Watson School, the best girls' school in New York. She was considered a thrilling teacher, demanding and imperious, although everyone understood this was a mask thrown up by shyness, and that her heart rejoiced and bled at the triumphs and failures of her girls. They adored her; they fell in love with her. She grew, with middle age, into a surprising voluptuousness: her field hockey player's body somehow suddenly understood itself. Men looked at her, as she left her thirties, in the dangerous way they'd looked at her mother, a way that, before this time, she'd tried to forestall.

But as she approached forty, it began to seem pointless to forestall it any longer. She had a series of enjoyable but otherwise pointless affairs. One day she was in the back of a cab, changing under her coat from a silk blouse to a cotton shirt. She'd left the house in the cotton, to keep Brad from suspecting, and had changed into the silk in the cab on the way to the hotel. Now she had to change back, and wipe the perfume from her neck with a Handi-Wipe. She caught a glimpse of herself in the driver's mirror and felt grotesque. She was only thirty-eight; she'd been married eighteen years, she'd done all right with her marriage. The apartment was elegant, they had a nice house for the weekends in Dutchess County. But here she was, changing her blouse in a cab. Her youthfulness seemed like a gift and a challenge it would be not only foolish but ungrateful to ignore. She knew Brad would be hurt, but she imagined it would take him about a year to remarry. He was shocked, at first, mainly by his failure to foresee the breakup. He was more hurt than she knew, but she was right that, within a year and a half, he'd married again, a Swiss woman who sometimes wore little hats to dinner parties, and who ruled his social calendar with an iron hand.

For several years, again to everyone's surprise, Lavinia didn't settle down. Then she met Joe Walsh, who was so clearly *the wrong type* that everyone knew it couldn't last, not long anyway.

But it went on for fifteen years. He was a "player" in the Koch administration, nobody was exactly sure what he did, only that it was something that had something to do with City Hall. When Koch lost, he kept doing whatever it was he did for Dinkins, which was unusual, people thought, and must mean that he really knew what he was doing, whatever that was. As all Lavinia's friends began drinking less in the late eighties, Joe didn't. For a while, people thought it was just that he was drinking as he always had and they noticed it more because they'd stopped. But then they had to admit to themselves—they wondered if Lavinia had admitted it—that Joe was, if not an alcoholic, then a problem drinker. He also kept smoking when everyone else had quit, and even took up cigars. One night, after a dinner at the Morriseys' on 119th Street, he earned Richard's enmity forever by putting his cigar out in the water of a glass bowl Helen had filled with nasturtiums. Richard had grown used to the transgressions of his friends, his children, and his children's friends, but he adored his wife as if they were new lovers, and seeing her face when the cigar sizzled in the nasturtium water, he knew that she felt violated, and this he could not forgive.

It was soon after that night that Lavinia decided she'd had enough of Joe. Fifteen years of feverish arguments followed by feverish lovemaking, sour-mouthed morning accusations, resolutions and recriminations seemed suddenly to settle in her spine like the aftermath of a debilitating fever. She realized that this feeling of bruised exhaustion had become so habitual that she hadn't noticed it. But she noticed it now. And so the next time Joe did something mortifying—he insulted one of their guests on the new color of her hair, asking her who, for God's sake, she thought she was kidding—Lavinia simply said, "I've had enough." It was her apartment they were living in. She gave him a month to find a place to live.

❧

Of course, she would have to go somewhere while he was still in the apartment, and she didn't have time to make plans. But plans had to be made. That was why she was crying when she ran into Rachel on the subway platform. "My parents would love to have you, I know they would," Rachel said. "I'll phone them tonight. You're still at the same number?"

Lavinia said yes she was, that was what was ghastly about it. She was sleeping in her son's room, in the bottom bunk of his childhood bed.

The next morning, Helen phoned as if she knew exactly the right moment to call; it was eleven in the morning but Joe had just left for work. She said that of course Lavinia must come to them, only she'd have to get herself to Bishop's House from Shannon. It was only forty-five minutes, but anyway, Helen said, she'd be happier with her own car, she'd want to see the countryside and not be dependent on the Morriseys to shepherd her.

Lavinia left two days after she spoke to Helen. She slept five hours of the six-hour flight, so she hadn't a lot of time for speculating about what her stay at Bishop's House would be like. She knew it would leave her feeling quiet and without malice—all passion spent was the phrase that kept going through her head. She reminded herself that Helen and Richard were eighty and eighty-two, and was prepared to do a lot of the cooking.

The drive from Shannon was as easy as Helen had said it would be. Lavinia had never been to Ireland before, and kept trying to resist making clichéd remarks to herself about the quality of the greenness. But she couldn't help it; it was so purely green, so without blue or yellow, or purple even, that she wanted it in her mouth, which felt scalded from recriminations, or against her eyelids, which had been abraded by hot tears.

She'd brought a dozen bagels and two pounds of hazelnut coffee, which she knew Helen especially liked. They'd be pleased by the gift, its cheapness, its knowledge of their habits. The coffee smell seeped through the shiny fabric of her suitcase and made her anxious for arrival, anxious to feel at home.

The front of Bishop's House was white stucco; it was surrounded by old trees, elms and chestnuts, at once domestic and venerable. The kind, Lavinia thought, you just don't get in America. There were two cars parked in front of the house, a small white Ford and a black convertible sports car. It was a 1965 Kharmann Ghia, Lavinia knew, because Brad's parents had bought them one as a wedding present. It was in perfect condition and Lavinia wondered if restoring old cars was a hobby Richard had taken up. It seemed unlikely.

How wonderful they looked, Lavinia thought, both of them opening their arms to embrace her. They were so American, the best of America, forthright and reserved and generous. They became more themselves as they grew older, softer and more tolerant. Tears of love came to her eyes and she buried them in the wool of Richard's shoulder.

"I'll take you to your room," Helen said. The huge black front door opened to a hallway, tiled black and white. Almost directly behind the door was a wide mahogany staircase with a red stair carpet that had faded in places from the sun. Lavinia's room was the second door from the staircase; she knew from Rachel that Bishop's House had six bedrooms.

"You look done in," Helen said. "You probably want a sleep, but I'd resist it. Try to stay awake till nine or so, get yourself on Irish time. I'll make coffee and we'll have a walk."

"Look what I've brought you," Lavinia said, flourishing her Zabar's bags.

"Hazelnut," said Helen. "You're a perfect angel, as always. I'm afraid I'm not, neither perfect nor an angel. I'm afraid I'm a bit of an old fool, I've allowed something stupid to happen."

Lavinia's heart sank; she was afraid Helen was going to

tell her that she was ill, or that Richard was, and that she'd have to leave because one of them was going to the hospital. She couldn't bear the thought; she could have taken the illness or death of one of her own parents more lightly than Helen's or Richard's. It was absolutely essential to the well-being of the world that they be in it.

Helen sat down on the bed and patted it so that Lavinia would sit beside her.

"Do you remember our friend Nigel Henderson?"

"I'm afraid I don't," Lavinia said.

"You must have met him one time or another. He and his wife Liz lived next door to us for three years. He was on lend-lease to Columbia back in the seventies. They're English. Perhaps you were too busy with the children."

"I'm not young enough for you to be erasing whole decades," Lavinia said.

"Nonsense, you're a baby. It's just that you're getting over a love affair. It makes everyone feel ancient," Helen said, making Lavinia wonder, for the first time, if she'd been unfaithful to Richard.

"Poor old Nigel," Helen said. "He's sort of a mess. Liz left him for a woman, and he stopped taking an interest in teaching. He shacked up with one of his students and took early retirement. They were going to live in Bali or something but it never came off. She took off instead. Anyway, here he is, no job, no girlfriend, and I'm afraid he's just been told he has terminal cancer."

"How terrible," Lavinia said. "How old is he?"

"Fifty-six."

"My age," Lavinia said.

"So you see when he phoned two days ago, really sounding desperate, asking if he could come over on the car ferry, we didn't feel we could say no."

"Of course not," Lavinia said.

"He's always been a bit pathetic, one of those overgrown boys, but this is really dreadful."

"Dreadful," said Lavinia.

"And dreadful for you. You come here to be petted and recover your spirits and we turn you into an angel of mercy."

"Maybe it'll be good for me," Lavinia said. "Put my own trouble in perspective."

"And there's always the Irish countryside. Nothing can spoil that."

The kitchen was in the basement and was dark, but Helen had made it cheerful with flowering plants and brightly colored pottery. Richard was at the stone sink, filling an electric kettle.

"Angelic Lavinia brought us some hazelnut coffee," Helen said.

"Good God," a voice said from the other darker end of the kitchen. "You Americans can never leave well enough alone."

"This is Nigel," Helen said. "We make him go to that dark corner if he has to smoke."

There are some bodies that belong to a particular time period, Lavinia thought. Medieval bodies, eighteenth-century bodies. Nigel Henderson's was the sixties' model. He was long-legged and narrow-chested; his jeans were tight and he wore sandals with a leather ring for his big toe. His hair was gray and wavy and he wore it to his shoulders.

He walked toward her. "Somehow in all my ghastly years in New York we managed not to meet, which made them even ghastlier."

His eyes traveled from Lavinia's breasts to her thighs in a way that made her feel the time difference. It was four in the morning in New York and she wanted to be asleep.

"I'll just help Helen with the coffee," she said. "We all know Richard's useless."

"Unfair, unfair," Richard said.

"Perfectly true," Helen said. "I only put up with him for his conversation."

∾

Helen walked with Lavinia through what she called "our field." Nothing grew there but grass, and Helen apologized for that. It made her feel like a tourist, she said, wasting the country's riches, but she really wasn't up to raising cattle or even keeping goats.

"I think it's all right, Helen. The country's lucky to have you."

Helen frowned and said something that Lavinia couldn't hear though it sounded like "humbug." She hated being complimented, and Lavinia knew that and felt slapped or slapped down.

"I wouldn't be surprised if Nigel tried his charms out on you. I suppose it's understandable, given what he's facing right now, but it might be a bore for you. On the other hand, it might be amusing for you. I can never tell."

"Tell what?"

"What, or who, young women find attractive. Or anyone, for that matter. Of course he's attracted to you. I suppose it's unfair of us, offering him a bed down the hall from such a sexy girl."

"Hardly a girl, Helen," she said.

"That's how I think of you and I'm sure Nigel does, too."

For a moment, Lavinia liked thinking of herself as a young girl, walking down a street, her step bouncy with the knowledge that all eyes that fell on her desired her. But only for a moment. Then she realized her body was tired, worn out, dried up, and what she wanted was not sex but replenishment and rest.

"Oh, God, Lavinia, I'm afraid we've put you in an awful spot. I hope at least he'll leave you alone to read and walk. And the lake just down the road here is lovely for swimming, if you can bear the cold, which I know you can because of your summers in Maine. I know he can't stand it. He's always complaining about the cold. And he's a late riser. So get up early with me, we'll have breakfast together. I'll make a lunch for you and you can pack it on your back with a book and be on your own. And thank God you have your car."

It sounded like a good plan, a refreshing plan, and Lavinia knew that was what Helen meant. But it made her feel a little sick, both fearful and ashamed, her childhood feeling when she was being packed off somewhere, sent off for someone else's idea of her pleasure.

Richard and Helen didn't modify their policy of leaving their guests to themselves because Nigel had terminal cancer, or because when he was left alone he seemed to do nothing but take over the sofa in the pretty sitting room, empty Richard's whiskey bottles into his Waterford glasses, and fill the clear air with the smoke of his cigarettes. He left the packets—Silk Cuts—in the grate of the fireplace. They collected there until someone—Helen probably—removed them. It was summer, no one was lighting fires. Did he think, Lavinia wondered, that his packets just disappeared? She wanted to say that to him and she wanted to ask him if he thought it was good for someone with terminal cancer to go on smoking, or didn't he feel that all that smoking had brought him to this pass. But she didn't say anything because she didn't want to upset Helen and Richard, who could only go on as they did if they believed their guests were getting on just fine.

Nigel wanted attention—from the Morriseys, from Lavinia—but he went about getting it exactly the wrong way, as wrongheadedly as a child who will never win his parents' love and whose every gesture leaches what little sense of duty they might have. Helen walked in the mornings. Lavinia sometimes joined her but only sometimes, on the days that Helen specially asked her to. She knew if Helen didn't ask her it was because she wanted to be alone. In the afternoons, if it was warm, she swam in the little lake and she did want Lavinia's companionship. Richard didn't swim, but she made him come with her if no one else was swimming, in case "I got a heart attack and disappeared."

She said it matter-of-factly, as she might have said, "In case there are no bananas in the market today." This was the way the Morriseys dealt with their age. Nothing was blinked, but nothing was dwelt on longer than it should be. They always made you feel, Lavinia thought, that they knew how to live. That was why it was good to be around them, and that was why Lavinia said nothing to Nigel, even at his most unpalatable.

She said nothing when she opened the door after her bath and found him leaning on the wall right across from the bathroom, slouched against it like a juvenile delinquent, smoking one of his endless cigarettes. And she said nothing when, one night, he'd had too much wine to drink and went on a tirade about what he called today's woman. "Womb-man. They have a womb but they want to be men.

"I mean, for God's sake," he said. "Anatomical differences count for something. Men have more strength. Women can bear and nurse children. I mean, shouldn't that tell us all something? Or am I quite mad? Perhaps I am quite mad. That's what Liz thought. No, I'm wrong. That's not what she thought at all. She just thought I was stupid. Plain stupid. 'You think with your cock,' she said. That was her greatest insult. And precisely that dyke's greatest asset. Made her brain clean: no cock to cock it up."

"I'll just make coffee for everyone," Helen said.

Richard suggested that perhaps one day soon, if the weather was good, they might all drive up to Coole Park, where Lady Gregory had lived, and see the tree where Yeats and Synge had carved their names.

"I mean really that's what it was all about with Liz. She couldn't stand that I had a penis and she didn't. That's what it all came down to. She rejected my penis out of her own bloody envy at not having one."

"I think that's been considered, and rejected as a theory," Lavinia said. She looked at Richard's disappointed eyes, and wished that she'd kept her resolve of saying nothing.

"Wall, wot wuz yer problem," Nigel said in what he thought was an American accent. "Was your husband's cock too big or not big enough?"

"Nigel, you must go to bed now," said Helen. "You seem overtired."

He covered his face with his hands. Lavinia thought that his hands were his best feature; he should have covered his face with them all the time. Then she could see that he was weeping. His shoulders shook and he began sobbing loudly, with no impulse to silence himself or to stop.

"I'm not overtired, Helen. As you perfectly well know. I'm drunk, and I'm dying."

It would have helped if there were some background noise: the ticking of a clock, the rumble of a dishwasher. Even the chirping of a cricket. But there was no sound in the room at all; it was a mark of how simply the Morriseys lived. And simply, they had to sit in the tumult of noise Nigel was making and endure it, unadulterated. Then Nigel stood and shook himself like a wet dog. He walked up the stairs, saying good night to no one.

"Oh, God," Helen said after she'd heard his door close. "I behaved like a fool. The poor, poor desperate creature. He's dying and he has not one real human connection. And I made it worse."

"No, Helen," Richard said.

"Well, I didn't make it better."

"That's as may be," he said. "But you didn't make it worse and there's a difference."

"And you did make it better, both of you," Lavinia said. "He feels less alone here. Less as though life were ridiculous, or hopeless or absurd. You make everyone feel that."

"Well, we could all use a rest," Richard said, pointing the way up the staircase, which Nigel had climbed in the dark.

Lavinia couldn't sleep. There was a full moon and the muslin curtains didn't keep it out. It made a pool of not quite light—but illumination—on the oak floorboards. She thought of all the people who'd slept in this room before. Most of them long dead. And Nigel was facing death alone. What was it like for him? Was he looking down a long, dark corridor? A tunnel? Or into an endless sky or into an endless well? She wondered if he was terrified or numbed. She wondered what it would be like for her.

I would be different. She would have her children, her friends, students whose lives she'd touched. It wouldn't be what it was for Nigel: that horrible aloneness, that sense that you'd been given a life, that it was being taken from you and you'd done nothing with it but make a mess.

She was thinking of him so intensely that she wasn't surprised when she saw the knob turn, and the door open. He stood in the doorway, framed by the light from the hall.

"Do you mind?" he said.

"No, not at all."

He walked directly to the bed and sat down on it. She propped herself up on her elbow. He kissed her; his mouth was rough from cigarettes and wine. His hair was a little unclean and she could smell his armpits, not dirty, exactly, but unfresh. None of that mattered. He was alone and he was dying. She could give him this, if this was what he wanted. They both knew that it could be his last time.

He nuzzled her breasts halfheartedly, he knew what he was after. He didn't make much attempt to arouse her, they both knew it wasn't about that. He finished, and lay on top of her a few moments. Then he said, "At moments like these, I need a cigarette. Do you mind if I turn on the light?"

She put on her nightgown and looked around for an ashtray, but of course there wasn't one.

"It's all right, I'll flick it out the window."

"Careful," she said. "We don't want to wake Richard and Helen."

"What's the matter? You don't want them to know what you've been up to?"

"No, I don't want to disturb their sleep."

"What do you think they'd say? That you were a nasty girl, or an angel of mercy? Jezebel or Florence Nightingale?"

"There's no need to be unpleasant."

"I don't do it out of need. I just seem to be rather good at it. Which is why I find myself alone most of the time."

He was challenging her to meet his eye, but she wouldn't.

"It's remarkable how many friends a death sentence brings you. For instance, yourself. You'd never have let me have you if you didn't think I was on my way to never-never land.

"That's not true."

He snorted. "Oh, get off it. You're not going to tell me

you're fond of me, or that you found me strangely irresistible. You fucked me because you think I'm going to die."

"Nigel, there's no need for this."

"You're feeling quite good about the whole thing," he said. "You feel generous and mature, and womanly. You gave of yourself. The supreme sacrifice. Like wartime. Give him a little of what he fancies before the cannonball gets him. But suppose I told you it was all bullshit? Suppose I told you the biopsy report came back and I was given a clean bill of health?"

"I don't believe you," she said.

"Oh, my dear, it's quite true. I did have a tumor. You see here." He took her hand and made her feel an indentation in his thigh. "The quacks said it was quite possibly malignant. Well, I was scared at that, and I fell apart, rather. And I told people, I thought, why the hell not. And people were wonderful. I mean, fucking heroic. Better to me than they'd ever been. And of course whose parental bosom did I want to rest my head on but good old Helen and Dick? Normally, I wouldn't have had the nerve to invite myself. But I called up, told them the news calmly, like a good soldier. So they said, of course, dear, come right over on the fucking car ferry. Only just before I left, the doctor called. Quite thrilled. Benign, old chap, he said. Apparently I'll live forever.

"Well, I couldn't tell Helen and Richard that. Think how disappointed they'd be. Dying, I had a certain tragic interest. Healthy, I'm just a pathetic pain in the ass. And think how they've always loved being the still clear pond for the world's lame ducks. Why, they wouldn't know what to do with themselves if everyone's lives were shipshape. They must know it. Certainly you know it. Still, they are a couple of old dears. And not as young as they once were. Which is why I know you'll keep our dirty little secret. Won't you, love?"

He reached over to kiss her.

"You're disgusting," she said.

"That's as may be, but I've just fucked you, haven't I?"

"Get out," she said.

"Right you are. And I'll clear out in the morning. Everyone will understand that I'm abashed after my little weeping fit last night. And I'll let them know you were a real help. A great comfort."

∾

She wanted to go to the bathroom to brush her teeth. Her mouth felt foul from his foulness. But she didn't want him to hear her doing it.

She wondered if it were possible to make him believe that the whole thing meant nothing to her. That she went to bed with anyone, absolutely everyone, because it was easier than saying no. But she had no idea how she would do that.

He wasn't stupid. He seemed to understand things very well. He'd even made her see the Morriseys in a way she must always have known was possible, but had always avoided. Were they parasites, feeding off the misery of others for their own prosperity? Was the misfortune of those they called their friends the elixir that kept them safe? That kept them from the kinds of risks that could distort or wreck a life? The kinds of risks she'd taken, and her parents had, and

Nigel and his wife and his wife's girlfriend? But not the Morriseys. And not their children.

She'd have to stay a couple more days so it wouldn't appear that her leaving had to do with Nigel's. Perhaps the day after tomorrow they'd all go to Coole Park. She'd take them out to a good restaurant. They'd talk about Nigel, the pity of it, the waste. They would say she must come back to Bishop's House again soon. Perhaps next summer.

But she wouldn't. She couldn't now. And when the Morriseys came back to New York, what would happen then? They were getting older. They'd be needing help. But there would be hundreds of people who'd want to help them, grateful, eager people. They wouldn't need her.

After a while they might say, "We haven't heard much of Lavinia lately." They'd assume it was because she was happy.

The Facts of Life

❧

Katy Hayes

I opened up the door. They stopped unpacking and stared at me. The blondy one looked friendly, but the dark one didn't.

"What di yi want?" said the dark-haired one.

"I want to know which is my bed?"

"Yir bed?" And they looked at each other and then looked back at me, horrified. "Yir ti young ti be in here wi us. What age are yi?"

"Eleven. But I'll be twelve next month. Aren't we supposed to speak Irish?"

"Yi only haf ti speak airish when someone's listening ti yi," said the blondy one.

"Yir ti young. We're fourteen. We can't haf a young one in her wi' us," said the dark one.

I hung my head. I felt my cheeks hot up, and my eyes start to prickle and I knew I was going to cry. Cry like an eight-year-old. My mum had told me to behave like a big girl, but how could I when these girls knew by looking at me that I was young? And I hadn't wanted to come to Donegal to learn Irish. I was sent on account of my mum being sick after the new baby.

"What's yir name?" said the blondy one, kindly.

"D-d-d-deirdre," I said, doing my best.

"Mine's Mary, but here in the Gaeltacht, it's Máire. And this is Róisín."

"She's ti young," said Róisín. "We want a girl our own age."

"I prefer hir," said Máire. "I like hir hair. It's real long. I can practice on it." And then she turned to me. "I'm going to be a hairdresser when I leave school."

Her own hair was lovely. It had those big curls that you get from using rollers.

"I haf a curlin' tongs. I'll do yir hair in the morning before yi go ti lessons. I need all the practice I can get, 'cause I'm engaged, secretly, ti my boyfriend Marty, he's eighteen, and in two years time, when I do my O levels, I'm going to leave school and marry him but I'll need a job. I can't practice on Róisín's 'cause hir ma won't let hir have long hair 'cause a nits."

"I want ti be a nurse," Róisín said.

"I want to be an actress, or an ambulance man," I said.

"That one is yir bed," Máire said.

"Where are yi from?" Róisín asked.

"Dublin," I said.

"We're from Belfawst," they said together.

&

From then on, they were dead nice to me. Máire cried a lot, but this was because her brother got killed in the Troubles only two months ago and she wasn't over it yet and her ma was having a breakdown. Máire was the youngest and she had six older brothers, and one was in the H Blocks, and one was on the run, and one was in a wheelchair after being shot joyriding, and one was killed by loyalists.

"Pigs," Róisín said.

"Who?" I asked.

"Dirty Protestant pigs," Róisín said.

I was afraid to tell her that I had a cousin who was a Protestant because my auntie Jean had turned into one.

"Di yi know that they wash themsels in their own urine?" said Róisín.

"No." I hadn't known that. My mother was cross when my aunt Jean turned into a Protestant. Maybe this was the reason. But I had never seen Auntie Jean wash herself in anything but water. Still, Róisín knew more about Protestants than I did. Maybe it was only Northern Protestants who washed themselves in their own urine.

Every morning, Máire brushed my hair and tied it back, and on Tuesday for the céilí she did my hair with the curling tongs and tied it up on top of my head with ribbons. She had loads of jewelry in a box that played a tune when you opened it and she lent me a necklace and earrings to go with my good dress. Máire and Róisín were giggling and laughing a lot before the céilí and winking at each other because a boy had asked Róisín to go with him. Máire wouldn't go with anyone because she had to be faithful to Marty, back home in Belfawst.

"Did you know that Marty looks like Bruce Springsteen?" said Máire.

"Oh," I said.

"Yes," said Máire, "he has the same hair and the same jeans."

"I like Bruce, but I love Elvis," said Róisín.

"I love Elvis ti," said Máire.

Róisín had a tape that she'd made off the radio and she played us some songs every night. There was Bruce Springsteen and Elvis and the Beatles and "Tubular Bells." Elvis sang "Are You Lonesome Tonight" and we loved that, and Bruce Springsteen sang "Born to Run" and we loved that too.

Róisín liked the boy at the céilí and danced with him all night. He asked her up for the Bolli Limini. I asked Máire what this was, and she said that it was Irish for the Walls of Limerick. Róisín was being walked home by the boy, which was great because I wanted to get Máire on her own. When we got to the crossroads we could see that there were boys and girls in the field there, lying in couples, kissing, I think. We tried to see was Róisín there but it was too dark. We had a right laugh, and drank our Coke and ate our crisps. And it was so dark we nearly couldn't see each other.

"I wonder did he buy Coke and crisps for Róisín?" laughed Máire.

"Should he?" I asked.

"Yes, definitely," said Máire. "A boy should buy a girl Coke and crisps. If he doesn't, yi shouldn't kiss him, 'cause he'll never appreciate yi."

"Does your Marty buy you stuff?"

The Facts of Life

"All the time. He has a job, he works at Shorts like his da, so he has the money ti. Yi haf ti be treated right, or it's no good."

"Máire," I said, glad it was dark 'cause I was embarrassed. "Would you tell me about the facts of life?"

"Yi don't know?"

"No. Because I've got no big sister to tell me things."

"Yir eleven, aren't yi? That might be a bit young. I'll tell yi what. I'll ask Róisín what she thinks, and if she agrees, we'll tell yi."

"Thanks, Máire."

"Di yi know anythin'?"

"I know that babies come out from the mother's tummy. I've felt our babies kicking about in there. I don't know how they get in there though. That's what I want to know."

∽

I loved sharing the room with Róisín and Máire, and I was dying for them to tell me the facts. A few days went past, and they didn't say anything, but then one day they called me out to the stream for a chat.

"Deirdre," Róisín said, "Máire was tellin' me that yi want ti know the facts, and we're sorry but we think that yir ti young. Eleven is ti young for the facts."

This was terrible news. For the first time, I felt really angry with the two of them. It was just so mean. I felt my cheeks get hot and my eyes start to prickle.

"But ti make up for it, we haf some good news for yi. There's a boy wants ti dance wi yi at the céilí and walk yi home. He asked me ti ask yi."

161

"What boy?"

"His name is Declan Moore and he's from Galway. He's staying down in McGinleys', he's their cousin. Y'iv seen him. He was in front of us at Mass, and he wears Adidas runners."

I had seen him. He was a nice-looking boy. He had smiled at me in Mass and I had smiled back.

"He's twelve," Máire said. "Just the right age. A boy should be one year older than a girl."

"Well, your Marty is four years older than you," I said nastily, "so he must be too old."

"That's what my mother said, that's why our engagement is a secret, but I love him," Máire said.

"She really loves him," Róisín said.

I felt mean, getting at her like that.

"I never showed yi the ring, because I don't show it ti people until I get ti know them well," Máire said. "Would yi like ti see it?"

"Yes," I gasped.

She put her hand down the front of her dress and pulled out the ring, which dangled on a golden chain.

"Would yi like ti touch it?"

"Yes, yes please."

"It's called a solitaire," she said. "That's when there's a single diamond."

"It's beautiful," I gasped.

"Would yi like ti try it on?" she said.

"I'd love to."

She slid the ring gently along my finger. It was too big, but the metal against my skin sent shivers down my spine.

"He had ti save up for a whole year. He had a post office book, and eight weeks ago, a week after our Jimmy got killed, he took me out ti buy it."

I handed her back the ring.

"So he's still savin', now for a house, 'cause he wants us to live away from the Troubles, so that's why I need ti get the job in the hairdresser's."

Máire put it on her finger and then wandered off toward the stream, looking sad.

"I don't know how she'd keep goin' without Marty," Róisín said. "She really loves him."

I didn't mind anymore about them not telling me the facts. I had a friend who was engaged!

∾

I met Declan at the céilí the next Tuesday. Máire and Róisín had spent ages getting me done up, and my hair was lovely. He was nice, and he asked could he walk me home. He didn't buy me Coke and crisps, though, I had to buy that myself. But I didn't mind. I even kissed him, on the lips. On Saturday, when we had no lessons, I met him down by the stream. We lay down on the bank, and he kissed me on the cheeks.

"Declan," I said, "do you know the facts?"

"What facts?"

"The facts of life. Where babies come from and all."

"From their mothers' tummies," said Declan.

"I know that, but how do they get in there?"

"I dunno," he said. "Why do you want to know?"

"I just want to know."

"I'll ask my cousin Kevin. He'll know. He's fifteen."

I had seen Kevin at Mass. He was tall and cross-looking, and his clothes were dirty. Sometimes he smiled at me and said hello. He was good-looking like Declan, but rougher.

∾

The next Tuesday, Declan never showed up at the céilí and the next Saturday I went to meet him at the stream and he didn't show up there either. Kevin came instead.

"You're Declan's girl."

"Yes," I said.

"He's gone. His mother came to collect him."

"Oh."

"Declan said that you don't know the facts of life."

"No," I said, "and I've been trying to find out for ages, but nobody will tell me."

"What age are you?"

"Thirteen," I said, telling a lie. "Would you tell me?"

"I might," he said, and he smiled. He was quite good-looking.

"I'll meet you at the céilí next Tuesday, and I'll walk you home and I'll tell you then."

∾

I was delighted. I couldn't wait. At Mass the next day Kevin looked around at me and winked a few times. I told Máire and Róisín that I had got myself a boyfriend on my own.

"Who is he?" Róisín asked.

"He's Kevin McGinley. He's a cousin of Declan."

"But he's too old for yi. What age is he?"

"He's fifteen," I said.

"Cradle-snatcher," Róisín said.

"Máire, will you do an extra special job on my hair next Tuesday and lend me a dress?" I asked. " 'Cause I want to look sophisticated."

"He's ti old for a wee girl of eleven," Máire said.

"Well, if he's too old for me, then your Marty is too old for you," I said.

"Máire loves Marty," Róisín said.

The next morning, while Máire was doing my hair for school, she said:

"Deirdre, I've been thinking, and I will help yi get ready for Kevin. I was eleven when I met Marty, so it wouldn't be fair if I didn't help yi."

"Thanks Máire," I said.

"But don't say ti much about it ti Róisín, 'cause she's not romantic. Who knows, maybe yirsel' and Kevin might get engaged in a few years time."

ॐ

Róisín and Máire had a row over me and Kevin, and Róisín wouldn't let us listen to her tape, but it had blown over by Tuesday. I didn't like to be the cause of a fight between them, so I was glad that the tape was playing while Máire was curling my hair. Elvis and Brucc and "Tubular Bells." Máire gave me a blue dress. It was a bit big, but it looked all right with a cardigan. And she put blue eyeshadow on me and pink lipstick.

"Noi yir set," said Máire. "Isn't she a picture?"

Róisín grunted.

"Thanks Máire, it's lovely. I'm so excited," I squealed.

"Gawd. I was like that when I was yir age. It's lovely ti be young," and Máire sighed at Róisín. Róisín relented.

"Aye."

∽

I danced with Kevin for the Bolli Limini and for a few more dances, and we left early because I was afraid that Róisín might stop me if she saw me. Kevin bought me a Coke and crisps and a Mars, and I ate them as we walked along. It was the middle of August, so it was getting dark earlier.

"That's a lovely dress," he said.

"Thanks."

"Is it your own?"

"Yes."

"Good," he said.

"Why?" I asked.

"It might get messed in the field."

"The field? What field?"

"The one by the crossroads. We'll go there."

"What about the facts?"

"I'll explain them to you there."

∽

We got to the crossroads, and Kevin jumped down into the field.

"Jump," he said.

I could see nothing, just blackness in front of me.

"Jump," he said. "I'll catch you."

So I closed my eyes and jumped. Sure enough, he caught me.

"We're the first here," he said. "There's always a big crowd down here after the céilí."

He took my hand and led me to the far side of the field.

"Lie down," he said.

He lay down beside me and leaned over to me and kissed me. Then he stuck his tongue into my mouth. It was disgusting.

"Did you like that?" he asked.

"No," I said.

It had made me want to vomit.

"You'll get used to it."

Then he started doing something to himself, but I couldn't see in the dark. He was moving his hands real fast up and down and there was a noise like the sea flapping onto the beach. Then he started to grunt and lay on top of me and wriggled and grunted and wriggled some more and then stopped with a loud grunt, and he flopped on top of me. For a moment I thought he was dead. Then he said:

"Thanks."

I had no idea what he was thanking me for.

"So, that's the facts, but I didn't go inside 'cause you're too young. This is what's called 'not going all the way.' "

What was the facts? Was I completely stupid that I couldn't cop on to these facts?

He was still flopped on top of me and he kissed me on the lips and stuck his tongue in again. Disgusting.

Then slowly I started to get cold. He got off me, and I realized that the field was damp. The back of my dress was wringing wet and I was covered in grass. Máire would be furious. And maybe we lay down in a cow pat for all I knew. I wanted to go home. I was glad it was dark, so he couldn't see me.

Kevin walked me as far as my house, and he pushed me up against the cowshed and I opened my mouth to say good night, and in shoved his tongue again and I swear I nearly bit it, I was so sick of this tongue business.

"Good night, you're a lovely girl," he said. "Dublin girls are the best."

Best at what?

I turned toward the house in dread. Máire was going to be raging about her dress. Maybe I could manage to sneak it into the wash without her seeing it.

I tiptoed to our door, and I could hear sobs from inside. Oh no, I thought, another of Máire's brothers had been shot.

I opened the door and the two of them were sitting there, tears streaming down their faces.

"What's wrong?" I asked.

Both of them gulped and started to cry again.

"What's wrong, what's happened?" I said, and I shook Róisín by the shoulder.

But she was sobbing so hard she couldn't speak.

"Elvis died," Máire said.

"Elvis died!"

"Yes Elvis is dead, he died of a heart attack in Memphis this afternoon." And Máire started to cry again.

"Ohno!" I cried.

"Play it again," said Róisín.

Máire pressed Play.

Are you lonesome tonight, do you miss me tonight, are you sorry we drifted apart? Does your memory stray, to a bright summer's day, when I kissed you and called you sweetheart? Do the chairs in your parlor seem empty and bare? Do you gaze at your doorstep and picture me there?

And both Róisín and Máire started to howl.

Is your heart filled with pain, shall I come back again? Tell me dear, are you lonesome tonight?

"Elvis is dead," howled Róisín.

Elvis was dead. I wrapped my cardigan around me to cover the dress and I cried too.

Son, Moon and Stars

༄

Jennifer Johnston

The room was dark; dark walls, dark furniture and the curtains were pulled over, only a narrow crack of light lying across the floor. The old lady lay on the bed staring up into the darkness of the ceiling.

Kate wondered what she saw up there.

Nothing very interesting, was Kate's considered opinion.

Apart from anything else she had never considered her grandmother to be a very interesting person.

Kind, generous, loving; not very interesting.

About three out of ten, Kate would have given her for being interesting.

She pulled at the corner of the curtain with a finger and thought how mean she was to be so critical of her grandmother.

The sun was shining and across the road on the strand she could see four men on horses galloping by the frilling edge of the water.

Below them their reflections galloped upside down among the reflected clouds.

Now, that was quite interesting, she thought.

"Don't fidget," said the frail old voice. "You make me nervous when you fidget."

Kate sighed inside her head and let go of the curtain.

"My head hurts. When I get nervous my head hurts."

"I'm sorry."

She moved across the room and sat on the chair by her grandmother's bed.

"What day is it?" The words rattled in her throat, like as if they didn't want to come out into the air.

"Sunday."

"Are you sure?"

"I only come on Sunday, Granny."

The old woman turned her head slightly toward Kate, but her eyes still remained fixed on the ceiling.

"Why?"

"That's the arrangement. Every Sunday."

"Why?"

"I don't know. I go to school the other days. You know . . . Monday to Friday."

"Monday to Friday."

The eyes were pale. They had been blue, Kate remembered that, but now a milky mist covered their brightness.

Abruptly they closed and the old woman appeared to be asleep.

Quite silently, unbreathingly asleep.

Kate stared at her; the mountain of her under the crumpled bedclothes.

I hate this. I hate these Sundays. I hate being frightened. That's what she's doing, she's frightening me. She's pretending to be dead. If she died and I was sitting here beside her, I think I would die too.

Death would invade the whole room. Aunt Millie would find us both here when I didn't answer her call to come down for tea. The eyes opened again and resumed their perusal of the ceiling. Kate took a deep breath; the black bat of death had flown away for the time being.

"I don't know who you are."

"Yes, you do, Granny. I'm Kate. I'm Kate. I'm Derek's daughter."

"Derek." The familiar name lay happily on the old lady's lips for a moment. A ray of sunshine caught the beveled edge of the dressing table mirror and a rainbow danced in the air. "Where is my son? I need my son."

Kate didn't quite know what to say. She, too, needed to see her father.

She had written him three letters. She had given them to Mummy to post. She had had no reply. "I think he's in London. Yes. He's been over there for ages."

"I need to see him. All is not well here. You know that, of course."

"I'm sure he'll be home soon."

"I need to see him." Tears bubbled from her eyes and began to course their way through the furrows of her cheeks.

"Need," moaned the old woman. She raised a heavy hand and began to rub at her face.

"I'll get Aunt Millie." Kate stood up and headed for the door.

"No, no, not Millie," shouted the old lady. "I don't trust Millie. I don't want Millie interfering. I want Derek. Here, you, person, come back and sit beside me." She banged impatiently on the bed with a hand. Kate obeyed, reluctantly. A hand was clamped around hers. "Millie thinks I don't understand."

"Don't understand what, Granny?"

"Anything. About the boy."

She realized that her grandmother was staring at her, her eyes blue slits in the crumpled flesh of her face. Was she really a wolf in a grannie's clothing? Hardly. Not too many wolves in Ireland. None, to be precise. Except of course in the zoo, skulking meanly behind wire. They looked a bit moldy, longing no doubt for the Rocky Mountains or the vast forests of the Russian steppes. Anywhere, but not here in Dublin.

"Do you know about the boy?"

Sometimes, Kate thought as she studied her grandmother's face, she does this on purpose. She is watching me, laying a trap of some sort for me. I don't like that. It's like being at an exam, everyone watching you to see how much you know.

"What boy?" Or don't know. That was more like it. Don't know. I don't know what she's getting at this time. The finger twitched impatiently on her arm. It must be nearly teatime. Kate crossed her fingers and willed Aunt Millie to plod up the stairs.

"That boy. I don't remember his name. Can't remember. I can't remember anything these days. Nothing. I must get up." She gripped Kate's arm and tried to shift herself across the bed.

"You'll have to help me." She gripped and pulled.

"Granny . . . You can't get up. You know that. I'll call . . ." Two hands now clawed at her arm. The old lady's face had become red with the effort she was making to throw herself out of the bed. "Please," said Kate. "Please Granny, you're going to hurt yourself."

The old woman let go of Kate's arm and lay back into the pillows, panting, her breath grating in her lungs. Her eyes turned once more toward the ceiling, as if up there in the darkness she could see her secrets. "I want to see him. He tells me about little things he does in school. He brings me the pictures he paints. He is my little love."

Downstairs the doorbell rang. Kate could hear Aunt Millie's steps on the parquet floor of the hall. Oh dear God, please don't let this arrival delay tea, she prayed inside her head.

"That would be them now." With an effort the old lady raised her right hand to her head and patted at her thin hair. Kate remembered only a couple of years back, her grandmother sitting on the chair in front of the dressing table brushing her long hair with the heavy silver hairbrush, before plaiting and winding it into a bun at the back of her head. She remembered the way on winter days the sparks crackled as the brush passed down the length of hair. She remembered the flickering fingers, braiding, the hair thick and soft, and then twirling it round with one hand as she plucked the hairpins from Kate's outstretched fingers with the other.

Voices murmured in the room below.

"Who, Granny?" she asked.

Nobody usually came on a Sunday. Sunday was Kate's day. It had been so for ages.

Before Grandpa died, before Granny had retired to her bed with her broken heart. Sometimes Daddy would come too and he would swing her up onto his shoulders and gallop like the horses along the edge of the sea.

She wondered again if he had got the three letters she had sent him. Probably not, she thought. Mummy was not very reliable when it came to things like posting letters.

"Them. He. The little pet. Your father's son."

Kate laughed. "Daddy doesn't have a son, Granny. He only has me. I am his son, moon and stars." The joke, one that she always loved when he said it in his deep laughing voice, sounded silly now, spoken by her. The old woman's eyes glittered for a moment.

"No," she said. "Oh, no, no, no. We have a secret. I mustn't tell the secret."

There was silence in the room. Kate wondered about broken hearts. When, a couple of months ago, she had knocked one of Mummy's Venetian goblets off the mantelpiece, it had lain in the hearth like a spiky pool of blood, sparks of light had glittered gaily, and the powdered glass had been like snow. "Don't touch it," someone had said as she bent down to get a closer look. "You'll cut yourself." It's probably a bit more disgusting than that, she thought. A bit more like a butcher's shop.

The old woman was scrabbling again to raise herself in

the bed. "You, you child help me. I have to get up. I have to."

Kate put out her hand and touched her grandmother's soft arm. "You can't get up, Granny. You know that. If there is something you want, I'll call Aunt Millie."

"I have to." She began to scream; a thin, frightening sound. She hauled herself around until she was lying on the very edge of the bed, one more move and she would be on the floor. She screamed again. "I have to see him. Will no one let me see him?"

Kate ran to the door and threw it open. "Aunt Millie. Come, come quickly. Please. Granny's . . . oh, please come quickly."

Footsteps scurried in the dark hall and she saw her great-aunt's alarmed face at the bottom of the stairs, and behind her another figure. The old woman continued to scream. Aunt Millie's breath came in little hiccups as she ran up the stairs. Snail, thought Kate. Crawling snail. Hurry, snail. Aunt Millie pushed her aside and ran into the room. Kate recognized her mother's alarmed face at the bottom of the stairs; her hand lay white on the banister. There was no certainty in her stance.

The light came on behind her and her grandmother's voice became dizzy in Kate's head. Aunt Millie called out "Una. Una. If you could come up . . ."

Her mother started on the journey, up the stairs; the hand on the banister coming closer and closer.

". . . just a few minutes. You could give me a little hand. She's so heavy. I can't . . ."

Her mother touched Kate on the shoulder and went into the bedroom.

"No," shouted Granny. "I won't have that woman in my house." Her voice was clear and unequivocal. "No. I won't have her near me."

Someone closed the door and Kate was left in the dark. Slowly she went down the stairs and across the hall. She opened the hall door. The sun was still shining. The tide was sweeping in across the sand in great arcs, leaving wrinkled sand hills bare and forming pools and swiftly running streams in the hollows. The horses were gone. The reflections now were sky and clouds. Birds pecked on the sand. Soon they would be gone and the sea would wash against the granite wall.

Softly, wash softly. Today, softly. She could imagine it now in her head, a sad noise. Today every noise would be sad.

She sat down on the top step and leaned her head against the railings and thought about the son, moon and stars and the little boys bringing presents and broken hearts and brushing long crackling hair and the sea that kept coming in and in and softly washing the granite wall.

"What on earth are you doing out here in the cold? Piles. You'll get piles." That, of course was Aunt Millie. Always fuss, fuss, fuss.

"Kate?" Mummy's voice was fractious.

"And no coat." Aunt Millie.

"It's time to go home, darling. Get your bike, there's a good girl." Kate got up. Her behind was numb and slightly damp from sitting on the steps. Was that how piles started?

What were piles anyway? Why did no one ever tell you anything? Why did no one answer letters? Why did people say silly things they didn't mean?

She went down the steps and round the house to the back door where her bike lay against the wall. She could hear their voices murmuring, whispering secrets. She could hear the grass growing. She could feel herself getting old. Her mother was waiting at the gate.

"Say good-bye to Aunt Millie, darling."

"Good-bye, Aunt Millie."

The old lady waved cheerfully from the top of the steps.

"Say, 'see you next Sunday.' "

Kate's eyes filled with tears. "Say it," her mother whispered fiercely. "For heaven's sake, Kate."

"See you next Sunday," she called out.

"Lovely, dear."

Aunt Millie went and closed the door.

"It's not their fault," her mother said as they got onto their bikes. After that they pedaled in silence for a long time. The chain on Kate's bike needed oiling and made a little scrunching sound each time she turned the pedals. They cycled toward the setting sun. To see, you had to hold one hand up in front of your eyes.

About halfway home her mother spoke.

"Daddy's not coming home, you know. Perhaps I should have told you before, but I . . ."

Kate dropped her hand down to the handlebars and the sun suddenly seared into her eyes.

". . . didn't. I didn't really know what to say. I didn't want to . . ."

Gasp, scrunch, squeak. Her bike seemed to make the only sound in the world.

"Aren't you going to say anything?"

"Never?"

"Never. You'll see him all right. No problem about that. You'll see him. He . . ." Her mother cleared her throat.

"He loves you. He won't ever stop loving you."

Son, moon and stars.

"Granny . . ."

"Granny's sick, doesn't know what she's talking about. Sick. Old. I'm sorry that happened. I'm sorry you were frightened."

"She said about the boy. He brings her the pictures he paints. He is her little love." She could feel the tears in her voice.

"Yes," said her mother after a long time. "Yes. That's something I should have told you, too. I haven't been very clever, have I?"

"That's true. That's not a joke?"

"Not a joke."

Kate wondered what she should say next.

"Is your heart broken?" She asked the question quite politely.

Her mother laughed. The front wheel of her bicycle wobbled for a moment.

"Heavens, no. Hearts don't break, darling. They get pretty bloody sore, but they don't break, thank God." She put her head down and her feet whirled on the pedals and she shot on ahead of Kate. She was black between her and the sun. Scrunch.

Kate didn't try to catch up with her.

Scrunch.

I suppose he won't ever answer my letters anymore, thought Kate. Love or no love. I suppose I am no longer his son, moon and stars.

Excuse me, she said to herself. Sun, moon and stars.

Late Opening
at the
Last Chance Saloon

❧

Marian Keyes

"It's no fun being a thirty-one-year-old woman without a boyfriend," complained Pamela.

"Stop whining," said Maggie. "I'm thirty-two."

"Are you? Already?"

"Yes, you big thick!" Maggie was exasperated. "What did you think all that was about last week? The two bottles of wine each? The dancing to Kool and the Gang in my front room at three in the morning?"

"Oh, of course, your birthday," said Pamela. "God," she sighed deeply, "we're getting old.

"Come on," she urged. "Let's go into town tonight and get jarred and meet fellas."

"Oh no," Maggie said. "Please don't make me."

"Maggie," insisted Pamela, "you're no fun anymore."

"But Pamela!" Maggie exclaimed. "It'll be full of teenagers, and I feel quite good about myself here but the minute I get in there I'll feel old and spinsterish and like my clothes are dowdy and the music will be too loud and I won't know any of it and everyone'll be looking at us and saying, 'Who's the pair of auld hags in the corner, shouldn't they be in sheltered housing?' and the only men who'll have anything to do with us will be ancient losers who are married but have no intention of leaving their wives or else fifteen-year-olds who want to lose their virginity and think we'd be desperate enough to oblige.

"Anyway," she added, relief making her almost giddy, "I have a boyfriend."

They both fell silent at the mention of Ian. Maggie had a dreamy smirk on her face. She got one every time she even thought of Ian, much less spent time with him. She was mad about him. She thought he was gorgeous—good-looking, intelligent, thoughtful, her first "older man." So much more experienced in the riding department than a man in his twenties. And he was so kind to her, he never once complained about her plump thighs.

Pamela was also thinking about Ian. Except she didn't have a dreamy smirk on her face. Far from it. She was thinking about Maggie's birthday when Ian had gone to bed at an outrageously early hour. Only to appear some time later, in the middle of Ladies' Night, to complain about the racket. As he stood in the doorway like a bad-tempered apparition, wearing only his underpants, he looked more like seventy-five than forty-five. Less of a sexy boyfriend and more of an old man, with his hair wispy and sticky-up, his legs skinny and white.

Pamela was kind enough not to remind Maggie of this.

"Never mind Ian," said Pamela. "And stop being so negative. I refuse to believe that there isn't an eligible man in his mid-thirties left in this city."

"There isn't," insisted Maggie. "I've checked."

"You mustn't have looked properly."

"I've torn the place asunder. And so have you—what's with your sudden burst of hope?"

"Desperation, I suppose," Pamela said gloomily. "I haven't had a ride in over six months. And a man hasn't bought me a drink in twice that."

"But you're not going to meet an okay man in a pub or a club."

"But where do I meet one? Where do I go?"

"An evening class?" Maggie suggested tentatively. Pamela rolled her eyes. "Yeah, right. Take up car maintenance and find the class is full of other thirty-something women like me, looking for a fella. Any other suggestions?"

"Friend of a friend?"

"We've met every friend of every husband of all our friends and they're all awful," Pamela pointed out. "Anyway I don't think I could cope with another dinner at a married person's house. All that talk about curtains, it does my head in. Jo used to be a bit of craic until she landed that eejit, Conor."

Pamela stared at her knees, sunk into gloom. Maggie tried to think of something to say to cheer her up. The onus was on her because, after all, she was the lucky one, she had a boyfriend. "Do you think we'll turn into boring wagons like

Jo and Gabbie and—who else do we know who's married?—Anne—when we get married?" Pamela asked.

"Time will tell."

"Do you know something," said Pamela, "it probably won't."

There was a horrible silence, while the thought flashed in Maggie's head, she's right.

"There is a finite number of men in this country," Pamela, the prophet of doom, continued. "There are more women. The men are. All. Fucking. Gone. All fucking taken. I've played the musical chairs of life and I'm the last one left. I've missed the boat.

"I could emigrate, I suppose," she went on. "I read about some town in America that's full of men. I nearly had my notice handed in when I saw a picture of some of them."

"Disgusting?" asked Maggie.

"Disgusting. They all had those funny beards that have no moustache, do you know that sort?"

Maggie did.

"And they were fat and weird and wore dungarees."

"Oh Pamela!" Maggie tried hard to sound upbeat even though she could feel depression steal over her in a cloud. "I met Ian, doesn't that give you hope?"

"Remind me again, where did you meet him?"

"Talbot Street."

"Whereabouts?"

"I drove into the back of his car."

"I see," said Pamela thoughtfully. "But no," she added, "that would never work for me."

"Why not?"

"I haven't got a car."

"No, you spa." Maggie forced herself to laugh. "I just meant that I met him by chance. I didn't have to arrange it in any way."

Pamela shook her head. "I haven't got time to wait for a chance encounter like that. My biological clock is ticking so loud I'm nearly deafened by it. They search me going onto planes."

"But you don't want to have children."

"That's not the point. I might want to.

"Anyway," she continued, "never mind the sprogs, I'm just talking about my looks   such as they are—in general. Any day now, my jugs will be down around my waist, my thighs will be down around my ankles, my crow's feet will be on my chin. I'm slipping, Maggie, I'm going. I can feel it. I am sitting on a barstool in the Last Chance Saloon, I'm nearly the only one left, they're shouting last orders, and if I don't get a man soon, it'll be all over. It'll be maiden aunt time for me."

"But . . ." Maggie couldn't think of anything nice to say. Everything that Pamela said was true and she thanked God that she had Ian. Someone to hold up as a shield against desperation and loneliness. Ian was her visa out of Failure-Land. Granted, things with him were far from perfect. But making-do was the name of the game and Maggie and her friends were no strangers to compromise.

"You know, we're intelligent, strong women, we don't need men," Maggie said, although her heart wasn't in it.

"That's crap!" Pamela spat. "I'm sick of pretending that

I'm not lonely. I'm a human being, I wasn't meant to be on my own."

Maggie was about to tut and proceed with the "We don't need men to be happy" speech, but she didn't bother. She didn't believe it either.

"Call me pathetic," said Pamela, "but I'm being honest here, I want a bloke, a partner, long-term commitment. I want the 'M' word."

"Marriage," she explained to Maggie's confused face.

"You're pathetic," sighed Maggie. "And so am I."

"I'm not ashamed to say I want to get married," insisted Pamela.

There was a short silence.

"Oh, all right then," she said. "I am. But I still want it."

"You're not the only one."

"So can we go out tonight?" asked Pamela.

"Er, no . . ." Maggie wavered.

"What are you up to?" Pamela asked suspiciously.

"I'd like to see the results of the referendum, it'll probably be on the news tonight. . . ."

"You want to stay in and watch it?" Pamela was surprised. "But it doesn't make a blind bit of difference to either of us, seeing as we're not married and not likely to be."

Then she understood. "Oh, I see. Fair enough. Although, if I were you, I wouldn't hold out too much hope."

"Why not?" Maggie demanded defensively.

"Because the priesteens have been threatening everyone with hellfire and damnation if they vote 'yes.'"

"Oh, I see." Maggie's face changed to one of relief.

"Why? What did you think I meant?" asked Pamela.
"Nothing."

∞

Maggie was delighted with the result of the referendum. Straight after the news she went round to her mother's to play Annoy the Catholic and gloat and gleefully predict that Catholicism would have all but died out in Ireland by the turn of the century.

Nuala Collins greeted her eldest daughter by saying, "What are you doing here on a Saturday night? Shouldn't you be out taking E's and getting off with boys in Leeson Street?"

"Ma, I keep telling you, I don't do E's."

"Maybe you should," muttered her mother. "You might address a civil word to me once in a while."

"You don't even know what an E is," Maggie pointed out.

"Yes, I do, it's a drug and it puts you in good humor."

"And I don't need to go to Leeson Street and get off with boys because I already have a boyfriend," Maggie continued.

At the mention of Ian, Nuala raised her eyebrows and the temperature in the hall suddenly dropped a couple of degrees.

"What's up with you, anyway, you narky oul' wagon," Maggie asked agreeably, marching into the front room. Although she knew exactly what was wrong.

"This country is gone to the dogs," Nuala announced.

But according to her the country had gone to the dogs whenever milk went up a penny so it was hard to gauge just how upset she was by the news that divorce had finally become permissibleish in Ireland.

"To the dogs, Nuala, to the dogs," agreed Maggie.

Her mother shot her a surprised look. And well she might—not only did Maggie never usually say "Gone to the dogs." (Instead she said terribly vulgar things like "The whole thing is shagged," or worse even.) But, more confusingly for Nuala, Maggie had made it her life's work to disagree with everything her mother said. And then she usually added insult to injury by lovingly saying, "Ma, it's for your good."

So why now the sudden concord on the canine element in the state of the country?

"Yes," Maggie went on, with a wicked smile that made her mother's heart do an abrupt U-turn and clench with dread. Maggie wasn't agreeing with her at all, was she? She was going to hold forth, again, about the poor priests being child abusers, wasn't she?

She was.

"What kind of country?" asked Maggie, with great rhetoric, "says it's okay for men in dresses to sexually assault little boys. . . ."

"Here we go again." Nuala crossed her eyes, stuck a thumb in each ear and waggled her fingers. Despite herself, Maggie giggled. Her mother and herself had had this "discussion" so many times now, it was a ritual that was almost comforting.

" . . . Or for men in dresses to use the church's money to go on expensive foreign holidays," said Maggie as she watched her mother's face for a reaction. "Or for men in dresses . . ."

"Cassocks!" exploded Nuala, unable to listen to her beloved church being thus pilloried.

"No, Ma, it's true," said Maggie.

There was the sound of the front door slamming.

"Here's Dad," Maggie said.

"Fergus," Nuala shouted from the living room. "In here." Maggie's father stuck his head round the door.

"Hi Dad," sang Maggie.

"Hi Dad," sang Nuala in the same tone of voice. "Will we get divorced?"

"So they finally shoved it through, did they?" asked Fergus as he lingered by the door.

"About bloody time," snorted Maggie. "This country has been in the stranglehold of those hypocrites and perverts for far too long."

"Don't speak like that about Our Lord's messengers on earth," said her mother automatically.

"Oh come on," exploded Maggie. "Wake up and smell the K-Y jelly. . . ."

"Are you two going to have a row?" asked her father nervously. "Do you want me to slam a couple of doors for you, Maggie?"

"No thanks, Dad, I can do it myself."

She looked at him and his anxious face. "Dad, I'm joking. Come in and sit down, would you."

"I'm a nervous wreck," complained her father. "It's not my fault. I've been psychologically scarred by having two daughters and a wife who never stop screeching at each other."

"Oh, Dad," laughed Maggie. "That's all in the past. We're civilized and grown up now. Well, at least Caroline and I are. You'd really want to do something about that religious maniac you're married to. Stick her on HRT or something."

Fergus forced a laugh.

"Who was in the pub?" asked Nuala, as she always did.

"The usual," said Fergus, as he always did. Then he muttered something about putting the kettle on and sidled away.

"Who did you expect to be there?" demanded Maggie of her mother. "Jack Charlton? Bill Clinton? Liam Neeson? What a stupid question to ask!"

"Oh, shut up!" Nuala said. Maggie was beginning to annoy her. It had been friendly sparring up till then.

"And what was that thing you said? Wake up and smell the what?"

"Nothing, Ma. Settle."

"Maggie, how come you're so bold?"

"Dunno. Genetics, I suppose. Probably your fault."

"Tell me, was I a good mother?"

"A good mother?" said Maggie aghast. "No, you were awful. The worst!"

Her mother looked stricken.

"All that praying you made us do," complained Maggie. "And making us go to Mass. And starving us on Good Friday. Although why it's called Good Friday is beyond me. Crap Friday would be a better name for it. And making us feel ashamed of our bodies and guilty about absolutely everything. No, Ma, you were the pits."

Nuala glowed with pride. Truly, she had been the best of Catholic mothers. "Never let it be said," she smiled, "that I didn't give ye a good Catholic upbringing."

"That's right," said Maggie. "It's not your fault that I'm a fallen woman."

A shadow passed over her mother's face and Maggie bitterly regretted what she had said. She'd pushed it that inch too far.

"But, Ma, now it's all all right," she said, a nervous fluttering in her stomach. "I can get married! I'll be married."

"Not in the eyes of the Lord," replied Nuala, quick as a flash.

"I'll have a ring on my finger, I'll be called Mrs. Ian Keating, I'll be respectable."

"You'll never be respectable," said her mother, with sudden bitterness. "He'll never marry you. Why would he bother when he's already getting what he wants from you?"

"Getting what he wants from me?" Maggie forced herself to laugh. "You're like something from the Middle Ages."

"Go on, go home now," Nuala said. "You're annoying me."

"Oh, Ma, be nice to me."

"No, go on, you couldn't wait to leave when you lived here. Now you're never out of the place."

"Ohhhh, Maaaa!"

"Where's Mr. Keating tonight?" Nuala eventually asked. "He's not much of a boyfriend if he leaves you on your own on a Saturday night."

"He's got his kids with him this weekend."

"And what about his wife?" demanded Nuala. "I suppose you never give her a moment's thought."

∾

As it happened, at that exact moment, Ian's wife, Veronica, was clinking a glass and drinking to her freedom. She would not have appreciated Nuala Collins's concern.

"To divorce," she said to her friend Anna.

"Divorce," agreed Anna. "Speaking of which, have you seen Ian, the shithead, recently?"

"Yes, unfortunately. He came over earlier to collect the kids. I tried to be out, but he was late arriving."

"How is he?"

"Pathetic, as always. His clothes are getting younger and younger. Soon he'll be wearing onesies."

Anna laughed. "Has he a girlfriend?"

"When didn't he?" Veronica drawled. "Yes, the kids say he has some poor girl hanging around. God love her, whoever she is. Isn't it hard to credit that once I was like that? I thought the sun shone out of his arse—back in the days before I found out he was sticking his lad into anyone who'd let him."

"A good Catholic wife turns a blind eye to such activities," Anna said in a put-on voice, which was, had they but known it, uncannily like Nuala Collins's. "Remember your wedding vows."

"Wouldn't they make you puke?" Veronica asked. "Judgmental oul' hoors. Offer it up, they say. Let him ride rings around himself and publicly humiliate you and you'll get your reward in the next world."

"At least he never hit you," Anna pointed out.

Veronica spluttered. "I'd like to have seen him try. And what are you doing making it sound like that's some sort of bonus?"

"Ah no," protested Anna. "I didn't mean that."

"I can't believe the attitude in this country," Veronica complained. "Where people think that if your husband belts you black and blue you have to put up with it—for batter, for worse. You can be damn sure that if any of those Good Catholics ever got a good thumping they wouldn't be preaching 'stand by your man.'"

∾

Three and a half miles away, Ian was with his three children, squashed into Ian's bachelor flat, which bore a startling resemblance to the flat he'd had during his student days twenty-five years previously. The similarity depressed him unutterably. What had all the hard work been for? If this was how he ended up? But he hadn't any choice. The children lived with Veronica in the home formerly known as the marital one. And he didn't have enough money to run two proper households.

This kind of lifestyle didn't suit him at all, he thought bitterly. And he hated having to look after the children on his own. Especially his fifteen-year-old daughter, Jessica.

If he and Veronica hadn't split up, would Jessica be such a difficult, spoiled little bitch?

But the facts were they had, and she was.

Although, when the result of the referendum was announced, Jessica lost her aggressive, scornful attitude and went pale. Even her lips went pale beneath the thick slick of lip gloss she was wearing.

Every time Ian saw her she was wearing more and more makeup. Earlier that evening he had tried, yet again, to forbid her from wearing it, but Jessica had just laughed and told him that because he had abandoned her, he had no right to tell her to do or not to do anything.

"I did not abandon you," he exclaimed. "Your mother threw me out."

"Nice one, Dad," she said sarcastically. "That's very mature, to try and turn me against Mum. As if I'm not traumatized enough."

"I wasn't, I only . . ."

But all her bravado disappeared as she watched the nine o'clock news.

"Will you and Mum be getting divorced?" she asked.

"Maybe," Ian said awkwardly. Definitely.

And another thing, Ian thought fervently, I'm never, ever getting married again.

∾

Maggie decided to call round to Pamela's in the hope that she might have given up on the idea of going into town on a man-mission. Maggie's mother had upset her and she wanted someone to complain to.

I mean, it's not as if I fell in love with a married man on purpose, Maggie thought bitterly, as she marched through the darkened streets. Would anyone do it on purpose? Not unless you liked never seeing your boyfriend. Not unless you got a kick out of him never having any money because he has three children and a wife to support.

But Ian had been all that was left.

Sure enough Pamela was in, with her sister Adrienne, her friend Louise and several bottles of fizzy wine.

Spirits were high. Immediately Maggie felt better.

"We're celebrating!" Pamela announced. "The people of Ireland can now get divorced!"

"It's a triumph of civilization and modernism," slurred Louise, waving her glass around. "Now Ireland will be able to hold its head up in the real world, without having to apologize for its medieval laws."

"Never mind that," spluttered Pamela. "The most important bit is that all we have to do is sit back and wait for everyone's first marriages to break up!"

"Exactly!" Maggie agreed joyfully. "Do you know what freedom to get divorced means to me? It means that now I can get married!"

Instead of everyone spontaneously rising to their feet and cheering wildly—which Maggie felt would have been an appropriate response to her happy news—the room fell suddenly and uncomfortably silent.

They all knew Ian. Better than Maggie did, in some ways. Certainly everyone seemed to be better acquainted with Ian's fondness for Maggie's friends than Maggie was.

Luckily no one was drunk enough to laugh out loud and openly ridicule Maggie's vision of her future as Mrs. Ian Keating, but it was touch-and-go.

"There's a certain irony in that," Pamela said, hurriedly

recovering her aplomb. "You know—being able to get married because you're able to get divorced?"

"Maybe," said Maggie defiantly. "But I don't care."

There was another nonplussed silence, followed by mildly frantic efforts to get the drunken, celebratory repartee back on track.

"It's not that I'm that fussed on getting married," Adrienne declared energetically, flashing them a forced, twinkly smile. "But now that every man in the country will be getting divorced, it'll be nice to have lots of available men around."

"Exactly," said Louise, violently upbeat. "I'm not interested in playing the little wife, but I wouldn't mind a half-decent relationship, with a man I could sometimes depend on."

Despite such valiant attempts a depressed air slunk through the room. Everyone was vaguely aware that it was coming from Maggie.

To Pamela's horror, she suddenly found herself saying, "Of course, all men are still bastards. And after a couple of years they'll be trading us in for even newer models."

Everyone looked stricken. Especially Maggie. Her mother's words about Ian's wife echoed in her head—"if he can do it to her, he can do it to you." Which was a stupid thing to have said, Maggie thought, seeing as Ian's wife had kicked Ian out. Ian hadn't left anyone.

Pamela was appalled at what she had just said.

Well, sort of.

It's for Maggie's good, she thought guiltily. Couldn't she see that Ian wouldn't ever commit—she hated that expression, it was so Californian—to her, divorce or no divorce? The sooner she realized that, the better.

"Janey, I never thought about it that way," muttered Adrienne. "Now we might be able to get married, but there's no guarantee that it'll last. Unless you're lucky enough to get a crap, ancient man that no one else would want anyway."

The words were out before she realized what she'd said. In case Maggie thought she was talking about Ian, Adrienne thought it was best to avoid looking at her for a while.

"There was never any guarantee that anything would last," Pamela said. Guilt made her try to cheer Maggie up. "Men were breaking women's hearts left, right and center even before divorce was allowed. It's the nature of things."

Oddly enough, Maggie didn't seem uplifted by this bit of news.

"Why is it the nature of things?" she demanded. She sounded perilously close to tears. "Why do men hold all the cards?"

Although Maggie used the word *men,* everyone knew what she actually meant was *Ian.*

"I don't know." Pamela was genuinely surprised. "Human nature, men being hunter-gatherers, having to sow their seed wherever they can.

"Or maybe we're wrong," she added. "Maybe some men feel women have all the power."

"They don't," Maggie said quietly. "Only the bearded, sandal-wearing, vegetarian types. And they only say it—all that shit about sympathetic period pains—they don't actually mean it."

No one disagreed with her.

"Why, Pamela?" Maggie asked plaintively. "Why do men seem to have the ball permanently in their court?"

Pamela waved with a vague flourish. "Men are from Cadbury's, women are from Disneyland, that kind of thing. Anyway, what about last year, Kevin Garvy was mad about you. You were certainly in the strong position there."

"Garvy," Maggie said quietly. "He made my skin crawl."

"I think," Pamela smiled at Maggie, desperately trying to pull her out of the trough that she had pushed her into in the first place, "I think the problem is just that there are more women than men. It's as simple as that."

Everyone looked downcast.

"Would you settle for just one man if there were millions more gorgeous ones, desperate for your attention, all over you?" Pamela cajoled.

"Yes," said Maggie stoutly.

Pamela arched an eyebrow.

"Maybe not." Maggie sighed.

"Exactly," said Pamela. "I don't think that men and women are necessarily fundamentally different, I don't think that's why a lot of men are so restless and a lot of women crave security. I think it's just the simple laws of supply and demand—"

"I'm going to turn into a complete bitch," Maggie interrupted with sudden, bitter passion. "I'm sick of men having all the power, so I'm not going to care about them anymore. And then they'll all be mad about me."

Everyone nodded knowingly, but not unsympathetically.

They waited for her to say that she didn't need a man to be happy.

"I don't need a man to be happy!" Maggie announced.

Everyone waited for her to say that she might even become a lesbian.

"In fact," Maggie threatened vehemently, "I might even become a lesbian."

Adrienne patted her shoulder awkwardly.

Silence descended. And hung around for a while.

Maggie wasn't feeling too good. It was something to do with Ian and the referendum of divorce, she realized. Something to do with her friends' lack of enthusiasm, lack of conviction, in her future with Ian. It was one thing for your mother to disapprove of your boyfriend—after all, you'd be worried if she didn't, in fact, you'd go off him if she didn't—but it wasn't very reassuring when your friends were wary of him.

Maggie had always explained away Ian's offhand attitude to long-term plans with her with the excuse that he was married—how could he make her any promises when he was trapped in a legal union with someone else? But soon Ian would be able to extricate himself from that marriage. And then what would happen?

Suddenly Maggie wasn't so sure that she and Ian would ride off into the sunset. Desolation hovered over her. She had thought that the arrival of divorce would fix her life. But maybe it wouldn't? She had thought that the arrival of divorce would change everything for her. But maybe she was going to get the wrong sort of change?

"Come on," Pamela said to the circle of miserable faces.

"We're celebrating! Look on the bright side, if we get married, they'll divorce us eventually, but at least we'll have had a couple of years of happiness."

"You're right," said Adrienne. "It's better than nothing. The day when we're completely on our own is being put off for a while."

"What you said earlier today is true," Maggie said sadly. "We are in the Last Chance Saloon. All of us." Including me, she left unsaid.

"Maybe we are," Pamela agreed kindly. "But it's had a bar extension. It's late opening at the Last Chance Saloon!"

Commencements

Mary Leland

The academic gowns swish through the atrium. Midmorning does not seem a likely time for wine, but this is a celebration and the glasses are refilled with gusto. The new graduates whose commencements ceremony this is swirl the bottles with the expertise born of the work which expanded their college grants.

There are people here who can identify the collars. People who can interpret the ermine trim, the scarlet cowl, the dark blue ribands. The law graduates are shawled in white fur. More than half of them are women. What will happen to these young women now? What are they hoping for, or planning? Have they, like this daughter here, a hope of the Bench, an eye on the path toward senior counsel?

The bright winter morning is a smoky gloom inside, but the atmosphere is energetic with gratification. Everyone has tried to make the day memorable. The college with its dedicated speeches, the long, articulated Latin phrases, the careful naming. Parents, guardians, partners and friends wear smart clothes, bear flowers, champagne, talk of bookings for lunch, flash their cameras.

Enjoying the day for what it is I let others preserve it. Who knows, who can tell, what is memorable? My glittering girl may remember this ceremony as her taking-off point but there is no guarantee of that. I may remember it as the period to a contract, the contract signed in the blood of her beginning. I look for nothing more than this hubbub of happy strangers, her glee, my relief.

She comes back to me through the throng, gasping, she says, for a cigarette. The mortarboard is at a rakish slant, its tassel swinging like her earrings. Her collar has slipped to reveal a shoulder, a vulnerable pale bone. Her hands flaunt the rosy wineglass.

We make for a corner in the sun outside. As we move a man catches my elbow. Kindly he says: "There's no reason why you should remember me."

Pretending a confusion of handbag, parchment scroll, wineglass, I do not stretch out my hand. He is a stranger.

He explains: "I once lived with you in Kerry."

The wine lurches from my daughter's goblet. We both laugh, this is a mischievous introduction.

"No!—I mean, we both shared the same guest house in Ballyferriter. One summer. Dun Ciomhain—do you remember Ballyferriter?"

Thirty years ago. Ballyferriter. Baile na nGall. Smerwick Harbour, the Three Sisters. The broad white sweep of glittering beach and Dun an Oir, the townland of gold, of death.

I don't remember him. He gives a name.

"You don't remember me. It's a long time ago. But you haven't changed much. I would have known you anywhere—you were there for three weeks. Always with your head in a book."

Suddenly my daughter recognizes me in his memory. She looks at me with amused fondness. Whatever past this stranger was going to call up with his reminiscences is annulled into literature. I am the woman she has known. This is not a shadow of her father who has left our lives. This is safe, a visitor from beyond her world of absences. "Some things never change!" she laughs as she turns to greet her brother.

They both smile kindly as that Kerry holiday is unrolled like a map to a country they will never visit. My past, not theirs. A place with no photographs to haunt them.

This is a man from thirty years ago. We knew each other's name and no more. We may have danced together at the céilí at Bruna Graige or walked home in separate but affiliated groups along the dimming summer roads, swishing at the fuchsia still glowing in the dark high damp hedgerows.

We may have met as we shook rain from sweaters and sneakers in the dank hallway. Departing on malodorous buses to different ends of the country—his accent has a Northern tinge—we may have wished each other well, and meant it.

It is as though someone has touched my heart's flesh with a finger. Let me have been nice to him, I pray, as if the prayer could make me have been so.

I gaze at him helpless with amazement. With awe. The space between us contains our imagined lives, what we have achieved or endured. What we have obtained without intention. What we have become.

He must have been as tall as this even when he knew me. Now the hair is gray but not sparse. He is a little stooped, but looks well dressed. Well-to-do, which appeases my heart. A boyish look, open as he awaits my recalcitrant memory.

I have no recollection of him at all. Nothing in the flood of awareness his words undam brings him back to me as a youth. How can it be that his mind has me in it and mine excludes him? In his kindness he acknowledges this; there is no reason, none at all he says, why I should remember. Perhaps this is true.

There is something I can offer: hadn't he been one of the lads who had spent so much time with Sean O Ciomhain?

Yes! His smile is a beam. My guess is a good one. Yes. He had spent a lot of time with Sean. It was important to talk as often as possible with Sean, whose Irish language was so pure despite the many years in Massachusetts.

He speaks easily, glad to have found himself. Yes. He talks of Sean's life in America, in Springfield. A Gaeltacht in itself, an image of the landscape of language we had been trying to encounter in Kerry. Wasn't that amazing? We shared that wonderment of the Irish-speaking ghetto in Massachusetts.

Ah—isn't this amazing? My smile is no longer blank. Our eyes engage although there is nothing to read except the mystery of this meeting. His children, my children, our offspring, are somewhere on the periphery of our shared vision. Amazing, to speak again together of Sean O Ciomhain and

Massachusetts. To breathe with the words that blowing mist off the headlands, its drift of turf-reek and salt.

Our eyes graze the boundaries in between. Years knotted like grass in the ditches. We look at one another, a look which must last us now as long as we have already survived, undulating like the long walk across the cliffs to Slea Head and Ferriter's Castle.

The profiles loom with the slant of the Three Sisters. With the long, noiseless silver curve of Smerwick Harbour.

Amazing! To be here. As old as we are. To have children as old as they are, as good, as acclaimed, as they are. We are caught in the square shape of the sun in the atrium. A winter sun, but something warms us.

His family—an engineering graduate to congratulate—reclaims him. An attractive wife, her face bright. I am grateful for his air of well-being, of completion. He does not question my solitariness; who would, these days, if I do not? And yet, for a blank second, I almost wish for, almost desire, his curiosity. Life has made us too polite.

His farewell is like a benediction. Long ago we must have wished each other well. I wish him well now. I hear his gentle blessing with gratitude as if it implies that our wishes, having once come almost true, will come at least as true again. Our adventures were not shared, but we survived them.

And what, demands my family—a lawyer to congratulate—was I doing in Kerry? They are almost proud of me, that my past has outlasted thirty years.

I am proud too. A past is one of the few things the old can have that the young might envy. I feel glad, without understanding why, that they have been reminded that I existed before they did, was known before they knew me. Before their father knew me.

What was I doing in Kerry? The same as he, that known stranger. Learning the Irish language. It was something we all wanted to do, then. I had not succeeded. I allowed distractions: the sweep of rain across Mount Brandon and the black crevices of Brandon Creek. The gray reeking ruins of Dun an Oir, a townland transformed into a slaughterhouse as refugee Spaniards sheltered hopelessly among its cabins. Walking the headlands I heard waves of music surge under the cliffs, the promontories.

Lines of poetry—we were very young, after all—rolled along the boreens as the fuchsia buds snapped open under my fingers, spilling pollen from the anthers. We would have been sixteen, seventeen. No more. In love only with what we imagined of ourselves. In touch with the rim of our lives, conscious of a beginning.

Those are my memories of Kerry, of Ballyferriter. Those, and my own conversations with Sean O Ciomhain, conversations in English about America. About the conflict between the life he had to live all summer long—host, professor, folklorist, storyteller—and the winter life of turf hoarder and herdsman, of rheumatism and the Christmas letter from Springfield and of silence and of rain. A conflict he was not equipped to understand or to explain.

There is, too, the memory of honey.

Precise as a dream I see the cabbage leaf, its clean green dimples upturned to form a plate and the comb thick with juice. Being a city child I thought of the honey as raw. Sean had brought it from the hive and took pleasure in my ignorance, my amazed fear of the thriving bees.

The hives were behind the house, in itself a featureless building common in Kerry, gray and spare and functional, imposed on the landscape rather than part of it. It was not the kind of house from which the emigrants had departed. It was the kind to which they returned, if they did return.

Sean had softened his with hollyhocks, blackcurrants, rampant fuchsia hedging the garden against the fields where sand grew. The milk had a salt taste to it; the honey swelling on the quilted cabbage leaf had a tang of flowers. Its aftertaste was scarlet.

I sat on the bank beside the house. I sat on clover and campion, butterwort, on scratchy sand spurrey. Warmth and damp invaded my skin. The sun was heating the drenched ditches. The honey steamed on the leaf. The light caught the veins twisted like briars on Sean's hand as he showed me how to scoop the honey with my fingers.

He was an old man but there was vigor in his hands, the energy of knowledge, the authority of custom. It was a delight to him to have such as I was—willing to listen, to respond to the continuing mystery of his life, where he had been, why he was here.

I should have learned from him the names of the wildflowers of the ditch but I never did. Sea rocket is rocket still, sandwort only that, the hedge parsley parsley forever.

I know the Irish word for honey: *meala*. From the Irish, sweetness. I think of the word with my tongue as I rock on the cobbles on our way out of the college.

There are other events to fill the day before our family

dinner this evening, the ceremonial union of what we call, what has become, our family. The one-parent family. There is a sweetness in this day's success. It is not all mine, but as I make my way to a seminar on women's studies it is relishable, more real now than the remembered molten honey on its honeycomb of leaf.

As women now we sit together, all our journeys joining us at the heart of a world we have made for ourselves. Yet we wait for transformation while a poet evokes her past. She offers us a memory of deliberately following in her father's footsteps to walk, as he had done, on forbidden grass. She parses the recollection into phrases. The rightness of it, its neatness as verse and as metaphor, its image of endorsed rebellion are all applauded. We are all, here, anxious for ourselves. We are all looking for the magic that will give us back the meaning of our lives.

Observer more than alchemist, for I have already found a mystery in my day, I admire the transfiguration of footstep to poetry. The investment of imagination in the real, the actual, the remembered.

There is the touch at my elbow. The apology: "You won't remember me. You were only three years old. . . ."

But this is not true. We have never met. This woman who must be much older than she looks does not remember me at all. Her memory is of two girls—the elder, the younger—and a baby brother. The components are of the family alive before I was. She had played, she says, in our garden. She thinks I must be the younger of the two girls. She speaks of the house I knew and of my parents. Her own mother had died, her father had remarried and she had been bitterly unhappy. A stepchild in a country where such a relationship occurred only through death and was rare enough to make her, among her peers, remarkable.

"Times change," she said; she would not be remarkable now.

Some kind of shelter and of ease had been available in our garden.

"Your mother was really lovely-looking, wasn't she?"

I think I knew that she was, but I did not know her then.

"She used to include me. She made those fancy-dress outfits out of crepe paper, and she made them for me as well."

She did not make them for me at that time. I was not born.

I am being introduced to my mother's life as my children were to mine. I try to explain, but this woman doesn't want to hear me. It is as if I have to be the person she thinks I am. Something is happening for which she has waited a long time. I must substantiate her memory.

A grief builds within me. If I had been that child I would have had more of my mother. The crepe paper dresses, the parties with singing and dancing in our small suburban garden with its apple trees, its lavender and Japanese anemones. I would have made different choices. I would have married differently.

In the confusion of my wish to reassure this stranger at my elbow, I think the baby brother she describes could have been the brother younger than myself. The brother now dead, a possibility unthinkable then and unbearable now. I want to say it to her. To confess that we were told to keep an eye on the pram but something happened, something terrible, not then but now, when we saw it coming and could not evade it. Now, when we felt, still feel, that we had taken our eye off the pram.

Instead I insist on chronology. We shake out the different members of the family and select, like children at a sweets counter, the siblings she names as alive before I was. My father walking to work. An uncle giving us backers on his bicycle. My grandmother accusing one of us of "shaping," showing off.

"And your mother. She used to give us little picnics in the garden. Bread and jam. Biscuits she made herself. She was the first person ever to give me honey, she put it in little sandwiches, tiny triangles with all that sweetness in them."

She stops. Her mouth trembles as if she were gathering herself for something else. "Once she said something to me. It went through me. I had a lovely little figure and your sister was very thin. We were in the kitchen. What can we have been talking about, or doing?"

Her face is tense. This has been a long anguish. All through her life she has remembered a time when not only was I not the child she recalls, I wasn't even born. A time when she was thirteen. Fifty years ago.

"I don't know. Maybe something happened to upset your sister. Maybe I said something or repeated something my stepmother had said. I remember how your mother looked at me and said: 'Margaret is just as womanly as you.' It went right through me at the time."

Womanly. It goes right through me. My mother's vanished admonition. This stranger's enduring pain. Out of the sunlit garden had come this sadness in the kitchen where the little picnics were prepared.

I think of the photographs in black and white with my sisters and a brother in them. An older girl who may have been this woman. The girls stand together in printed cotton frocks and cardigans. I remember the sharp sweet smell of the bolts of fabric my mother used to bring home, unrolling the glossy cotton on the dining room table where she did her sewing, the spread of flowers flooding the surface before becoming skirts and shirred bodices and Sunday frocks.

The little girls stand by the seesaw, the dresses tucked into the legs of their knickers. Who held the camera? Who preserved them in their play, their heads of curls tied with bows of white taffeta? The kind of ribbon, I remember, which shrieked when being tied.

Her life, she tells me, has gone well. A good job, a good marriage, she is a grandmother. But she had to speak to me when she saw me at this meeting on women's studies, seeing a face, hearing a name remembered from all those years ago.

It had not been me. My sisters, the elder, still-living brother. My mother. These had been real to her before I knew them. She remembered them from a time before my life began. There had been no me to remember.

Nor had there been a me in Kerry. There had been someone, someone, for the kind and successful man to recall. If I do not remember meeting him there, neither do I remember myself.

Incidents, yes. I remember the incidents. Memory is accurate enough on happenings.

We can't rely on it, though. How could it be that in this

one day I meet two people—one of whom I never knew, one of whom I don't remember—in whose lives I have somehow been held at anchor? Anchored by language, by my mother, and by a more retentive eye than mine.

All I remember is the shared garden. The rain, the smell, the honey. As if these were all there could have been. The absence of my self strikes me like a stubbed toe in holiday sandals. Where have I been all my life? What was I doing, my head in a book, my hair tied in ribbons? Walking the headlands, dreaming of a future, sea mist in my face, honey sandwiches among the blackcurrant bushes. From these I entered my life, leaving some traces of my passage.

Other lives were touched by me, more deeply than I touched these revenants. I have left my mark. My impressed bruise has lingered on landscapes long deserted by what I must still call, can only call, my self.

Going to meet again those whom I call my own, those in whom I will live only as long, and as accurately, as they remember me, I feel the swelling of regret. It hurts me now that I have never liked honey. It is too sweet. Too sticky, its traces lasting long beyond its taste.

Dwelling Below the Skies

❧

Liz McManus

"Do you know Graham?" Michael directs his question to me but his attention is fixed elsewhere. He lifts a glass off a passing tray. He does it so casually you'd never guess what a lush he is. The signals are so slight. I admire Michael. His drinking has subtlety. When he gets drunk his complexion turns pink and I swear his hair whitens although actually, his hair is a rather delicate ash blond. He can be talking quite distinctly, even making sense—as much sense as Michael can make, twenty years as one of Dublin's leading hairdressers makes for a lot of small talk—then, all of a sudden, his face folds up. He is too self-contained to cause a fuss. He doesn't cry or shout or laugh unduly. He just passes out. No more Michael. Being drunk is, I believe, an out-of-body experience for him. A reformed drunk we have all met in our time but there is something special about a refined drunk.

A man is standing beside Michael, a man with a fringe of well-washed hair falling onto a prematurely lined face. Do I know Graham? The answer is yes, even in the biblical sense. And the answer is also no. Graham Harbison. Even from here I can see that he has changed. Although, to be honest, I don't remember much about him. Long, cold limbs between lilac-colored sheets is about all I remember and a failed coitus.

The intimacy of it still shudders in the air. As memories go there is nothing to match the sexual act. You walk into a room full of people and you find yourself plummeting down a time tunnel. Like Alice chasing the White Rabbit, my past is chasing me. In either case the outcome is ridiculous. Oh, my belt and braces, not Graham Harbison! How embarrassing! What does one say after so long?

You look different with your clothes on. . . .

I do not wish to be standing here talking to this man. I don't like the girl who has her legs twined around his spindly thighs between the lilac-colored sheets. She is young enough to be my daughter and far too calculating to be me. Get out of that bed immediately! I want to shout at her.

A waiter with a tray of canapés creates a diversion. Sushi, crab claws, caviar, little heaps of pink glop. Mmmmm, delicious! Exploring these concoctions gives us something to talk about. A taste of dank rock pools fills my mouth. Last year's fashion in finger food is already looking tired. What is needed here is some culinary courage. Why aren't those vols-au-vent crammed with plump earthworms *marinés*? That would get the taste buds quivering.

There is less hair, less muscle, less flesh, less, all told . . . of Graham Harbison. He smiles wistfully. I am amazed we ever got as far as bed. I can't remember what happened before or after, if there was a courtship, or what kind of parting. And when I kissed him was I aware he had a tic at the side of his mouth? The tic pulsates as he asks me how I am and how my family is, and my beautiful mother. The men in my life invariably remember my beautiful mother. I realize that Graham Harbison remembers my mother a lot more clearly than he remembers me. This thought cheers me up. As we are now both reaching middle age, he and I can forgive those two young souls, clasped in their chilly embrace. Growing older gives us license to measure the depths of our ignorance with equanimity. We have something in common; we can afford to laugh at ourselves.

"My mother is very well," I tell him. "My parents celebrated their fiftieth wedding anniversary last month."

"Fifty years married!" He is dutifully amazed. "Half a century . . ."

He's not bad-looking really, there is a certain boyish diffidence. I'd forgotten that Graham was one of them; a Northern Prod like my mother. Only strictly speaking she isn't a Protestant. She comes from a family of non-subscribing Presbyterians, otherwise known as Dissenters, Aryans, Unitarians, or New Light Thinkers.

"Actually, we took her back for the celebration. Up North. She hadn't been back there since I was a child. Imagine!"

I am eager to tell my story but already Graham's attention has wandered. As he turns to Michael his expression changes.

"Are you all right?" Graham asks. A smile illuminates Michael's face. There is nothing drink-induced about it. His smile is so full of warmth that I'm envious of it. The signals are unmistakable; the body language; the leap in temperature; the secret code. These two are an item. They have no interest in the past and in particular, they have no interest in my past. They only have eyes for each other.

As a topic of conversation my mother has toppled off the edge. I carry her away with me to another part of the room. I don't wish to lose her so soon, particularly to a pair of old queens. But there is no one else who will listen so I stand in the window alcove and watch. By now the party is in full throttle and people are baying at each other. It's only when you stop and listen that you discover just how noisy the human species can be.

My mother by contrast, is a quiet woman. Conformist by nature if not by religion. A foil to my extrovert father. I have difficulty imagining my mother ever rebelling and yet she did once.

Nowadays nothing is sacred; men marry men; children divorce their parents; a mixed marriage hardly merits a yawn. But fifty years ago the world was a different place, particularly, our world on this small island. My mother did the unforgivable; the treacherous; she was the Juliet to my father's Romeo. By marrying him she put herself outside the tribe and delivered their future children into the papist camp. The rift in her family was never bridged and any loss she felt she kept to herself.

I realize now that she conspired as much as anyone to

bury her past. We two girls and our father formed a coherent unit while my mother was defined by what she was not. She did not go to Mass, or confession or Benediction. She would never have dreamt of offering anything up for the souls in Purgatory. Not that she interfered with her daughters' pious practices, but her silence was a challenge in itself. Secretly I prayed for her conversion because the nuns told me to. But it was so absolute, her refusal to engage in organized religion. The great procession through the church calendar—Christmas, Easter, Pentecost—passed her by. And inexplicably—despite His insistence that I go to Mass and wear holy medals and say novenas—God refused to strike her down.

I can see my mother kneeling down to examine a half-open crocus in the grass.

"*This* is truly miraculous—not Jesus changing water into wine. Nature is its own best miracle."

Jesus . . . miracle . . .

The words were profaned because they issued from *her* mouth. How little I knew! In the purple-and-white-striped heart of that flower I searched in vain for a bulwark strong enough to withstand the One, True, Roman, Catholic and Apostolic Church.

∾

We grew up. My mother grew old. Children were replaced by grandchildren. Her daughters became two middle-aged women who rarely agreed on anything, but our grumblings were usually harmless and we formed a truce easily. Time was running on. We did not have forever to breach the maternal reticence that stood between us and our inheritance. Our plan was hammered out over kitchen tables. We were determined to satisfy our curiosity in a grand nostalgic tour.

It was hard to know what she thought about it all, but there was no stopping us. On the map we located a farmhouse here, a birthplace there. Early on it became obvious that these places were no longer connected to anyone belonging to us. While the Catholic side had flourished the non-subscribing Presbyterian side had wasted away. Emigration, death and *Ne Temere* had done their work.

When the time came we traveled across the Border at Newry. Beyond the town an avenue of trees closed in around us, darkening the interior of the car. Then light broke, like a tall glassy arch shattering over our heads, and my mother spoke. For the first time she began to recount details of her early life. Discreetly she pulled photographs from her handbag. How well she had concealed them all these years! Portraits of women with long Ulster chins, wearing white linen aprons. Among them a dark pixie face peered up at the camera lens. The runt of the litter. Even in those days my mother stood out as different. After the photographs came a prayer carefully transcribed by her childish hand onto the flyleaf of an old school reader.

> *"From all that dwells below the skies*
> *Let faith and hope and joy arise.*
> *Let beauty, truth and good be sung*
> *Through every land, by every tongue."*

"How come you never showed us these before?" my sister asked, enchanted. Wonderingly mother replied, "But you never asked before."

∾

As the day progressed I began to weary a little of the whole idea. We were chasing dead people with whom we had nothing in common. Whatever spoor had been laid it was well and truly cold. Even the living were alien. We marched through farmyards and sat drinking cups of tea with silver-haired women in dark parlors decorated with certificates of the local Loyal Orange Lodge. A grandmother's house was a two-roomed cottage recently extended by a Belfast engineer called Cameron and his wife. The uncle's hotel had been transformed to a hardware shop.

We stopped for afternoon tea at the Kiltartan Hotel. Mock-Tudor decor with Toby jugs dangling from the rafters. The speciality was cream tea and muffins and a butler to serve it. The entire family sat down together, all twelve of us, grandchildren shrieking with excitement. As usual my sister and I had a falling-out. This time it was over seating arrangements but there was no rancor in our dispute. Later a cake was brought out and we all sang Happy Anniversary. My mother said she had never known such a fuss to be made of her.

Our last visit was to the school my mother had attended as a child. The headmaster, she told us, had a liking for homilies about the wonders of nature. To see its ruined buildings, derelict and overgrown, must have been hard for her and yet her recollections were lively. Her memories swept through the broken walls and along the exposed rafters like housemartins in summer. At one moment she stood in the corner of a classroom for punishment. At another she lifted her skirts to beat a way through the fields. Beyond the hazel trees a river slipped by where she went swimming with the Minnis girls and her best friend, Sara McCracken.

Beside the school stood a Quaker Meeting House where the children from the school went to pray. It was a shabby building, crumbling a little with age, but clearly still in use.

The interior was a square timber-boarded room. At the rear ran a small gallery, lit by sunlight straining through the narrow windows. A smell of damp and old polish clung to the rows of pews and on the lectern lay an open Bible. There was little else. Nothing to relieve the severity of contemplation. Yet the tongued and grooved boards and the whitewashed walls gave the Meeting House a plain, homely quality.

"I always sat here . . ." my mother said. The expression on her face was serene as she sat down. Any pain or grief was washed out by the sunlight falling across her skin. Only the joy of remembrance remained. It was easy to imagine the rows of pews filled with children. I could hear the murmur of their voices drifting through the still air.

I can recall every detail of that moment; the light on her frail head; a hair snagged in the collar of her coat; her patent leather handbag slouched against the pew-end. Up through the layers of experience comes an explanation of sorts. What discovery was I making? The wellspring of existence? The disclosure of a godly hand in the world?

Hardly. That is too simplistic a version of the truth. Full

of contradictions I have stumbled through life, swaying this way and that, under a burdensome, mongrel inheritance. You need to know where you are coming from, the proverb says, to know where you are going, but it is all a matter of guesswork in the end. When I see where the quarrel ends I will know my destination. In the meantime there are flashes of light; pinpoints in the dark to guide me through. Out of nowhere enlightenment comes, clothed in joyfulness and then, in the next breath, it is extinguished.

I don't know much. All I know is that there was a space for me among those phantom children. In that holy place, delineated by the absence of things, for a moment I belonged.

The sound of an argument brings me back to where I'm standing in the window alcove. A glass falls off the waiter's tray. It shatters into pieces. I hear Graham's voice shouting, *"No, no, no, you bitch!"* Michael is pink-faced and swaying. He tries to grab another glass of wine. Even at this distance I can see his empty drunken grimace. Poor Graham, he mustn't know Michael well enough to learn to love the unlovable in him.

How long it takes to know someone. I think of my mother in the car traveling south, out through the gap in the mountains and across the Border. She spent the journey staring out of the window, barely saying a word. It's hard to tell what she was thinking. But I think she was happy. Yes, I'm sure she was. As sure as anyone can be.

Lucy's Story

❧

Mary Maher

I didn't ask to be the keeper of Lucy's secrets. I was trapped into it when the first divorce referendum was looming, and the newspapers had begun to whine indignantly about giving a second chance to people such as herself, those in "anomalous situations," the remnant ends of old marriages now rematched to each other.

Lucy decided she needed counseling. "I'm not that kind of psychologist," I told her. "It's research I'm interested in." Surveys, questionnaires, analysis of human behavior in the mass. No trucking about in the inconclusive maze of individual human personalities as originally planned. I had my fill of that in the '70s.

I suggested Caitriona, who'd stuck with the original plan.

"No," Lucy said, and shook her head firmly for emphasis. She has tight, wood-shaving curls. They were black once but by that time were speckled with gray, as if she'd flipped a paintbrush over her head. The effect was nice. I suppose she is as white as a granny now.

"I trust you more than anyone," she said. "And trust is the cornerstone of counseling, isn't it? The key to effective therapy." Lucy has always picked up phrases like lint, usually not so accurately.

"That's not the point. We're friends, I know you too well."

"No, you don't. You just think you do."

She was right, but at the time I wanted to laugh; the idea of Lucy suddenly revealing unplumbed depths was pretty rich. She was easily the least complicated person I'd ever known, and I'd known her since she turned up at the drop-in center in the '70s, the early days of the movement. It was right after we opened and Tess was still frantically slapping up posters over the damp patches on the walls when this little vision appeared in the doorway: small, sweet-faced, itsy-bitsy voice. She told us she could come in to help every morning while her twins were in school. We took her on merrily, as we took on any woman who crossed the threshold, yea-ho and welcome, sister. It was part of the credo.

We were also desperate. We'd been besieged from Day One, and of course none of us really knew what we were doing. But it rapidly became clear that compared to Lucy we were all Mary Robinsons. She was hopeless. She forgot messages, lost folders, and couldn't take a phone call without getting into a seminar on the meaning of life with the caller. Her command of the alphabet wasn't up to filing—dyslexic, almost certainly, but we wouldn't have understood that then. Anything with numbers flummoxed her. The week we tried her on appointments the cards went out telling people to come on the 4th of the 6th when it should have been the

6th of the 4th, that kind of thing. When we got the coffee bar going we stuck her in there. I remember Tess snarling, "Well, for Christ's sake, she is a housewife, she ought to be able to manage that much." But Lucy invested herself in chatting to the customers, and the second time she burned the element out in the fiendishly expensive urn, Tess asked her if she'd mind just being on general call near the front desk while we reorganized.

We put her on the agenda for a council meeting. Apart from her hazardous impact on the work—we were deeply self-important about the work—she was as irritating as a bluebottle to the workers. She sang advertising jingles. She washed ashtrays. She clasped her hands to concentrate. She said "conscienceness-raising." She'd named her twins Peter and Wendy because she loved *Peter Pan*. She herself tinkled, possibly a subconscious identification with Tinkerbell; her voice, her clothes. She wore clinky bracelets and earrings and those long, full-sleeved Indian dresses with miniature bells at the collar and cuffs, over color-coordinated polo necks. We wore, to a woman, elephant flare jeans and sweaters. And clogs, they were almost uniform, too. I loved those clogs, they were strong, free and noisy. Lucy wore black patent flats. Worst of all, she was one of those wives who invoked her husband's name at every word's turning. Edward says, Edward thinks, Edward likes, Edward hates.

But apart from moaning about what a nerd she was, we didn't know what we could do about her. Even Tess accepted that dumping her would demand a lot of tact, something none of us possessed in surplus. In the end we did nothing, hoping she'd get bored. No chance. We went on clattering up and down the rickety stairs, herding people into waiting rooms, climbing over kids, and Lucy went on tinkling about, smiling vacantly.

She produced Edward in his august person at our first fund-raiser. It was our standard effort, basement lights low and Abba tapes loud, pipes ineffectively camouflaged with crepe paper and tables loaded with bottles of dire plonk smuggled in cheap from Belfast. He was not, as Caitriona and I had imagined, short and pompous, but a big, good-looking fellow with bold, adulterous eyes. We already hated him, now we hated him with lust and anticipation. But he disappointed us and didn't dance with anyone. He steered Lucy to the wine table and took over the waitering masterfully. She stood in his shadow, Tinkerbell with her lights modestly dimmed.

After that we were kinder to Lucy. We were no kinder about her, because we needed her for light relief. Caitriona and I used to collapse laughing, leaning against the wall and snorting until our sides were sore, at the sight of Lucy in her floaty frock gravely studying that poster about the male contraceptive that was inserted into the penis. She never asked, and we never told her, it was a joke. If she saw us, she would smile hopefully and ask if she could do anything, and then Caitriona would have to fend her off.

Caitriona was the real director. It was Caitriona who put up the weekly rosters, the "Womaning Rotas," and scheduled the workshops on self-help, self-defense, assertiveness. She built up the list of phone referral numbers that grew over the years, for the Well Woman, Rape Crisis, Battered Wives, Children's Assault, Pregnancy Advice, Free Legal

Aid. The last thing Caitriona needed was Lucy, which is why Lucy came to nestle under my reluctant wing. My job was information. I got Lucy to sit next to me and listen to statements as I read them out. If she wasn't a help, neither was she a burden, since she thought anything I wrote was superb.

But as the months wore on we were far too busy with people to idle over words on paper. We were the hub of the universe, and the universe was there every day, usually in tears, sometimes in full-scream hysterics. Tess never believed the way we went through boxes of tissues, she always complained somebody was swiping them.

And slowly we began to see what Lucy was good at. She was a natural frontline comforter. She could sit quietly for as long as it took, her whole little body curled in sympathy, while some raw-faced farmer's wife or poor young one in a crumpled school uniform went to pieces over a positive pregnancy test. Certainly I wasn't up to it. I was rigid with impatience and rage. But I did have the wit to see that Lucy was a godsend, and I pushed the others to create a special role for her. Tess finally agreed. We asked her to sit at reception and wait for crises, like a little fireman. She was so happy and proud and humble to be there, we were touched. And amused.

But if we laughed at her, we also began then to love her in earnest; and Lucy, divining that it was I who had enabled her, all but lay before my clog-clad feet in fealty.

All that and more of the past was between us when she came to see me for counseling about Joe; I couldn't really refuse her. I agreed to a few sessions in a cafe off George's Street, near her genealogy job, on Monday mornings. It was quiet, and I could go from there into college. She could pay for breakfast, but that was all. "It isn't really counseling, Lucy," I insisted, "and if I say you should really be seeing someone on a proper basis, you have to promise me you won't get annoyed and think I've let you down."

"I promise. I know you have to follow your ethics," she said.

She began that first Monday as most people do, picking her way around. "Everything is so perfect with Joe, it *scares me.* Do you know what I mean?"

Yes.

"I mean, I never, ever thought I'd ever meet anyone like him," she said. Her smile was what you would have to call rapturous, and I realized that I hadn't ever seen that before. "He's so good to me! And we have such a good time together. I keep waiting for something awful to happen. I'm afraid it will all come crashing . . ." and so on.

Yes, yes, yes.

I felt confident I wouldn't be called on to do more than nod attentively between mouthfuls and was just laying into my second sausage when she said, "I think sex might be the problem. We don't have simultaneous orgasms, and I suppose I shouldn't worry about it, given the way things turned out with Edward, but I don't have experience. What do you think?"

I swallowed so much sausage my eyes watered but I managed to stay po-faced. During all those ardent meetings in the center when we pondered the Shere Hite report and the myth of the vaginal orgasm, Lucy had never, not once, said diddley-boo about sex. She used to sit in clasped-hands mode with that blank frown Tess called her I'm-a-serious-feminist face, and you had to keep reminding yourself that she must be following some of the discussion because she did, after all, have two children.

I drank some coffee, remembering to keep eye contact unwavering. "How were things with—what was it like with Edward?" I asked.

She told me. It was contemporaneous combustion with Edward from the very first time, stretched before the two-bar electric heater in her bedsit on Lower Pembroke Street. Before that she hadn't been at all sure about him. "He was very sure about me right from the start. He was such a powerful, kind of overwhelming person—well, you know what he was like."

"Indeed. And by Jesus, Lucy, you know far better."

"I do, yes." The smile vanished, she looked across the room blankly. "I was awfully flattered by Edward. I did know that, you know. I used to say to myself, 'now Lucy, don't get swept away by sweet words.' But when we had finally had sex, well. It was—oh, Lord. It just *blew out my mind.*"

I laughed, I couldn't stop myself, but she only smiled, happy as always to please.

"That changed everything. I felt that something like that was a definite sign. A destiny sign. And I don't feel that way yet with Joe. Now I think maybe if divorce comes in we'll be able to get married, and I keep worrying that it's not quite right yet."

I sat back and poured us both more coffee. First we could deal, as swiftly as the executioners he deserved, with Edward. I asked her how long this idyllic state of sexual congress continued into their marriage and Lucy said well, always, until of course things went wrong.

"You mean until he started knocking you about for real. That does wreak havoc with the old response mechanism."

Lucy nodded and looked away again.

Edward had finally gone a blow too far and slammed Lucy down on the ironing board with the iron. The Indian dress was scorched through in a precise stencil of an iron, replicated on Lucy's shoulder blades. The hospital twigged, since there's almost no way you can back into a hot iron, and she finally named me as the one to phone. When I came tearing in, breathless with remorse for my blind stupidity, Lucy sat up on the bed, a little troll with a hunchback of dressings, and wept and wept. "Why? Why couldn't I make my marriage right? I don't want anything else. Even though I'm a feminist. I never wanted anything else. I believe in marriage." She was bewildered and sad and not even slightly angry. I handed her tissues and kept my mouth shut.

Edward did a runner. Caitriona and I moved Lucy and the twins back home to her mother. It was winter and miserable, and home was in one of those bleak towns that you'd speed through on wet Sundays, grateful that you don't have to live there. A hardware shopfront jammed with dusty tea sets and hot-water bottles, the dingy chemist, dummies with hollow tubercular faces in Lily's Dress Shoppe window.

From the backseat Lucy said tremulously, "I wonder if there'd be a women's group here?"

Despite all the assurances on her mother's doorstep, our paths promptly diverged. I got married, had a baby, finished college, had another baby, started my master's. I saw Lucy a couple of times when she came up for the Women Against Violence marches. She stayed with us and always rabbited on at Frank about how brilliant and wonderful I was. I'd say, oh come on Lucy, for heaven's sake, but I was pleased. It didn't do any harm for Frank to see me as mildly heroic instead of muddled and fearful, as he usually did. She hadn't changed. The bells were gone and so were the polo necks that had hidden Edward's ministrations, but she still wore dresses, and Tess would have said she still tinkled. I wasn't on great terms with Tess during those years, the bickering at the center had turned venomous.

Lucy's life was even grimmer than I'd feared. She was looking after her mother, who'd got Alzheimer's, and struggling with the twins, who were difficult, Peter especially. Sometimes I'd get at her about looking after her own life, saying there were fellows out there like herself, men whose marriages had shattered, born-again bachelors. Lucy would shrug, well, maybe when the twins were older. Having done my sisterly bit, I let it go.

Then Edward surfaced, via a solicitor's letter from Birmingham announcing divorce. He was under pressure to marry again, a poor sod of a woman who'd produced another set of twins on the strength of his double-tailed sperm. The injustice of this was cruel. Lucy was wiped out, as badly as if there'd been nothing but bliss between them. She confessed—to me, to Caitriona, to anyone who'd listen—that yes, she'd been nurturing the prodigal-husband-returns fantasy all along. But the bank of outraged sympathy that should have been hers to draw on was constantly depleted by the hilarity—the absurdity—of the situation. We felt guilty about it, but we couldn't stop sniggering and punning about double takes and double joints, doubling up and come again, come again.

She got over it because Peter diverted her. After he landed in juvenile court on a drugs charge, Lucy spent her days tearing from police stations to courtrooms to rehab centers. Wendy finished school and went off to college in England, after delivering a speech on Lucy's pitiful failure as a parent. Neither twin was at Lucy's mother's funeral.

She moved back to Dublin then. We met fairly often, sometimes with Caitriona, who was still hanging in at the center, fighting to keep the free support services open. Lucy made friends with our children and never talked about her own, but the day Peter came home she was suffused with joy. He'd been through several programs before he finally emerged, pale and vague but drug-free. He stayed until he discovered the Hare Krishnas, then shaved his head and went off in a pink caftan to live in a commune. Wendy had already taken herself and her degree to Australia.

Lucy didn't crumble. She went out and found a job with a man who'd started a family-tree-by-post operation and needed someone to hunt down ancestors in the Births, Deaths and Marriages Registry on the basis of information supplied by third-generation Irish Americans. Even though Caitriona and I were genuinely delighted for her, we couldn't stop laughing uproariously about all the trusting Yanks mounting their family tree charts, full of all the wrong O'Malleys and Sullivans. But Lucy loved her work, and the Yanks loved Lucy. They sent her presents and took her out for dinner when they came on their package holidays.

And then Lucy's boss decided to update their technology, and Joe strode into her office and her life, wearing a magician's top hat and cloak. He was as amazing as he looked— an actor turned computer wizard, one of those early geniuses who could do outlandish things on screen when everyone else was fumbling with cursors and discs. When he wearied of the keyboard, he went back to the boards and performed for children: magic shows, puppet shows, clown acts, fantasy productions full of mythical creatures in preposterous costumes.

The relationship flowered tenderly. Joe's story wasn't unlike hers. He'd been bewitched into marriage, chosen inexplicably from the shambling flock by the village princess. They set up home in a cottage by the sea, where Joe tried to fan the enchantment. But his bride had capricious inclinations, and she vanished with a playwright to an island off Donegal. One weekend Joe even took Lucy to Cork to retrace his past, to the church where he was married, the cottage off the rainy coast road. Lucy offered a return tour of her life, back to the midlands, to the home she'd fled from that wretched winter day in Caitriona's car.

Certainly they were holding nothing back. Caitriona and I approved. We also approved of Joe; we absolutely loved him. He was zany, fanciful, inventive. Our husbands dismissed him, but they couldn't help liking him too. He had a gift for endowing us with light hearts, and when Lucy and he had parties we laughed like children until we were giddy and staggered home exhilarated in the dawn.

❧

Hard to accept there were real sex problems there, I thought that Monday in the cafe, but who knows? As it happened, I did know something about simultaneous orgasms and I knew exactly where the information was. It was in a back issue of *Cosmopolitan*, jammed into my sock drawer with a pile of other magazines also offering tips on enhancing life's various dimensions, none of which I'd mustered the courage to attempt.

But in keeping with best counseling practice, I said nothing just then and encouraged Lucy to talk away. I thought it might be unfinished Edward business that was the actual difficulty. She blathered agreeably, about love, hope, romance, commitment, but mostly about Joe. Edward's only relevance seemed to be his participation in the mystic mating sign.

The following Monday I handed her *Cosmo* and said, "Start reading this while I go and order." It was an article about coital alignment technique, with briskly salacious instructions on how to work out the required position. We went through it together, Lucy puzzled but alert. "Lucy, this is something people can learn, you and Edward just discovered it accidentally," I said. "It's nothing significant at all. It's not a sign of destiny. Not even a sign of compatibility." She nodded doubtfully.

I turned briefly to geometry, fulcrums and so forth, but

abandoned it. "Look, it's a physical trick," I said. "Alignment, aligning, it's just a matter of two people adjusting the way they—"

"I know, I get it," she said abruptly. "I see." She closed the magazine, looking completely at a loss. "I did always wonder if it might be something like that."

I am no use at being nondirective, one of several reasons why I didn't go the psychotherapeutic route. I snapped "Lucy!" and then I asked her was there anything specifically wrong with sex with Joe, and was she having orgasms, or what?

No and yes, in spades, were the respective answers. "We're very sensately focused," she said, and smiled again and began to rattle away about aromatherapy and candles and "effervescent" massage, until I cried halt.

"Listen to me," I demanded. "What are you really upset about? It isn't really sex, is it? There's something else bothering you."

She looked down at her hands, clasped as always, and was silent a moment before she sighed. "I know. I just don't know what it is. There's something I can't put my finger on. But I knew it was unusual about my simultaneous orgasms—I did listen to things, you know," she added, flashing me a look, just faintly reproachful, "and I thought, well, sex is always an interesting thing to talk about and maybe in our sessions I should start there and after a while eventually I'd see something. . . ."

After a lot of coaxing she agreed she'd have to see someone else, a real counselor. I gave her some names.

When she phoned a couple of nights later I was hoping to hear that she'd found somebody, the right person. What she said was come over now, please, as fast as you can, I have to talk to you, something crazy has happened. I flung my raincoat over my tracksuit and drove over.

Her face had a caved-in, faraway look. "Joe's not married," she said. "He never was. I looked him up in the Registry this afternoon."

I was so relieved I fell into her rocking chair laughing. "Lucy, you made a mistake."

She watched me. Quite shrewdly, I realized later. "I knew you'd think that," she said. "But I do know how to do this. I looked, and he's not married to anybody and he never was."

It had been an innocent investigation. Rainy afternoon, not much research to be done, she was in the right section of the Registry. She just wanted to see Joe's name, enjoy that peculiar satisfaction of seeing names that belong to your life recorded in official documents, there for an uncaring posterity to see.

"I promise you, it's there somewhere," I said, rocking lazily. "You just missed it."

"Come with me tomorrow, I'll show you."

I went. I had a hundred other things to do, but I met Lucy at the Births, Deaths and Marriages Registry off Pearse Street, full of indulgent good humor. She was right. We ransacked the records, five years in either direction of the named date, several townlands either way of the named place. We found birth certificates for Joe and his putative bride, right where they should have been, but no evidence that either had married anybody, not in Ireland.

We eventually went out and into the first dingy pub we came to on Pearse Street. Lucy had coffee she didn't touch, I began drinking gin and tonic. I said this was silly, there had to be an explanation. All she had to do was ask him. If we'd overlooked something and he really was married, as I believed, they'd laugh about it. Lucy sat silently, shaking her head over and over as if to clear her mind. Finally she said, "I knew there was something. This is what it is."

All right, I said, if you think that, that he'd concocted the whole thing, you need to know why, and fast. There were men—Adulterers Against the Amendment, we called them—who liked things the way they were in this country, with marriage as a shield against the complications of dalliance. Joe didn't seem the type. But if he invented this story, told such massive lies, he was in bad trouble—sick, mad, evil? What else was there she didn't know?

Even as I talked I could feel Lucy growing stiller and more remote. "I know why he lied," she finally said. "And it's not any of those things, sick or wicked. He lied because he wished it were true. That girl is real and he really loved her, I know he did. She wouldn't marry him. So he made it up the way he wished it had been, even if it had to have a sad ending. He's had it so long it's true for him."

"Lucy, come on. Please."

"I'd do that," she said calmly. "I have done that. Why can't people do that? If you have dreams about how happy you could be if only a certain thing would happen, why can't you have dreams about how happy you could have been if it had? And now it's just as over with as it would have been if it really had happened."

"You're not making sense, Lucy. Stop it."

"I'm not going to ask him anything. It would spoil everything if I did. I'm just going to adjust to this. Align myself," she said. "And besides, this old divorce referendum won't get passed anyway. So what difference does it make?"

I lost my temper. This is infantile, Lucy, I said, clinging on to dreams, it's fantasy, rubbish; people aren't that way, life is full of deceit and disillusion; face facts for a change, grow up and live in the real world like the rest of us. I was seething, ranting in a furious hiss, when she suddenly stood up and put her coat on. She said thank you for being my friend, even if we can't agree. "You won't tell?" she asked, and then added, "I know you won't, it's all in confidentiality. But if you like you can tell Frank. Everybody tells a secret to someone, even counselors, so I don't mind if you tell Frank my story. But no one else?" I said certainly not, huffily, and sat there and watched her leave.

The referendum was held a few months later and divorce wasn't passed. By then Lucy and Joe had moved to Sligo. They're still there. Caitriona keeps in touch with them and says they're gloriously happy. I know Caitriona wonders what happened between Lucy and me, but she doesn't ask. Caitriona and I aren't that close now, either. We depressed each other too much for too long, bitching about Tess, the way she destroyed everything to set herself up in business servicing professional women's health needs, making her name.

I've never told Frank. I might someday. I'd like to. Just

say to him, listen, I want to tell you this case history, Lucy's secret case history; if I thought he would say the right thing. I don't want him to say, I would hate him to say, any of the things I said that night in the pub, the last time I saw Lucy.

Clods

❦

Mary Morrissy

Clods hit the coffin lid. It was a country funeral. They
didn't go in for covering up the grave with what looked like
a carefully cut sod of golf course.

"Thanks," Louis said.

"For what?" Norah tugged at his sleeve playfully as they
turned away from the graveside.

It was an unruly day of spring, blustery and gray, the
new-leaved trees tossed as if by grief. The wind shivered as
they led the mourners down the ragged path between the
furred gravestones. She wasn't sure if she should link him. It
seemed too proprietorial; he no longer belonged to her, after
all. Neither had she been sure of whether to wear black.
Would that be laying claim to a grief that didn't belong to
her either? (In the end she chose a Lenten purple.) Norah
had not cared much for Louis's mother but only because she
sensed his mother did not care much for her. It had been the
first time she had encountered hostility for its own sake.

The mere fact of her, Norah Elworthy, had been enough.

And, of course, she was spiriting away Mrs. Proctor's only son.

~

The noonday pub smelled of damp coats and the night before. There was a further round of condolences as neighbors came up and pumped his hand, saying simply "Louis," as if his name were an incantation of mourning. Norah went to sit in a corner under the dartboard. He caught her eye above the knot of people gathered at the bar and cocked an eyebrow, part query, part apology.

"A hot whiskey," she called.

He clapped his thighs in search of his wallet, then hitched up the tails of his overcoat and rummaged in his pockets. If Norah missed anything from her former marriage, it was the knowledge of those trademark gestures, so familiar, so typical, so male. These too had once been hers.

Nobody approached her, though Cora behind the bar had waved a vague greeting to her as she came in. The intervening years had reduced Norah to a once familiar face which could not be instantly placed. But then her memory of those who had peopled her young marriage had also dimmed. She recognized the postmistress (what was her name?) who used to beam at Norah as if she were visiting royalty. And there was Louis's uncle Ned, haphazardly shaven and bow-legged, leaning against a stool, his chest softly growling as he tried to draw breath.

Louis's boyhood friend, Ray, whose approval had once been so important, was handing out fistfuls of whiskey, a cigarette clamped in the fork of his thick, scored fingers. He had smiled shyly as he passed Norah earlier in the church. She was sitting several pews down on the groom's side while he had stood beside Louis at the front, a brotherly arm around his shoulders. She had watched the back of Louis's head, his hair curling over his collar, his ears, large and defenseless, the soft bulk of his back, and felt a choking sort of sadness. Not for him, but for the ancient loss of him.

∽

"It's Louis," he said when he rang with the news.

From his new life in America. She still regarded it as his new life though it was hardly apt. He had been away five years now. She had considered it running away. That was not her way. Hers had been to dig in deeper, to disappear into the debris of their marriage, to live among the ruins.

"Louis Proctor," he added hastily, as if there were a danger she would confuse him with some other Louis.

In the early days he would ring regularly at odd hours of the morning because he couldn't get the hang of the time difference. She remembered those conversations and the poignant intimacy they achieved over the transatlantic hiss, the comradely solidarity of two people who had survived a calamity as if their broken marriage were an external event, a natural disaster like a hurricane in which they had both been hapless bystanders.

Then the phone calls petered out and she knew he had found someone else. He had settled in Ann Arbor, a place that sounded to Norah like the name of another woman. Safe in the arms of Ann Arbor.

"It's my mother. . . ."

In the background she could hear the disappointed cadence of airport announcements.

"I was wondering . . ." he had started.

"The funeral?" she prompted.

There was an audible sigh.

"Would you?"

She had agreed heartily; it was only now, sitting in the albuminous wash of a lounge bar afternoon, that she wondered what she was doing here.

❧

Louis finally broke away and brought her the by now tepid whiskey. He took off his coat and slung it on a stool beside him. She resisted the temptation to lift its arm trailing in the sawdust and to fold it carefully. Even when they were married she wouldn't have done so; it would have been too wifey. They had prided themselves on not being conventional even as she marched down the aisle in white. To check one another they had used pet names. "Now who's being Agatha?" he would taunt when she complained about having to pick up his dirty socks from the bedroom floor. "Bangers and mash, George," she would bark when he would ask what was for dinner. She smiled now at the bragging childishness of it, as if they had been involved in an intricate board-game, and saw the fierce denial at the center of it. George and Agatha. He had boasted to friends that he wouldn't have a rolling pin in the house because theirs wasn't that kind of marriage, which meant that Norah had to use a milk bottle. For baking, that is. All her piecrusts had *Premier Dairies* imprinted on them.

❧

"Well," he said, "this place hasn't changed."

She wasn't sure if he meant the pub or the country.

"You look well," she offered.

And he did. The sun had given him a glossy, cosmetic air. His clothes—the neat, dark jacket, the tastefully somber tie, the stiff white shirt—bore the hand of another woman. She tried to imagine the woman at the other end of his life, roused in the graveyard hours by the death of someone she had never known, standing in her slip at the ironing board pressing his good clothes while he called reservations trying to get a ticket.

"I'm knackered, to tell you the truth. I haven't slept in days."

The pub was clearing slowly. The postmistress (Mrs. Baines!—the bane of our life, Louis used to say) came over to shake his hand. She was a stout, raddle-faced woman with small, pert lips.

"Your poor mother, Louis," she said, peering at him with an inquisitive sympathy. "All alone at the end."

Louis shifted uncomfortably.

"And with no family here, but Ned, and . . ." she paused and turned to Norah, "your good self, of course."

Norah did not know whether to feel complimented by this, her first official inclusion, or to be offended by the obvious reproach.

"If she were at home, itself. They go downhill once they go into those homes."

There was a moment's silence.

"You'll be selling the place, I suppose. Nothing to keep you here now."

Norah felt oddly, bleakly disowned.

&

She had visited Mrs. Proctor once at the nursing home, after Louis had gone away. She felt she owed it to her; it was a last-ditch attempt to be liked, she realized now, though it was less likely under those circumstances than any other. It was an old manor house set in half an acre of rutted parkland. A modern annex had been built on with floor-to-ceiling windows which gave on to seeping, foggy fields. Matron directed her to the rec room; in her mind's eye Norah saw a dry dock full of rusting hulks.

Mrs. Proctor was sitting in a large circle of plastic chairs, as if a group therapy session were about to start, or an afternoon tea dance. Only one other chair was occupied, by an old man in a cap with a leathery face and chipped teeth. He had no legs; he sat there like a lewd version of a nodding children's toy, his stumps swaddled in a tartan rug, grinning broadly and winking at Norah.

"Mrs. Proctor?" Norah whispered.

Her mother-in-law was sitting upright with her hands firmly planted on a walking frame, but in fact she was fast asleep.

"Mrs. Proctor?"

Startled, she awoke, and seemed ashamed as if Norah had come upon her having a secret tipple.

"It's me," Norah said. "Norah."

Her mother-in-law's sight was failing.

Clods

Norah drew up a chair beside her.

Mrs. Proctor registered no surprise at her former daughter-in-law being there. Just as she had barely reacted when Louis told her they were separating. It was as if their lives were inauthentic in some way, Norah had thought, as foreign and as passively regarded as a television soap opera.

"Did you come down today?"

"Yes, on the train," Norah replied, wanting to elaborate but finding nothing more to say. There had never been much small talk between them.

"I find the days very long here," Mrs. Proctor said after a while. "I can't get round, do you see. I can't get round like I used to."

"Have you heard from Louis?" Norah asked. She was still hungry for news of him then, or even to talk about him in a kindly and abstracted way.

"In the summer you can walk in the garden, but with my pins I've seen the last of the garden, I'd say."

"Does he write?" Norah asked gingerly.

"Timmy there." Mrs. Proctor gestured conspiratorially to the man with the amputated legs. "Timmy there is always asking me how much land I have. I think he's after me."

Norah abhorred this flirty gaiety; it revolted her. She preferred the patients who sat sunk in a primeval gloom lost in the sepia musings of long ago. A restive silence fell between the two women.

"It's nighttime there now," Mrs. Proctor said suddenly.

"Nighttime where?"

"Where Louis is," she said quietly. "I count the hours. . . ."

As did Norah, frequently. It was a kind of mental house-keeping. Before going to sleep, she would do a quick calculation and think, without rancor or envy, he's probably leaving work now, or going to the movies, maybe. It was a way of placing him, of rendering him fixed.

"And neither of us have him," his mother said.

∾

The key turned stiffly in the lock and Louis stepped into the small hallway which smelled of damp disuse. It was icy, as if the cold fingers of death had edged their way into the place. The kitchen of the small cottage had been "improved" since Norah had been there last. There was a fridge now in place of the bucket of cold water outside the back door for milk and butter. The fireplace had been bricked up and in its place a two-bar electric fire with mock coals had been installed. Louis stooped and plugged it in. It cast a phosphorescent glow on the parquet-look lino which had been laid over the old flagstones. The only sign of life in the place was Louis's two bags opened and spilling out their contents onto the floor. He fished out a woolen sweater and put it on. (It was true, Norah thought, exile makes people soft.) Then rummaging further he retrieved a bottle of duty-free whiskey. He hunted around for glasses, sliding back one door and then another of the kitchen cabinets, which released musty little bouquets of neglect. He found two dusty tumblers with bees painted on them, free offers with a honey promotion.

"So," Louis said, setting the bottle and beakers on the kitchen table. In this setting, two near strangers sitting on hard chairs in a darkening room lit only by the sickly hue from the fireplace, the scene could have been one of interrogation.

"So," he repeated, "how have you been?"

She felt she had so little to offer. Years of recuperation, a steady but mean renewal of her life. She spoke about her job, she was head of her department now with her own office and a car. She did not talk about men. It was an unwritten rule between them, a kind of deference. He inquired about Patricia, the baby sis, he always called her. And her mother, of course, who was slipping slowly into senility.

"The poor old bird," Louis said refilling their glasses. "Who's looking after her?"

"I am," she said.

"Oh, I see, the dutiful daughter."

"I couldn't just abandon her."

"Like I did, you mean."

The accusation sat between them in the gathering dusk. Louis narrowed his eyes over the plume of spirits in his glass. Norah watched him covertly. She could barely see him in the deepening shadows, so she had to imagine his bog-colored eyes, those big soft hands, the fluttering nerve in his cheek. As she had done for five years.

∾

She remembered, once, shortly after they separated, finding a note from Louis in the kitchen. He still had a key to the house. She had never got round to asking for it back. The kettle had been broken and he had scribbled a message to her on the back of an envelope.

What you need, it read, *is a new element.*

For a moment she thought he was being philosophical and she remembered standing there contemplating this proposition, basking in his new wisdom about her, as if he were offering one last remedy in a gnomic code.

Then, stung by her own foolishness, she crushed the note into a tight ball and set fire to it in the sink.

Darkness fell. The reproachful silence between them blossomed into a mournful but easy complicity. Too easy, Norah thought.

"I really should be going," she said.

"You can't drive with all that drink in you," he said. "Stay!"

He put a restraining hand on her wrist. It was the first time he had touched her since they'd met.

"I can't, Louis."

"Why not?"

"Not here."

"You mean people will talk? Hell, let them. I mean, technically, we're still man and wife."

He cupped his hand over hers. They sat like that for several minutes, like children making a solemn pact. She could feel goosepimples rise on her forearm. She attributed the stirrings within her to the artificial heat and the whiskey.

"Don't, Louis, please."

She disentangled her fingers.

"The Big No," he said in mock basso.

She rose and shrugged on her coat.

"Is this it, then?" he asked.

Clods

❧

It was she who had asked that question when they had parted. After the breakup (she favored the term *breakup;* it suggested a dramatic shipwreck as opposed to breakdown, which was like an engine running out of steam) she felt obliged to remove the framed photograph of their wedding from the mantel, but she still kept a holiday snap of him stuck into the corner of the dressing table mirror. There had been no final ritual—no death, no divorce—so he remained there like some lost figure, a hostage or a pilot missing in action. They were still, after all these years, just separated, as if only time and circumstance were keeping them apart. The Ex, she would say jokingly if anyone asked who it was. The ultimate abbreviation. The Ex.

Shedding the ring had taken longer. It took until Louis stopped wearing his. She had met him by chance on the street. It was the first thing she had noticed, the naked finger. He had rubbed at it self-consciously.

"I didn't see the point," he had said.

She had felt betrayed. Somehow, she had always thought that this was something they would do together. She had imagined some grand gesture, the pair of them standing on a bridge and flinging the gold tokens high into the air and watching them dazzle briefly before falling into the waters below.

❧

They made love desperately on his mother's bed. She had thought it would be like a gentle stroll through a childhood haunt; a marveling at the orchard's windfalls, an easy climb to the dark aperture of the old barn, a cushioned fall in the springy hay. Instead they clawed at one another, all fingernails and spittle. They wrestled greedily, their sweaty flanks slapping against one another, both of them bellowing and braying, joyously aghast at this suddenly unleashed appetite. They lay afterward on the candlewick bedspread, smelling of semen, their good clothes crumpled and gaping. If they had been naked it would have seemed less illicit, Norah thought. And yet as they lay there, fingers barely touching, eyes locked in the questioning embrace of aftermath, she realized that this was the first time she had desired Louis. It had not been a matter of comfort. Her own, or his.

An hour passed in a grave, sprouting silence.

"I'm an orphan now," Louis said finally.

He had broken the spell. She had forgotten his weakness for lofty self-pity. She pulled herself up and wedged several pillows behind her. His hand rested lazily against her thigh. She listened as his breathing grew quieter, steadier, and he drifted into sleep. She wanted to reach out and stroke his hair or touch the blue-veined skin around his temples, but she was afraid of her own tenderness now. And, anyway, she would only wake him and what was the point in that?

∾

It was the early hours of the morning before she slid from the bed. She wrapped her coat around her and stepped into her abandoned shoes. She stood for a moment in the doorway before picking her way through the dark kitchen.

"Bye, bye," she called out softly as she pulled the front door to. There was no reply.

As she drove through the moonlit countryside she thought of him lying on the littered remains of the conjugal bed. Like an undiscovered corpse. Dead, dead to the world.

Passover

Mary O'Donnell

Practically every night since the first exhausted ones when the blood leaked out onto her damask nightgown, Rosanna dreamt of still, pale seas. Like a child, she would run breathlessly along the cliff paths, seeking a way to the water's edge. It was a sunny dream, with scattered tribes of summer visitors below on the sand. Children's voices were whirled high on the light wind; a brown and white terrier ran after a ball, and Rosanna's body was bent on immersal in that sea. Sometimes Henry was with her, part of the dream. She accepted his presence without question.

One Saturday afternoon when the baby was eight weeks old, she drove over to Henry's place. It was her first visit in the six months since they'd met. Her mother had taken the baby for the day.

She'd spent the morning drifting through the warm crowds on Grafton Street and she was still free, free, free.

Accelerating across the canal bridge, she overtook a slow-moving scooter, then admired the exultant light that cascaded through the trees onto the windscreens of oncoming traffic. Not once did she relax her excited clench on the wheel. She adjusted her Ray-Bans, sniffed at the tang of a new leather jacket draped over the passenger seat, then looked quickly in the mirror. Her hair flew in loose blond wings around her shoulders, her cheeks were drawn and hollow as if with a dark energy. Her eyes were shining and gray. As she scrutinized herself and the car wavered across the white line, an oncoming driver sheared past, horn blaring, then disappeared down Heytesbury Street, a snort of gleaming red, his face maddened. She swerved, barely missing a cyclist. The sound of the red car, followed by the sight of the cyclist's raised middle finger, jarred at her high excitement. Her whole body stiffened in the car seat, then slumped closer to the steering wheel. "Jesus Christ," she whispered to herself, "when will it end?"

The only place she could get a bit of peace and quiet at the hospital was in the baths, especially the demi-tubs. That was her hideout, three or four times a day after the birth, a gushing, echoing haven which contained two such tubs and a standard long one. Conversation between the women, on the occasion that all three alcoves were occupied, was random and sporadic. The walking wounded, she remembered, would sink their bruised lower parts into a warm swirl, sigh and grow still behind plastic curtains.

She had never had a Turkish bath, but back in Washington, Marlene once told her of the exquisite release of handing one's careless flesh over to the hands of women who slough away every trace of time's recent deposits.

Marlene rarely exclaimed about anything. She had traveled from Timbuktu to Termonfeckin, had boated down the Yangtze as well as the Corrib, never forgot her portable computer, her razor, her vibrator and an antispasmodic pill called Imodium. During labor Rosanna thought fleetingly about Marlene's accurate yet unhelpful advice that every contraction meant you were one stage closer to the finishing line.

As she sat in the demi-tub, she would listen to the other women on the far side of the partition as they bathed. They were like escaped animals, stunned but functioning. When the water cooled, Rosanna would open the taps and blast more anodyne around her thighs. Sitting there, she sometimes thought about Henry, about the way his forehead had puckered with disbelief, fascination and less nameable emotions, the moment he'd laid eyes on the baby.

At the hospital, the ward orderly who emptied bins and mopped residues with sodden towels from the delivery ward floor, told her he had once been a pork butcher. The nurses behaved toward him as if his maleness alone accounted for the condition of all the women in the hospital. "Testosterone overload, if you ask me," one of them said in an offended voice, "brings me out in a rash, he does."

Rosanna did not dislike him. He understood some of the pangs of mind and body. She knew by the way he had flirted so casually the night before her induction, acknowledging what everyone else seemed to have long forgotten. He was perky. She imagined him down at his local, boasting about the things he knew about women.

The married women in the ward, awaiting sections and inductions, were surrounded by husbands, mothers and sometimes children. She rested for the last few hours of her pregnancy, blood pressure soaring, fingers tight and puffy, and sparred with the orderly. She did not feel alone. Henry had brought chocolate-covered Brazil nuts and a damask nightgown, then left for a night shift at the pathology department up in James's.

Later, the blinds and curtains on the flats opposite were drawn, late spring blizzards ripped across the roofs of Dolphin's Barn, then cleared to reveal a mother-of-pearl moon fixed to a frozen sky. Rosanna could not sleep, anticipating the next day's certain events.

One morning nine months before, she'd invited the child's father back into bed. What she remembered now was a pink aura in the bedroom as sunlight washed through the slats of the blinds, rather than an act of any particular pleasure. She had hooked him around the waist with her arm, without knowing why, without thinking of possible consequences. The reasons for the gesture, she concluded, sprang from some prehistoric place of keen animal perception which never slept, alert to every pharmaceutical ruse designed to outwit the rhythms of the twentieth-century female body.

After the birth, they'd left her in the delivery room for a while, wrapped in cotton blankets, a dimmed light behind her head. The orderly chatted about his last job. Rosanna relaxed and flexed her feet gently beneath the blanket, propped her head with her left arm.

"So it's yerself." He nodded, recognizing her.

"How's the pork butcher?" she whispered by way of a reply.

"Ex–pork butcher," he corrected, squeezing a mop.

"Pigs bleed like hell," she said quietly.

"Yeah, bleedin' like a stuck pig, as they say."

She watched as he mopped and squeezed, mopped and squeezed, pictured him slicing a dead, bled pig down the middle with a glistening cleaver, splitting the sternum, separating a symmetry of ribs and pelvis until the animal lay in halves, like an enlarged, Technicolor Rorschach image.

"Have you ever looked into a pig's eyes?" she asked drowsily. He paused, his gaze earnest. One of the nurses poked her head around the door.

"Are you nearly finished in here yet?" He raised his eyebrows and made a clicking sound with his tongue as the door swung closed.

"Nice girl that. Don't know what's wrong with her. Now where was I? Oh yes. Pigs. They're as intelligent as dogs," he went on. "Me missus has this bitch and I swear there's no difference between her and some of the pigs."

"The dog?"

"Jayyzzz . . ." he snorted.

"Did you mind doing it?"

"What?"

"Killing them."

"They hardly know they're gone."

She could see why he was at home in the maternity hospital. Women coming and laboring and going, one of life's greatest emergencies crafted to a medical art.

❧

The first time she met Henry, he was poring over a newspaper in a cramped restaurant off Fownes Street, hungrily cramming a chocolate Swiss roll into his mouth. Rosanna was five months pregnant. Something about the ripples on the chocolate as it disappeared into his mouth reminded her of the day she and Marlene visited the Hirschhorn Museum and Sculpture Garden at the Smithsonian. She'd bought a Georgia O'Keeffe print called "Black Hills with Cedar," which the artist painted while living in New Mexico. Back home, it aroused mild consternation, even embarrassment. Her choice of souvenir unsettled and amused some of her friends.

In time, it became a source of bawdy conversation at parties which had reached the point of no return. Initially, Rosanna had only seen hills fringed by a slightly ominous clump, unaware of O'Keeffe's alleged tendency to turn flowers and mountains into florid genital representations.

On the Day of the Chocolate Swiss Roll, she recalled the Hirschhorn's fabulous bronze antiwar sculptures. One in particular showed the heads and bodies of hundreds of soldiers mounted on a huge phallus.

While in America, she wasn't aware of pregnant women, unlike at home where they were very much in evidence. Marlene wrote soon after the birth, in response to Rosanna's hastily scribbled SOS.

"Rosanna, dear, Your letter arrived and the exhaustion

you report is, alas, normal. Particularly when one is over 18 and without a man. I remember thinking I wouldn't survive it, but I did, and you will also. And life goes on. Despite everything (and maybe because of it) life goes on."

The living and the dying, the about to live and about to die, held the world to ransom. Coming into life was like visiting a season. Perhaps when God created the world, he had imagined a season and called it Eden. Eden first announced itself to Rosanna while she sat in the demi-tub at the hospital. Now she dreamt about Eden every night between the baby's feeds. It had all the flora and fauna of springtime in the Northern Hemisphere. Blackthorn hedges prowled, crows cawed, poplar trees shivered, sturdy seaweeds trailed the piers of ancient estuaries, and a vernal light danced on every surface, seeking apertures, crevices, dusty corners.

It was as if she had been reborn. She brimmed with something imponderable. Whatever it was, it felt dangerous. Yet she still pushed Henry away, gently but firmly. He'd call by on his way from the laboratory, freshly scrubbed after a day dissecting cadavers, removing organs bequeathed in advance of death. His attention, on top of everything else, was almost too much. When her visitors had left, after swamping her with good wishes, flowers and teddy bears, Eden would overwhelm her again. Sitting in the tub, she knew she'd been cut away from the past, had survived a primitive journey across a river of casual slaughter.

Rosanna slid beneath the surface of the water, felt it lap up along her neck, over her ears, finally over the top of her head. Beneath the surface, the sensation of warmth throughout her coiled body was so pleasurable that she realized she would have to postpone drowning in lieu of pleasure. She surfaced, took a deep breath and again submerged herself. It obliterated everything, the thundering sound of water pouring into cisterns somewhere above, random echoes from the corridor, the laughter of visitors come to scrutinize the newborn.

∾

Seven months pregnant, she'd cycled to the shop late one evening, skidded and fell on a patch of ice. Monstrous ice-laden mists rolled up the river. For a split second, her head reeled as she lay on the road.

"Are you all right?"

It was Henry. For a while she said nothing, afraid to move until the child turned inside her again. He pulled her in as the traffic thundered across a nearby intersection.

"I'm fine," she eventually replied, as near to tears as she had ever come in those months. "You keep—turning up," she added.

"This is my beat. Pathology's just up the road," he said, helping her to her feet. He insisted on walking with her the remaining stretch to the shop, wheeled the bicycle with his left hand, guided her elbow with his right. Up the hill at Christchurch, bells pealed through the freezing fog. Traffic was at a standstill, each driver locked in an elongated metal capsule, breathing dampness and sulphur, bent on the homeward trail, thoughts focused on fires, television viewing, the prospect of rest. She bought three Walnut Whips and two bars of orange chocolate. There were pink blotches on Henry's cheekbones and she caught a whiff of spirits from his breath. He paused once and turned to her, placed his hand gently on her stomach. To her surprise, she felt blessed by the touch of this near-stranger.

Then, embarrassed, she asked him about his job.

"Nobody," he said, turning puce, "has ever before asked me why I do what I do."

"I wonder why."

"Bodies. People are afraid of dead bodies."

She laughed. "So they think you've a vested interest in death?"

"Something like that." He continued to guide her from the shop, until they stopped outside a cafe. The smell of fish, chips and vinegar raged warmly from within Burdocks along the queue that wound around the street corner. Her stomach rumbled.

"Come on. You need something to steady yourself."

In Kennelly's Tea Rooms, she smelt soda bread and clovey apple tart. For the first time since she'd become pregnant, the aroma of strong tea did not make her stomach heave. She rested her chin in her hands and smiled at Henry.

She and Marlene visited the famous site at Appomattox. Marlene had rambled on about her ex-husband, whose new wife had the IQ of a piece of wallboard, was very sweet and perfect for him.

"Why do we do it Rosanna, why the heck do we bother with 'em?"

"Because they are different. Because they are other," Rosanna had speculated.

The pork butcher–turned-orderly would be more impressed with Appomattox than some of the people who came to view it before whizzing off to Monticello, President Jefferson's specially designed home. It was he who had worked ambivalently for the abolition of slavery while retaining his own retinue of black workers.

"How come you're no longer a butcher?" she'd asked in the delivery room, after the midwife took the baby to warm up in an incubator.

"Business went bust."

"So what brought you here?"

"It's a job." He shrugged, then cocked his head and looked at her quizzically. "If you wanted to cook marrowfat peas, how would you cook them?"

"What?"

"Would you steep them overnight with the white tablet, or what?" He propped his chin on the mop handle.

"Ah, fuck off."

"Go on. Serio, like."

"What kind of a stupid question is that?" she asked, as the blood spurted onto the brown wadding the nurses had slipped beneath her exploded, new-stitched perineum. She regarded her hands, fingernails ridged with dried blood, her left hand and arm streaked with it. The smell was sweet as a balm.

"Just to see if you'd make a good wife," he muttered, and resumed his labors.

Unhesitatingly, she told him that she'd go right out and

buy a tin of marrowfats, precooked. He rolled his eyes, smiled sadly, then shook his head.

The ward orderly's experience would be welcomed between the covers of a hardback novel, or a slim volume of angry poetry, particularly if he dared to articulate it himself. Yet the difference between his written life and his lived one, was like the difference in distance between the Milky Way and Andromeda. Her most physical and violent work over, she watched him idly, imagined a future for her child, her daughter. Yet the future, she knew even then, could be terminally shocking. She took a deep breath. More blood spurted from her. Take it day by day, lady, she hushed herself. Enter Eden.

Remember Eve. In the weeks after the birth, she struggled to contain the panic of her love. She was wet with it, sweating with it, hot with it. Even her nipples pranced with it. Was it for the child alone?

There seemed so much feeling that the only way she could cope was by lavishing her excesses on Henry. If only he'd stayed away instead of pursuing her, she might have felt calmer. Yet she kept phoning him, at any hour of the day or night, whether he was in the laboratory or in his bed. One night when the baby almost choked because the teat on the bottle let the milk run too freely, she rang him in a panic, her body trembling uncontrollably. The child had gone purple in her arms. Rosanna had held her in the air like a doll, tried desperately to remember what to do. Was it the Heimlich method or did she hold the little creature upside down and rub her back vigorously? In the end, the baby coughed and spluttered, then cried, and everything was all right.

Henry came over anyway and slept on the sofa. Every time he smiled, she feared she might collapse against him or beg him to hold her and mind her forever. She wanted to be held. Yet she could not ask him, not yet.

She remembered Eve in Eden, what her first spring must have been like after the birth of those awful brothers.

❧

Rosanna and Marlene saw the servants' quarters behind houses dating from the Civil War—pristine, whitewashed little shelters which would have been stifling in summer and freezing in winter. They didn't look so bad until she heard how many black servants they housed at one time. Meanwhile, up in Monticello, Jefferson worked on his inventions. He had a bed built into the thick wall which separated the bedroom from the study. In that way, whenever an interesting possibility struck, he could leap straight from bed to study. Before, Rosanna used to quite regularly hop from bed in her nightclothes for preliminary work on some plan, a fan heater blowing across her bare feet as she sat at the computer. Now the central heating was on day and night for the baby. And she had to sleep.

In Washington, she'd sat in McDonald's with Marlene after a visit to the Torpedo Factory. The Smithsonian was High Culture and Torpedo Factory was hands-on but definitely Lower Culture. Marlene had talked about her plans to have a second family someday, she wasn't sure when exactly, but someday, if her biological clock hadn't stopped ticking.

"Who'll be the father?" Rosanna asked.

"More like who'll want to be father," Marlene grumbled. "The choice isn't limitless, I guess."

Outside, it began to drizzle. The last stifling fall days had ended. Temperatures plummeted overnight and Rosanna had bought a cardigan in a shop off Independence Avenue. In a matter of hours, the cicadas went silent, signaling an end to thirsty days and the beginning of freezing nights. The two women paused for a moment, their eyes drawn to the street outside. The silence continued longer than it should have. They watched, transfixed, as a wizened Vietnamese man tottered past the window, feet rag-bound and filthy, his body emaciated.

"In some parts of the world, people work magic in order to ease suffering," she told Henry. "Remember that bit in *The Right Stuff*?"

"A cinematic trick," he scoffed.

It was the film's climax, the critical moment when the astronauts are locked within their capsule, far from Earth. Images of bushmen chanting around a bonfire intersperse the high-tech action. At the point of maximum danger, one of the astronauts witnesses an inexplicable drift of sparks around the spaceship, brilliant as fireflies. The men are saved, because (the viewer is expected to deduce) the aborigines had intervened.

Rosanna had speculated about the aborigines, the Carmelites, and unorthodox priests banished to outposts of either Ireland or the Third World, psychics and healers within every community. Why, she wondered, could a blazing aboriginal bonfire, a pointed bone, or a possessed dancer leaping over hot coals, not relieve the hunger and pain of an ancient Vietnamese man thousands of miles from his home? During her delivery, when she had felt like a cornered animal, the thought of the aborigines flashed through her mind, but most of all the sense of having been conned.

❧

Now, she pulled up on the broad footpath outside a renovated building above the brewery, braked hard and switched off the car engine. She sat for a moment wondering if she should go home again.

Her gaze rested on a small holly hedge that scratched and tapped at the building's low windowsills. She had no right to be away from the child, out gallivanting with Henry. The blaring car horn, the accusing face of its driver, the cyclist she'd almost hit as a result, were still vivid. It took so little to make her feel small, to sense her energy in retreat to God knows where. The drone of traffic rose from below on the quays. It was too late to turn back. Henry stood in the doorway, making funny welcoming gestures. "Where's baby?" he called out.

She stepped stiffly from the car. "With my mother," she replied. "I didn't think—"

"Never assume anything, Rosanna. Never assume." He smiled, wagging his forefinger. "I wanted to see the little witchette, you know."

She shrugged and made an apologetic face. It was too late now. Once inside, she removed her jacket, tossed her hair back from her shoulders and looked around. She eyed the bottle of Bordeaux, two glasses, and the cheese snacks laid on a low table. Henry fiddled with the CD player, then turned as a thought struck him. "Do we need music?"

"I don't know. Do we?"

"Hmm," he deliberated. "Perhaps not."

She sighed, relieved. Atmospheric music might break her. The room had absorbed the odors of all the meals Henry ate while watching satellite television late at night. Despite herself she sniffed. Chips and spag bol, curry, eggs and toast and garlic. A musty odor that she could not quite define underpinned everything.

"Mice."

"Mice?"

"I saw you sniffing," he explained. "Mice. An interest of mine. No doubt you hate them—"

"Actually no. Never assume . . ."

They both laughed.

A scrap of bacon rind curled from beneath the table and a succession of yellow notelets stuck to the cracked glass panels of a bookcase. In Eden it was the apple that did it, not the serpent, she thought. Eve didn't need a bloody reptile to draw the attention of historians and scholars to the phenomenon of an exploring feminine conscience. Rosanna's body was tired. Leather boots kicked and marched once more within her breast. Henry passed her a glass.

"Hell, I shouldn't. It makes me want to sleep."

"You can do that here. Nod off," he said quietly, pouring, not looking at her.

She flopped back against a cushion. She had pushed a child to life, yet there had been a death. Despite that death, she would explore Eden, she must ascend to meet it. It was like choosing to love or not to love the child, to live or to die. There was no choice. "So what'll we do?" She smiled at him, stirring herself.

"Nothing."

"Nothing?"

"You're too exhausted."

Suddenly, the new leather jacket, the Ray-Bans, even her long hair, made her feel silly. Her skin was as slack as his but for different reasons. She wanted to be held, and she wanted to weep like a child battered for no reason, beaten black and blue with no court of appeal, ripped to pieces by the birth of a baby. Her baby. Child. Daughter. They sat and gossiped for an hour. He made no attempt to touch her. Gradually, she felt better.

Later, she drove away, hair disheveled, cheeks livid from wine and the unexpected exertion of hunting for an escaped mouse. Henry had blathered on about dominant and recessive genes. She chugged into the sunset, snared in the traffic near the estuary bridge. Unlike Jack Kerouac she wasn't on the road anywhere but to her mother's to pick up the baby.

❧

That night, for the first time in eight weeks, the baby slept right through. Rosanna slept and sweated. Sometimes her shoulders twitched, her eyelids rolled and darted as she dreamt about the hot bush country, watched shoals of sparks drift into a southern midday. Already, the future beckoned. Eden had come and the world was ablaze; the pylons and satellites, the pulses and connections were alive and singing above and below field and mountain. Night passed effortlessly into dawn. The angel of despair had passed her door without stopping, daubed as it was with the blood of new life. The baby snuffled and turned. Rosanna stirred.

"Let me hold you . . . I just want to hold you . . ." she whispered in the frail light.

She swung the baby from its creaking basket beside the bed, leaned into the warmth of its drowsy body; her lips brushed the down on its head. She inhaled the scent of her waking child.

Ripples

❧

Patricia Scanlan

June '96.

"Bit of frost there with the McHughs tonight," Mike Stuart murmured dryly to his wife Kathy as they stood at the front door waving off their guests.

"That's an understatement if ever I heard one," Kathy muttered out of the side of her mouth. "They'd have been at home in the Arctic."

"What's new?" Mike asked glumly.

They stood caught in the wide beam of the car's headlights as Barry McHugh reversed down the drive, giving a toot on his horn as he did so. Beside him, his wife, Alison, looked utterly pissed off. Kathy knew that the tight smile she gave them would be gone in seconds as soon as the car headed toward the main road.

Kathy gave a sigh of relief as the Lancer's rear lights disappeared into the night. Tonight had been a disaster. Alison had sniped at Barry continuously. At times he'd ignored her completely. This had been like a red rag to a bull and as her rage and resentment, fueled by several large Bacardis, over-flowed, she'd turned to her friends and said with pure venom, "I'm married to the biggest fucking bastard you could meet."

"Either take your go now, Alison, or forfeit it. You've been holding up the game for the last five minutes," Barry said coldly, his eyes like flints behind his glasses as he glowered at her.

"Get lost. I'll go when I'm ready. Just because you think you're *Mister Intelligence.* Well you're not you're just a cheat. I mean who else would try and get away with putting Monaco down and claiming it was a font? It's not in the dictionary so it shouldn't be allowed. And you shouldn't get a triple word score."

"Well if you weren't so *thick,* you'd know it *was* a font and I'll show it to you on the computer when we get home."

"Oh stick your bloody computer. You should have married one you spend so much time on that one in the office," Alison snapped as she slapped down her letters.

"Is that the best you can do? *Rat!* Pathetic!" Barry's brown eyes flashed with scorn.

"Well I'm married to one aren't I?" Alison riposted coldly. "Don't forget it's a double word score."

"The first one you've managed so far," Barry drawled as he wrote down the score.

They'd been playing their usual Saturday night game of Scrabble. A tradition that went back to the carefree giddy days of their early twenties when they'd all been newlyweds and the future had looked rosy. Now, fourteen years later,

Ripples

Barry and Alison weren't getting on too well, much to the dismay of Mike and Kathy.

Over the last few months things had got so bad that the weekly game of Scrabble, which they'd always looked forward to after a few drinks and a Chinese, was becoming a bit of an ordeal.

"I've never seen them as bad as tonight," Kathy reflected as she collected the dirty glasses and emptied the cold, congealed remains of the Chinese take-away into the bin.

"Why they ever married each other I'll never know. They're like chalk and cheese. And they always were. I mean Alison is always gadding about, and Barry hates going anywhere." Mike picked the bones of a cold sparerib.

"Put that in the bin, you glutton." Kathy grimaced. "They say opposites attract and maybe it worked at the start but it's not working now."

"Yeah well Alison made the big mistake of thinking she was going to change Barry and he'll never change. He's not even making the effort now. I don't think he really wants to come over to us on Saturday nights anymore. All he wants to do is go to his football matches and bury himself in his work. He lives in that office."

"Would you say Barry's got another woman?" Kathy eyed her husband quizzically. "I mean he can't be spending all those nights at work."

"Barry! Barry McHugh! Don't be daft, woman," Mike scoffed as he licked his fingers. "He'd run a mile if a woman came near him. Imagine Barry sitting down and having a conversation with a woman. It's hard enough for him to have a conversation with us and he's known us for years."

"Yeah, maybe you're right," Kathy poured Fairy Liquid into a basin of hot water. "He's great fun though when he's in form. He's got a real dry sense of humor. I feel sorry for him sometimes. Alison's always nagging him."

"Barry likes being nagged. He likes being told what to do. He never makes decisions. Alison makes them all. I mean did you hear her tonight telling him he was to get his hair cut next week? And telling him that she'd told Brenda Johnston that he'd tile her bathroom without even *asking* him? I mean what is he, a man or a mouse?" Mike picked up the towel and started to dry the dishes. "It's like he's the child and she's the mother. It's always been like that with them. That would drive me nuts. If I came home and found out that you'd told Brenda Johnston I'd tile her crappy bathroom you know what your answer would be." He grinned.

"Well Alison always was a bossy boots. And I wouldn't inflict Poison Dwarf Johnston on you. I'd know better." Kathy giggled. Brenda Johnston was Alison McHugh's best friend. Kathy didn't like her. She thought she was sly and she was always flirting with other women's husbands. Brenda, who was unmarried and in her early forties, had recently bought a house that needed a lot of renovation. She was an expert at the "Poor little me, I'm a helpless female" act. Every male of her acquaintance was being roped in to assist in her renovations. Barry was doing the lion's share.

"*Poison Dwarf* ! . . . Miaow! Brenda's not in the good books. What's she done now?"

"She had the nerve to say that I didn't know what stress was. I had you to provide for me and I could come and go as I pleased because I'm a housewife with very little to do."

"Well I do provide for you and you can come and go as you please," Mike said innocently.

"You know what I mean." Kathy flicked frothy suds at her husband. He flicked back and drenched her.

"Stop it," she squealed.

"Shush, you'll wake the kids," Mike warned.

"Well if the baby wakes up *you* won't be getting any nookey tonight because it's your turn to get up to her. And *I* intend sleeping my brains out . . . in the spare room if necessary," Kathy said smugly.

"We'll see about that." Mike dropped the towel, grabbed his wife and gave her a long, smoochy kiss.

"Let's leave the rest of the washing-up and the *two* of us can sleep in the spare room." He nuzzled her ear.

Kathy giggled. Even after ten years of marriage and three children, Mike still turned her on and she loved him passionately. Hand in hand they crept upstairs into the spare bedroom and thoroughly enjoyed themselves for the next hour.

Later, nestled in the curve of Mike's arm, Kathy said sleepily, "Would you say Barry and Brenda are having a fling?"

"Who in their right mind would want to have an affair with Bug-eyes Johnston? Are you mad? She wouldn't shut up long enough to let someone kiss her she loves the sound of her own voice so much. She's such a bloody know-all. Who'd want to listen to that one yakkin' in that squeaky little voice of hers and watch her flicking that lank greasy brown hair of hers over her shoulders the way she does."

"Well Barry didn't say he wouldn't tile her bathroom for

her. He's always doing bits and pieces for her. Maybe *he* likes her, and Alison's always telling her that she can have him. Big joke but I think Brenda thinks she's serious."

"She's bossy enough for him anyway, she's even more of a dictator than Alison."

"Ah, Alison's not that bad," Kathy defended her friend. "If she didn't nag Barry he'd never do anything except watch soccer and play with his computers."

"If I lived in their house that's all I'd want to do. It's like a pigsty. Housekeeping is not Alison's forte. You don't know how lucky you are, I never watch soccer and I don't have a computer," Mike murmured into her hair.

"And I don't have a job, like Alison. I'm always here to cook your dinner and have the fire lighting and have your shirts ironed every morning. You don't know how lucky you are, buster!"

"I know how lucky I am," Mike whispered as his arms tightened around her.

"Poor Barry and Alison, it's horrible isn't it?" Kathy said sadly.

"I couldn't stick a marriage like that. All that bitterness and anger and resentment. It's almost as if they hate each other now. Maybe they'd be better off divorced."

"Oh don't say that, Mike," Kathy exclaimed.

"Well it's true. What kind of a life have they got now? No life. The trouble with Alison and Barry, and I don't say this lightly, they're very dear to me, we've been friends a long time, but the two of them in their own way are very selfish people. There's very little give-and-take there. Barry should never have got married. He should never have had a child either. He's not prepared to make the effort. Poor Ciara's a nuisance to him. He thinks once he provides financially for her that his responsibility's over. He's not prepared to give any more. It's like our friendship. If we didn't have them over and keep in touch he wouldn't bother. It's too much effort. He's a strange chap."

"I wonder does our friendship mean anything to him? Or is it just habit with him?" Kathy mused.

"You never know with Barry. You never know what's really in his mind. Barry's very . . . how would I describe it. Sort of calculating, I suppose. He always was. Says nothing much, but takes it all in."

"He's very good-natured though. He'd never see you stuck. Maybe it's just a bad patch. Maybe they'll work things out."

"I hope so, because if they don't, I don't really want to go away for a long weekend with them. I don't want to have to sit listening to that for three days."

"Me neither," Kathy agreed glumly. "But I always looked forward to that weekend away without the kids. It wouldn't be the same going on our own. Remember the time we went to West Cork and we found out that the hotel was an out-and-out kip and Barry told the mad one behind the desk that he was from Bord Fáilte and there was no way he and his party were going to spend one minute there let alone a night and she'd better hand over his deposit fast. And he waved his union card under her nose and she believed him and gave him back the money. God, we legged it out of there so fast."

"Remember the time we were camping and Alison set the tent on fire?"

"Yeah, and remember the time we went on the Shannon cruiser and Barry caught a pike and chased you along the quay wall at Dromod with it and you tripped over a rope."

"I nearly broke my neck." Kathy grinned in the dark at the memory. "We did have fun though, didn't we?"

"Ah, maybe they'll get over it. Maybe a weekend away would do them all the good in the world," Mike, ever the optimist, declared.

"Maybe," Kathy agreed, but she wondered if they'd all ever have such good times again. The way things were going, it didn't look like it. Alison had told her in the kitchen that she'd got off with a fella she'd met at a dance and she'd enjoyed a mighty good snog with him too for good measure. If she met someone, she was off and Barry could like it or lump it.

That didn't sound like someone who was prepared to try and make a go of things. Poor little Ciara, Kathy's motherly heart went out to her goddaughter. She felt very angry as she lay in the dark listening to Mike's volcanic snores beside her. Couldn't either of them see what they were doing to the child? Couldn't they see how insecure she was? Always fighting in front of her. Ciara had told Sara, Kathy's eldest, that Barry had told Ciara that her mother was an imbecile. Imagine saying that to a child? Mike was right, they were bloody selfish and neither of them were taking any responsibility for what they were doing to their daughter. Kathy didn't like the crowd Ciara hung out with. Imagine letting a twelve-year-old go to a mixed slumber party. Sara had been asked and was in a mega-huff with her parents at the moment because she wasn't let go. She could stay in her huffs, God help her. Because no way was she going to any mixed slumber parties. It was very awkward though, Ciara was allowed to do so much. In Sara's eyes, Mike and Kathy were very strict and it was starting to cause terrible hassles.

Kathy sighed. Bringing up kids was no joke. Where did you draw the line between being overprotective and letting them grow up safely? At least she and Mike were trying. Barry and Alison didn't seem to have any such qualms. But then Ciara was very "responsible" for her age, according to Alison when Kathy had asked her how in the name of God had she agreed to let her go to this goddamned slumber party. Of course it suited Alison to think that. It let her off the hook when hard decisions had to be made. "Responsible" was not the way Kathy would describe Barry and Alison right now, she thought crossly as she gave Mike a dig in the ribs to stop him snoring before drifting off to sleep herself.

❧

I think I'll have a lazy day today, Lillian McHugh decided as she snuggled under the duvet and pulled it up over her ears. The bed was lovely and warm and she could hear the rain lashing against the window.

Lillian smiled. What bliss! Who would have ever thought that she'd be able to lie on in bed on a Monday morning and know she could do exactly what she liked all day. She could stay in bed all day if she wanted to. At seventy years of age she was a liberated woman!

"Thank you, God, for making me a widow." It was a

heartfelt prayer. Since her husband Tom had died two years
ago her life had changed completely. She'd discovered a
whole new lease on life. She didn't have to get up at the
crack of dawn anymore to cook a breakfast for a cantanker-
ous taciturn old man that she hated. And she hated Tom
McHugh, her deceased husband of forty-five years. He'd
made her life a misery with his moods and his meanness and
his vicious temper. Tom had been a most thoroughly selfish
man. He'd courted her for three years, married her, and she
like a fool had believed that life would be happy ever after.
She'd mistaken his quiet, reserved ways for shyness. The
relief of having a ring on her finger, saving her from spin-
sterhood, and the excitement of having a home of her own,
helped her overlook her disappointment in her husband.
She'd thought that they would do things together, go to the
cinema, the theater, or out for a meal now and again, but
once the honeymoon was over and they'd started living in
the small terraced house they'd bought in Fairview, her
dreams had quickly turned to ashes. Tom wasn't the slightest
bit interested in doing anything other than going to work,
reading his sports news in the paper and going to his football matches. He expected his breakfast on the table at seven
a.m. sharp. His dinner had to be on the table when he came
home from work in the evening. They had sex every Friday
night and that was over almost before it started. After a few
grunts and groans and rough fumblings Tom would roll over
and fall asleep.

That had been the pattern throughout their marriage.
They'd had one child, Barry. A quiet, introverted lonely boy
who'd left home as soon as he'd done his leaving cert. to live

in a flat in Drumcondra. He'd married a girl from Phibs-
boro, and they had one child. Lillian didn't see much of
them. They'd rarely come to visit when Tom was alive,
Christmas, Easter, that was it. And Lillian couldn't blame
them. Who'd want to come and try and make conversation
with the old grump sitting by the fire?

Well, Tom was dead and she was glad of it. She was in an
active retirement group now. She went bowling, and flower
arranging and they were always going on little trips to places
of interest. She was having the time of her life and she was
going to make the most of it as long as she could. But today
it was raining, the weather had changed and she was staying
in bed. Lillian picked up her library book, a steamy romance, and snuggled up for a good read.

∾

"You're a stupid cow, that's what you are!"

"And you're a scummy bastard, I wish you'd get the hell
out of here and never come back."

"Yeah, well maybe I will, ya bigmouth bitch. . . ."

Ciara McHugh pressed her thumbs into her ears. They
were at it again, shouting and roaring and ranting and raving. She hated them. Why couldn't they be like other parents? Why did they have to be fighting all the time?

Why couldn't her mother leave her dad alone? She was
always nagging him. Nag, nag, nag. He'd just ignore her and
that would make her worse and then she'd say something
that would get him going and then they'd be yelling and
shouting at each other and her dad's face would go dark
with fury and Ciara was afraid he'd hit her mother. It fright-

ened her. Sometimes she'd lie on her bed and her heart would be pounding so loudly she thought it was going to burst out of her chest.

Ciara heard the door slam so hard that it seemed to shake the whole house. She heard the engine of the car start. That would be her dad. He'd drive off and not come home for hours after a row.

There was a dull silence in the house. Soon her mother would come upstairs to Ciara's room and start giving out about Barry. She'd tell Ciara that Barry was selfish and cruel and that he'd never given her any support in their marriage, not like their best friend, Mike. Alison thought Mike was a great husband and father. "See how Mike helps around the house, and cooks dinners at the weekend instead of sitting with his nose stuck into a football match on TV.

"See how Mike helps his kids with their homework.

"See how Mike takes them out at weekends and gives them . . . *quality* . . . time."

Alison always paused before she said "quality" time and made it sound like something holy and reverent. She was always reading books about relationships and quality time and communication.

"Mike . . . *communicates* . . . with his kids. Your father can't *communicate,* Ciara. I've spent years, years trying to get him to talk to me, to share the way Mike and Alison share, and it's like banging my head off a stone wall. I tell you, Ciara, if I can make a go of it with someone else, I bloody well will. I'm not wasting any more time on that thick, squinty-eyed shit. Life's not a rehearsal, Ciara, we only get one go on the merry-go-round. Always remember that.

And if you've any sense . . . *never* get married. You don't want to end up like me, stuck with a selfish cruel callous bastard." She'd usually burst into tears at that point.

When her mother said she was going to go off with someone else it always frightened Ciara. She didn't want Alison to go off with someone else. What would happen if her parents split up? Where would her daddy go? She didn't think her dad was that bad. He didn't drink. That was good. Liz Kelly's father was always drunk. Once he even puked up his dinner in front of a gang of them who were staying over for a slumber party. Poor Liz was so mortified she just burst into tears. Her dad was good for giving lifts even though he moaned about it. When his team won and he was in a good humor, he sometimes gave her a pound. His team were doing very badly this season, so financially it had been a bit of a disaster for her, Ciara thought glumly as she doodled on the brown paper cover of her copy. She could do with some extra money. She'd been invited to another slumber party in a friend's house and it was going to be mixed. Alison said it was okay, but she told her not to say anything to Barry. Alison maintained that Barry was far too strict. She wanted Ciara to be independent and stand on her own two feet.

It was going to be a camping slumber party. They were going to buy some of that new alcoholic lemonade and get plastered. Ciara had tasted it at Sharon Ryan's barbecue in August and it had made her feel nice and woozy. She'd smoked three fags as well. She didn't really like smoking, but it was a cool thing to do and she wanted to hang out with the rest of the gang. She was the youngest—twelve—the only one not in secondary school. Ciara sighed deeply. She was starting secondary school next year. She'd have to do her assessment next February and she was extremely worried about it. Her maths were a disaster. She hated them. Sara Stuart was dead lucky. Her dad was a wizard at maths and he was great for helping her. Mike Stuart was a real nice dad even if he was a bit strict, Ciara thought enviously. Sara wasn't allowed go to the slumber party and she was freaking out about it. Actually, secretly, deep down, Ciara didn't really want to go to the slumber party. Declan Owens was going to be at it, and Ciara didn't like him anymore. Once she'd thought she fancied him, but he'd given her a French kiss and stuck his tongue down her neck and she'd thought it was *disgusting*! He'd touched her boobs once too, and that made her feel dirty. She wished she hadn't got boobs. She didn't like having them. She hated wearing a bra, but Alison had insisted. "You're a young woman now," her mother said. "Enjoy it."

What was so enjoyable about having fellas sticking their tongues into your mouth and touching you up? Yeuch! Ciara shuddered. Another horrible thought struck her. What if she got her first period the night of the slumber party? They could come any time now. Some girls in her class had them already. It was scary. What would she do? Imagine if some of the blood dripped down her leg and the fellas saw it. She wished that she could stay at home, but her dad was going to a match and her mother had arranged to go dancing in Tamango's when she knew Ciara was going on a sleepover.

Why, why, why couldn't she have normal parents like the Stuarts? Kathy Stuart wouldn't be caught dead in Tamango's. She was a *real* mother. She cooked bread and tarts and everything and she made proper dinners, not burgers and chips, Alison's idea of a dinner, Ciara thought angrily as she heard her mother coming upstairs. She didn't want to get an ear-bashing about the row she'd overheard between her parents. She jumped up, switched off the light and dived under the duvet still in her clothes. She heard Alison open the door and peer in cautiously.

"Are you awake, lovie?"

Leave me alone. Leave me alone. Leave me alone, Ciara screamed silently as she lay perfectly still, eyes scrunched tightly shut.

"Ciara?" Alison tried again, hopefully. Ciara knew she needed a shoulder to cry on. She always did after a row. It wasn't fair. It was very confusing. She felt guilty. Maybe she should comfort her mother. She was just about to sit up when Alison closed the door with a little sigh. Ciara lay in the dark and felt tears brim from her eyes in a hot wet waterfall down her cheeks. Her stomach felt tied up in knots and she felt sick and very scared. She couldn't do her maths, she didn't want to go to the slumber party and her parents were fighting. What would happen to her if her parents got a divorce? She didn't want them to get divorced. She just wanted them to be normal.

∾

Brenda Johnston smiled happily as she lay back in her lover's arms. She hadn't been expecting Barry to call tonight but he'd arrived unexpectedly just after nine. She'd been watching the news reports about the passing of the amendment for divorce. The relief she'd felt when, by the slimmest majority, the Yes vote had won and been enormous. Then the gut-wrenching fear when that senator and his cohorts had appealed the decision. Brenda had wanted to strangle him with her bare hands. Didn't the fool realize that this was her last chance? And the last chance for many like her.

She and Barry had been having an affair for the past three years. She knew Alison suspected. But Alison wasn't bothered by it. How many times had her best friend said, "You can have him I'm sick of him."

The trouble with Alison was that she didn't appreciate Barry, she'd never looked after him. Not the way Brenda did. The trouble between Barry and Alison had started when Ciara was born, according to Alison. She claimed Barry resented not being the center of attention.

Maybe it was true, Brenda conceded privately. She'd known Barry as long as Alison had, and Barry did like being the center of attention. Not in a flamboyant, in-your-face way. His way was much more subtle. He'd sit, shoulders hunched up, staring out from behind his glasses with his poor-sad-misunderstood-me-with-the-weight-of-the-world-on-my-shoulders look that you'd have to feel sorry for him and ask him what was wrong. He'd say "nothing." And then you'd have to keep at him. Wrinkling it out bit by bit.

Then you'd get a litany about the pressure he was under at work. Or about Alison and the state she'd left the house in. Once he'd said to her, "Look, Brenda, I'm a loner, I always have been and always will be, so don't even try and understand me." He'd been feeling very sorry for himself that night.

But of course she understood him. She understood him

more than anyone and she loved him very much. And if he'd let her, she'd make him happy. Much happier than Alison made him. It was just, she was never quite sure where she stood with him. He swore he loved her and he wanted to be with her. His marriage to Alison was over, they were just staying together for Ciara's sake. He promised that when Ciara was finished college in another ten years he and Brenda would be together for good. He had his responsibilities as a parent and he knew she understood.

It was very decent of him to be so concerned for his daughter, Brenda thought stoutly. He was a good, sound, honest hardworking man and she couldn't fault him for his taking his responsibilities so seriously. That was a good trait surely? But ten years seemed like such a long time away. She'd be over *fifty*.

Crikey! What a horrific thought. Brenda hastily banished it to the recesses of her mind as she stroked Barry's back. He had pale, pasty, spotty skin. Barry wasn't God's gift in the looks department or even in the sex department, come to think of it. But beggars couldn't be choosers. He was her last chance to have a man of her own.

Her bubble of happiness at his unexpected arrival was getting a little flat. Imagine even thinking like that. Was that how pathetic she was now? Why couldn't she have been like all the rest of her friends and acquaintances? Why couldn't she have met a nice man who would have courted her properly and bought her flowers and chocolates and held car doors open for her and then proposed and given her a day to remember with a beautiful white dress and veil and all the trimmings? Had it been so much to ask for? Had she just grasped at Barry because the years had been slipping by? Because she'd been so panicky and lonely that she was afraid of ending up a spinster on the shelf with no man to show for a lifetime of Friday and Saturday nights dolling herself up, to go out on the hunt to find a mate? Year after year, dance after dance, disco after disco, nightclub after nightclub.

Was she crazy to believe that Barry would divorce Alison and marry her? How happy she'd been to vote Yes. She could still remember how firmly she'd marked the X with the black pencil in the polling booth. How relieved she'd been to hear the news this evening, that the legislation was to be passed. She was sure he would have been pleased too. When she said it to him he'd just grunted and said, "One marriage is enough for me." They could just live together, it was much less complicated, he muttered.

Of course she'd agreed, but deep deep down she was scared. She wanted him to *want* to marry her. That was how it should be. What if he dumped her for some babe in the office. If he could cheat on Alison, he could cheat on her. The thought came unbidden. She buried it. Don't think about that now. He was here, in her arms. That was all that mattered.

He wouldn't have been here if there hadn't been a row. Another sneaky horrible little thought escaped and she shoved it back in the Pandora's box she'd opened this evening. What was wrong with her, for crying out loud? Another even more hideous thought erupted. Maybe she was starting the change of life early. Hell! That was all she needed. To become a dried-up old prune as well.

She thought of Eileen O'Neil at work. Eileen was having

an affair with a married man who had four kids. He spent from Friday to Monday with Eileen and the other three days at home. Eileen was nuts about him. She was so cracked about him, she'd even got in Sky Sports for him so that he and his pals could watch live football. He'd assured Eileen many times, that he'd marry her if he could . . . safe in the knowledge that divorce wasn't legal in Ireland. Well, it looked as if it was going to become legal now. It would be interesting to see if he kept his word. He was an out-and-out shit though. He couldn't be satisfied with one mistress, he had several strings to his bow. He didn't think being faithful to Eileen was a priority, and still she took him back and listened to his lies and believed him when he told her his flings were over. Twice, he'd deceived her with another woman and she just closed her eyes to it.

Brenda snorted. What a foolish woman she was. There he was, living with his wife, living with his mistress, seeing other women, having his cake and eating it. And Eileen was so desperate to keep the lying, cheating, two-faced creep, she'd got Sky Sports for him!

Never! Never in a million years would Brenda sink to such levels. She had her pride. Besides Barry *wasn't* anything like that two-faced rat of Eileen's. Barry had *integrity*.

Brenda felt a little happier. He'd change his mind about the divorce. She was sure of it. If only Alison would find a new man. That would solve everything, Brenda thought with renewed hope. Maybe it might happen next Friday night. She was going to Tamango's with some friends. Ciara was going to a party and Brenda was going to have Barry all to herself for a few hours. She was going to go to a football match with him. She wanted to share every part of his life.

"I suppose I'd better go," she heard her lover say. How she longed for the time when he could stay all night. That would be the most wonderful thing in the world.

❧

Ciara felt sick. One of the fellas had brought vodka in a 7-Up bottle to the party and she'd drunk some and it made her feel very odd. Then she'd smoked a cigarette and it made her feel dizzy. The music was very loud. She didn't really like Oasis. She much preferred the Spice Girls. Her friend's parents had gone off to the pub and two fellas that hadn't been invited had gate-crashed and they were causing trouble. Ciara wanted to go home. Declan Owens grabbed her.

"Let's snog." He leered.

"In your dreams," Ciara said in what she hoped was a sufficiently cold and sophisticated rebuff.

Declan ignored her and kissed her anyway. She thought she was going to puke.

"Can't wait to see you in your nightie. Whose tent are you sleeping in?" he asked hopefully.

"Not yours, for sure. Besides you know it's one tent for the boys and one for the girls," Ciara retorted. Declan winked.

"We're coming visiting."

"Get lost," Ciara slurred irritably. She didn't want to sleep in a tent. She wanted to be safe and snug in her own bed knowing that Declan Owens couldn't get near her. She felt most peculiar. Her fingers closed around her house key in her jeans pocket. She always carried a key. She got home from school at three, every day, and her mother was never home from work until after six and often later. She was used to being on her own in the house. She wouldn't mind being alone until her dad came home from his match tonight.

Ciara slipped out the side gate and hurried along the footpath, glancing around every now and then to see if anyone had seen her. She felt very sick and dizzy. Her knees started to shake. She felt scared as she hunkered down trying to take deep breaths.

"Ciara, Ciara, are you all right?" She heard Mike Stuart's anxious inquiry.

"I drank some stuff. I feel funny."

"Come on. Come home with me." Mike sounded very kind as he helped her up and she leaned against him. His house was just across the street and it was a huge relief to sink down onto his sofa and close her eyes.

"It's a bloody disgrace. Those kids are all half pissed down in Hennessys'. I rang some of the parents. How could Barry and Alison let Ciara go to something like that? They should be shot." Mike was furious.

"They don't care about that poor child. Do you know they left her on her own in the house after school with two men who were fitting a new alarm system? Maybe they were perfectly nice men, but who's to know these days? Have they no cop-on? Don't they worry about things the way we do? I wouldn't leave Sara on her own with two strangers for three minutes, let alone three hours. It's just not safe anymore.

Have those two lost their marbles, or have they any sense of responsibility? By God I'm going to give Barry and Alison an earful when I bring Ciara home," Kathy fumed. "She's out gadding. He's out at his match, and that poor child is wandering the streets pissed out of her skull. Haven't they a great life all the same, the pair of them?"

"Let her stay the night," Mike suggested.

"No, Mike. I want Barry to see Ciara's little white face, God love her. I'll bring her home in an hour or so, besides she wants to go home to her own bed."

"Okay, maybe you're right," Mike agreed as he handed his wife a mug of coffee.

An hour later Kathy drove her weary goddaughter home. She'd tried to phone to check that Barry was there, but the phone was engaged. So one of them must be there. She felt very sorry for Ciara but it was time that pair accepted some responsibility for their child, she thought grimly as she swung into the McHughs' drive.

Barry's Lancer was there and there was a light on in the hall.

"I've my key, the bell's not working properly. You can't hear it if the TV's on," Ciara said miserably. "Dad's going to kill me."

"No he won't. I'll explain. I know you won't drink again after this," Kathy assured her.

"I promise I won't, honest," Ciara said fervently as she slid the key into the lock.

Kathy followed her into the sitting room and heard Ciara's gasp of horror as she halted in her tracks at the scene in front of her. Wailing loudly, she ran from the room as

Barry cursed vehemently and Brenda squeaked, "Ohmigod, ohmigod," from her supine position underneath him on the sofa.

Kathy was so shocked she could only think, *What a hairy ass he has!*

"I . . . I . . ." she stuttered. "I'll bring Ciara home with me." She had to get out of here. This was a nightmare.

"Blast you, Barry, could you not have gone to her house," Kathy exploded. She raced upstairs after Ciara.

"Come on, love. Come and stay the night with me."

"I hate him. I hate him. I hate all of them."

"I know, Pet, we'll talk about it at home. Come on you need a good night's sleep." Kathy's heart bled for her. Ciara, just five weeks older than her own Sara, had just had her innocence and security snatched from her in the cruelest way imaginable.

Kathy had lost all respect for Barry. Having an affair was his business, but couldn't he have the decency to conduct it somewhere other than his own home. And Brenda was supposed to be Alison's best friend . . . some friend. She'd always had a thing for Barry, even before he was married. But then Alison had told her she could have him, and she was out on the manhunt too. It was crazy. The McHugh's marriage was well and truly over, that was for sure, Kathy thought sadly as she ushered the distraught young girl out the front door. Hard as it was on Barry and Alison, it was a thousand times worse for Ciara.

∾

January '97.

Thank God he was staying with his fancy woman tonight, Lillian thought with a sigh of relief as she plonked herself in front of the TV with a cheese and tomato sandwich. He wasn't coming home for lunch so she could watch *Twelve to One* in peace without having to worry about cooking a meal. She smiled at her favorite presenters Marty and Ciana as they read out the lineup for the program. What a lovely couple. Nice pleasant people. She wouldn't mind cooking a meal for Marty Whelan. He'd a lovely twinkle in his eye, not a bit like Barry and his scowls and bad humors.

What had she done to deserve this trial in her life? Lillian wondered angrily. It was almost eight months since Barry had arrived on her doorstep muttering that there was a bit of trouble at home could he stay with her for a while. Lillian had been dumbstruck, but what could she say? She couldn't turn her own son away, even if he was the last person in the world she wanted living with her.

He was so like his father, surly and bad-tempered. He'd moved in, bag and baggage, and the days turned into weeks, then months, and slowly but surely her precious hard-won freedom was eroded away. She had to wash and iron his clothes, and cook his meals for him. She couldn't even watch the programs she liked on TV anymore if there was sports on.

He had another girlfriend, he'd told her that, and he usually spent the weekends with her. But if they had a row, which they did frequently, he ended up staying with Lillian. She bitterly resented the situation but couldn't bring herself to ask him to leave. She'd never been good at standing up for herself, a lifetime married to Tom McHugh had seen to that. Now it was as if he'd come back to haunt her. She woke up angry in the mornings and went to bed angry at night.

The news came on and she heard the newscaster announce that the first divorce in Ireland was going through the courts. A little flicker of hope glimmered. Maybe Barry would get a divorce and go and marry that Brenda one. Lillian had never met her nor did she want to meet her, but if she took Barry off her hands Lillian would be eternally grateful. She wondered could she pray that Barry would get divorced and remarried. Hardly. It didn't seem right. Maybe she'd just pray that Barry would move out and get a flat of his own. He surely didn't want to spend the rest of his life living with her?

It was all so distressing. Lillian pushed away her sandwich. She wasn't hungry. Her life was a hard old grind again. Just like before. And she didn't have the guts to do anything about it. That was the hardest thing of all to live with.

∾

Kathy glazed the top of the chicken and mushroom pie and popped it in the oven. It would be cooked by the time the kids came in from school. She'd made it specially for Ciara. It was her goddaughter's favorite. Ciara was spending the weekend with them . . . yet again.

Kathy's mouth tightened into a thin line as she remembered how Alison had phoned with one of her rigmaroles about how she needed Ciara looked after as she'd just got a lovely offer of a weekend away with her new boyfriend and she couldn't ask Barry and Brenda to take her because it wasn't their weekend to have her and they weren't at all flexible in that regard. "And she just loves being with you and Mike. And Sara's her very best friend," Alison gushed as usual.

Poor old Ciara, she was just a nuisance to her parents, who were far too concerned with having a good time to worry about the effect it was all having on their daughter.

Kathy was so angry she wanted to really tell Barry and Alison what she thought of them. She hadn't seen Barry since that dreadful night when she'd walked in on him and Brenda. He hadn't had the manners to contact her or Mike once. It was as if they didn't exist in his life. Some friend he'd turned out to be. He didn't have the guts to face them. Or maybe he just didn't want to. He'd dropped them like hot potatoes when he didn't need them and all their happy times together meant nothing.

Kathy could understand why Barry couldn't face her, but she couldn't forgive him for the way he was treating Ciara. She'd never forget Sara telling her last summer that Ciara had got a postcard from her daddy and his girlfriend on holidays and she hoped they'd buy her a nice present.

He'd only seen her three times that summer. At least Alison had taken her away for a week. But Barry had taken his two weeks holidays and spent them driving around the country with his mistress. The best he could do was to send Ciara a postcard. Kathy had been incensed.

"It's neglect, Mike, that's what it is and I'm going to have it out with him. And with Alison. The two of them are off having the life of Reilly and it's you and me that are here worrying about Ciara."

"And if you cause a row, who's going to suffer? Ciara. Say nothing. It's not our place to interfere. All we can do is be here for Ciara as long as she needs us. If there's an argument they might stop her from seeing us. That poor kid has enough trauma in her life without that. Say nothing," Mike had advised.

Kathy knew he was right and she'd held her tongue, but she sizzled with resentment. She'd liked Barry and Alison as friends. They'd had a lot of good times in the past. Never in a million years had she expected this of them. It was quite obvious Barry didn't give a hoot about her and Mike, and that hurt.

Alison was using them at every possible opportunity. Emotionally blackmailing them by saying how much Ciara loved staying with them. Kathy was sick of it, heartily sick of it. Users, that's what they were. Only that she loved Ciara like one of her own she'd tell them to get lost, she thought angrily as she set the table for dinner.

Brenda sat in the staff canteen drinking coffee. The chatter and buzz and the rattle of china and cutlery was giving her a headache. She read the headlines. Once, the news of the first divorce in Ireland going through the courts would have filled her with joy. Now she just didn't know anymore.

Being involved with Barry left her feeling as if she were walking on a tightrope. One false move and that was it. Why didn't he want to marry her the way she wanted to marry him? Why wouldn't he commit to her? Why did he keep using Ciara as an excuse? It wasn't as if he was exactly Father-of-the-Year-Award material. Actually he wasn't as good a father as she had once given him credit for, that couldn't be denied. He admitted it, but he was too selfish to do anything about it. It was a side of him that Brenda didn't like, but she tried not to think about it.

If he was living with her permanently, Ciara could spend more time with them. The trouble was, Brenda knew he was happy enough living with his mother. He was well looked after. Better than when he'd lived with Alison. He had all the home comforts. And then he had her for sex when he needed it.

How could she compete with Ma McHugh? Barry had told her that his mother liked him living with her. "It made her feel more secure," he said. He wouldn't like to "desert" her.

That had chilled Brenda to the bone. Something drastic had to be done. She needed to make living with her a more attractive proposition for him.

Brenda got up from the table and marched upstairs. She flicked impatiently through the phone book, found the number she was looking for and dialed it.

"Hello, I'd like to make an inquiry about getting Sky Sports. How do I go about it?"

∞

Ciara sat in class listening to her teacher explain about the assessment test for getting into secondary school. It was like a huge big weight on her shoulders. It made her feel sick to think about it. She was going to stay with Sara this weekend. She'd ask Mike to explain simple interest to her. He was very good at explaining things.

She was glad she was staying with the Stuarts this weekend. She didn't want to go to Kilkenny with Alison and her new boyfriend. She hated seeing her mother in bed with another man, just as she hated seeing her dad in bed with Brenda of the knitting needle legs. She'd never forget the sight of those skinny legs wrapped around her father's white arse. Ciara bit her nails. They were down to the stubs. They looked awful, but no matter how hard she tried to, she couldn't stop.

Biting her nails made her think of food. She hoped Kathy would cook chicken and mushroom pie for dinner. It always tasted mega. Everyone thought she was dead lucky to have a mother like Alison. A mother who let her wear makeup and minis and who brought her into pubs and gave her sips of wine and who allowed her to have a TV in her room. Her friends thought Alison, who went to discos, and knew all the words of the latest pop songs, was dead cool. Ciara just wished she'd stay at home and cook real dinners and help her with her homework. Like Kathy. Kathy was a proper mother, Ciara thought enviously. Sara was very lucky.

"Are your ma and da going to get a divorce?" Sadie Flynn whispered. "Someone got a divorce today. It was on the news at lunchtime."

"No, they're just separated for a while, they're going to get back together," Ciara whispered back. She always said that, hoping against hope that it would come true.

"Oh!" said Sadie . . . disappointed.

The knots tightened in Ciara's stomach. She'd forgotten about this divorce thing. Now it loomed large and threatening again. Another great worry to add to the ones she already had.

"If you wanna be my lover, you gotta get with my friends," Alison McHugh sang to herself as she packed her toilet bag for the weekend. She was looking forward to the trip to Kilkenny immensely. She felt young and carefree, so different from the past few years. It was a joy to be free and almost single again. Not that she wanted a divorce, she decided as she folded her black lacy negligee. She'd given the matter a lot of thought.

No, she was happy as she was. She wasn't going to disgrace the family name with a divorce. Brenda could have the rat, but she wasn't getting her mitts on a half share of the house and whatever money would be divided between her and Barry if they divorced.

Alison didn't want Brenda to become Mrs. McHugh. That would alter the status between them too much. She'd always enjoyed being the object of Brenda's envy, and as long as she stayed married to Barry, Brenda would be the poor little spinster who couldn't quite get a man of her own and had to settle for used goods, while Alison would have the security of her wedding ring and still have men attracted to her like moths to the flame. It was almost like being a teenager again.

I'm quite the *femme fatale,* she thought giddily as she packed her sexy black suspender belt.

∽

Barry switched off the news and inserted his Elvis tape into the deck. So, the first divorce case was going through. No doubt Brenda would give him an ear-bashing tonight. Well, she was barking up the wrong tree there. He had no intention of ever getting married again. Once was enough. Besides, he was damned if that cow Alison was going to get her hot sweaty little paws on one penny of his money. He'd worked hard for that house. It was his investment. He wasn't going to split the profits for it down the middle so she could go and set up with her new toy-boy lover. Let *him* buy his own house and set her up in the style to which she was accustomed. Not that he'd let on to Alison that he didn't want a divorce. He'd keep her dangling. It was the best way to keep women. On their toes. Anyway he had Ciara to think about he thought self-righteously. He wouldn't inflict divorce on her. He had to be a responsible parent.

No, Barry scowled, divorce was not an option, and if people didn't like it, they could bloody well lump it. His life suited him just fine the way it was.

Polygamy

❧

Gaye Shortland

Last night I dreamt I was putting a young girl into bed beside my husband. We were here, in Ireland, but she was African—brown-skinned and slender with hair cropped close to her skull. Though she was naked, I was unsure whether her breasts were developed or not. But I'd been told often enough it didn't matter, they would soon grow. What hurt me was the way she nestled close to him, her head on his shoulder, as if it were the most natural thing in the world, and the way he folded an arm about her in the same inevitable way.

❧

Haro worked for me when I ran a restaurant in Africa for the Americans. I never asked his age—he probably didn't know it. His hair was a bit grizzled, his face lined, but he had the trim muscled body of a young man—a fact I took note of the day he stripped off and got into the pool to scrape the ever-threatening algae off the walls. His teeth were filed to sharp points. Strange that in all the time I worked with him I never asked how or when that was done. It wasn't a local custom, Haro came from one of the neighboring tribes. His skin was very black against the white uniform and slightly pitted, his hands leathery, nails ingrained with work and weather. I found him attractive. We were often in conflict, since money problems and a natural cunning led him into minor scams, but despite this we had hammered out a good working relationship, full of play and humor. He had learned how to manage me.

One day I stepped into the yard outside the kitchen and found a young girl sitting in state on an upright chair there, clutching a bundle of books and papers to her breast. No doubt I glared. Certainly she looked at me in great alarm.

"Issouf!" I stalked through the kitchen into my office-cum-store, a small windowless room where a decrepit table fan struggled to supplement an ailing air conditioner. The fan was for the ice-cream machine, which was threatening to break down or blow up. I swung the fan around and let it blow against me for a moment. Even the loose light traditional dress I was wearing seemed cumbersome and oppressive and, when I sat, the plastic seat of the chair felt wet through the thin cotton. It was the hot season before the rains.

"Madame?" Slim, doe-eyed Issouf, head cook, was my standby and negotiator in all sticky situations. He was leader in the kitchen, for all his quiet gentleness.

"The girl—who is she?" I asked in Hausa.

He smiled his lovely mischievous smile. "She is Haro's wife."

"Haro has a second wife?"

"He hasn't married her yet . . . but she has a belly. . . ." He gestured with his hand.

She was pregnant. Well done, Haro. "But she's a little girl! How many years does she have?"

"Fourteen, Madame," said Issouf, the laughter in his eyes saying what a gay dog Haro was. "Yes, she's a new girl!"

I moved on cautiously. "Is she at school?"

"Yes, it's her lunchtime now. That's why she came—she doesn't have the taxi money to go home to eat—she lives far out in Makami."

"But, Issouf, what about Haro's wife? Does she know?"

"She knows. She heard the news and she's angry."

I didn't want to deal with this. "Listen. Tell Haro if the Harrisons see the girl they'll make trouble. Tell him she's not to come again."

"All right, Madame." The light had died out of Issouf's face. It was curious how, without that light, the skin itself seemed to change and take on a gray cast. "You have truth."

Rob Harrison was current president on the board of directors and had very strong ideas about what was "appropriate." I was scared of losing my job. The guys were scared of losing theirs. I did my best to be a kind of bulwark for them but, in fact, we were all craven. If the Harrisons had thought segregated bathing "appropriate," I'd have had Haro putting up the notices.

But using Rob in this instance was a cop-out for me. Truth was, I was sick with anger. A fourteen-year-old! Maybe not even that. Jesus! He'd be jailed back home. And his wife! After eleven children, God knows how many miscarriages, a lifetime struggling and starving with him on their little scrap of money—away from her own people in a strange town.

I picked up my ballpoint and started to fill in the never-ending columns of figures straggling down my accounts sheets, the anger a tight little ball in the pit of my stomach. But what was the matter with me? What kind of cowardice made me let these things go? Linda Harrison would have stood in the kitchen and argued it out with admirable American certitude, made her point at least, done some good maybe—but me, my anger on such matters was so instinctive, so primitive, that it gripped me by the throat and made me fear I might do murder.

Some days later Haro had the audacity to request, through Issouf, that his girlfriend be allowed to spend every lunch hour in our yard. I turned this down flat. The girl didn't come again, but Haro's wife began to appear with greater frequency, leaning over our metal security gate, laughing, vivid, enormous, checking things out. No yard for her.

Time went by, and I followed my habit of shying away from any problem that wasn't exactly hitting me in the face. Survival tactics. Eventually Issouf told me Haro had paid the bride-price, God knows how—a loan, I suppose—and the girl was his. She was still living with her parents out in Makami so Haro had to travel between her place and his own, which was across the river at the other extreme of the town. He was doing this on the battered scooter which he also used to do all the shopping for the restaurant.

❧

That evening, after Issouf told me this and the guys had left, I finished off my bookkeeping, mixed the breakfast pancakes, helped myself to the remaining peanut butter cookies, locked up and—like every other day—drove to Sideka's place, the building site where he worked as a security guard.

Hadiza was sitting on a mat in front of the makeshift hut where they lived—the kind of temporary shelter they felt quite at home in, being nomadic people. I looked around, hungry for the joy that would rush in at the sight of Sideka, but he wasn't in sight.

Hadiza smiled her dazzling smile and waved a heavy golden arm. The baby, Zainabou, was on her lap grappling with a generous breast and little Moussa sat against her, sheltering under the fall of her black veil. I sat down beside them and handed out peanut butter cookies courtesy of the American Recreation Center. A blackened pot brimful of rice was simmering on the fire. Hadiza could do all her housework from where she sat. And sit she did, in the glorious relaxed way they had, solidly on her great haunches. She was so tremendously female she made me feel lacking. She was my friend.

I sat there on my own skimpy buttocks, the usual great contentment welling up in me, my body aching with relief and pleasure in the warmth of the late afternoon sun. I watched Hadiza. I wanted to be comforted too. I wanted to lay my head on her rounded thighs and breathe in that musky mixture of indigo and sweat and oil-based perfume— the smell of the tribe. I stared at her, feeling the intimacy and affection between us. What if it could always be like this? What if I were part of the family? If Sideka married me? Would Hadiza accept that? Would it be such a blow to her pride, after all? Granted, she was Tuareg, and they clung to their monogamy against all odds—but they were Muslims after all. And she had been in a polygamous marriage before, as a young girl, when her uncle sold her off down south. In any case, wouldn't her shrewd business sense win her round, if nothing else did? What price a rich infidel co-wife who could set her up in a proper business? I had no money—but she didn't know that. She ran a tough little business already, selling cigarettes, bread and tinned fish to the laborers and guards. She probably had more stashed away in her tin trunk than I had in the bank.

"Hadiza? That first husband of yours—the Ibo. He had other wives besides you, or is that not so?"

She pursed her lips. "He had."

"How many?"

"Two. Both of them Ibos."

"But wasn't he a Christian?"

"He was a Christian but they follow their traditions. You know, they were all pagans before. His uncle even had eight wives! What do they care!"

"Did you feel sweetness about that? Sharing him like that?"

"I was a little girl! What did I know? And afterwards I was used to it. I wouldn't agree to it now! At all! Every third night!" She sniffed her contempt, tossing back her glossy braid of hair and plunging a small stick viciously into the pot. She lifted out a few grains of rice and pressed them between thumb and forefinger. "Huh! Now—that would be the day I'd pack my things!"

And, indeed, she had already proved herself capable of that. She had run away from her Ibo, leaving three young children behind. The bra she had once worn, in her life as a smart young southern woman, now hung from one of the supports of the hut like a kind of trophy. She had come north and Sideka had fallen in love. I could remember well how lovesick he was, risking his job as nightwatchman to court her nightly and fend off the others who clustered around her. I used to drive him to her place. He and I were good friends, even then. So, she had married him and achieved a precarious happiness, which I was now intent on stealing from her.

∾

Payday came. I knew there was something afoot and it turned out to be a request from Haro for a loan, because of his extra expenses. I made some arrangement with him and then found Issouf still standing there, striking the sort of deferential posture I recognized. Money.

"Issouf?"

"Well, Madame, I have a small problem of my own. I want you to help me."

"Right. What is it?"

"Well . . . you know I had to send my first wife away?"

I hadn't known.

"You see," he said, shamefaced as if it were his failure, "they refused to live in peace with each other so I had to send her back home. But I kept my little son with me." He gestured with his hand. "He's only three years old."

The familiar anger fluttered. I tried to hold it down.

"Well, now I must send for her again because the young wife won't take care of him." His light voice had tightened and become more guttural, as it did with emotion. "She refuses to wash him and, you know . . ." he hesitated delicately, "she refuses to clean up after him—when he shits."

The anger surged. "Can't you *force* her?"

He smiled ruefully and shook his head. "Two wives, Madame—nothing but problems."

Serve you bloody well right. I made a big effort. "But, Issouf, why do you do it? What's the use of two wives?"

"Madame, it's good to have two wives! One can rest after she gives birth and while she's giving milk. They can share the work and keep each other company in the house!"

I knew all the arguments. I pushed on. "But look at Haro—he can't keep two wives—neither can you—and now he's going to make another family!"

"But that's good, Madame! If some of the children die there will be others to take care of him when he's old. . . ."

"Issouf. How many of your children have died?"

"None, by the grace of God . . ."

By the grace of modern medicine. I dropped my gaze, ashamed that I had trodden on forbidden ground: if one of Issouf's children should now die from a bout of malaria, it would be because Madame had put the evil eye on him. . . .

"If they agree to live in peace it is good, Madame! Look, it is nothing. Women—that's how they are." He laughed gently. "You know, that's why we call co-wives 'jealous ones.'"

I stared at my account sheets. I thought of the little boy. I thought of the mother.

"I'll talk to them," he said. "I'll show them that it is proper they should live in peace. Patience is everything. They must be patient and behave as is proper."

And what could I say to Issouf, who bore the trials of life with such exquisite patience himself?

I gave up my feeble argument and handed out the loan he needed.

༅

Hadiza joined me on the mat, plumping down heavily. She took Zainabou from me, tossing her over her head. "Hah!" she cried, pinching the child's genitals and then flicking the fingers open under her nose. "Perfume!"

I heard the bicycle before she did. Sideka. And suddenly all was right with the world.

He took a brown paper parcel from the carrier and approached with his long-limbed stride, pushing the veil down from his smiling mouth with a long finger. "Madame!" And the formal handshake with the secret little bite of a fingernail into the palm of my hand. When he handed the parcel to Hadiza, a huge piece of steak all but spilled out as she took it. "It's for you two. I must go straight to work. Eat it *all*!"

He was moonlighting, guarding a plant nursery outside the town.

Hadiza exclaimed shrilly over the meat, questioning him

about it. He answered her as he fumbled in his pocket and took out the knotted handkerchief that held his tobacco. I watched him as he stood there with his characteristic graceful tension, going through the little ritual of poising some tobacco and a few grains of potash on his lower lip before chewing it. All the while his quizzical gaze was fixed on me.

"Well, we thank you!" Hadiza cried after him as he finally rode off bedecked with a cheap Chinese flashlight, knife and traditional sword.

I would join him later, in the evening. My secret was a kind of power I had over her assurance.

"How will we cook it? On the stove?" And she cooked it by throwing it on top of the Primus stove. I had never seen that done before.

I remember eating that meat very well. It was surprisingly good—quite tender. I knew that as soon as we had eaten the last bite I would say, "Hadiza, I want to marry your husband."

My fingers trembled. I thought she must surely notice. Hadiza, save us all. Say you'll accept me.

She made sure the last piece of the meat went to me.

I ate it and said nothing.

ﻌ

The next day was Friday and the evening dinner was Mexican. And I'm thinking " 'twas far from Tex-Mex dinners I was reared" and I'm secretly proud I know how. Tex-Mex was always popular so we had to expect anything up to eighty people. I sent Haro to the market to do the shopping and get some more large cooking pots. I had hesitated quite a while, considering our straitened budget, but decided we couldn't manage without the pots. Haro didn't speak Hausa, so I had Issouf explain to him in Zarma exactly what we needed and he wrote it on his shopping list. He had taught himself to read and write in a rudimentary fashion.

Things were going badly. As usual. We were running late. As usual. It would all come together in the end but not without shoving my blood pressure up by a few notches.

The blood pressure began to soar quite early this Friday when I found Boubakar, a fly boy if ever there was one, asleep on a bench in the women's washroom he was supposed to be cleaning.

Haro arrived back an hour and a half later, staggering into the office under the weight of a huge cardboard box which he plonked down on the stone floor. Sweat stood out on his skin. It was scorching hot outside—two o'clock. A moment later I was amazed to see him pull a pair of long cardboard boxes from among the groceries.

"What are they, Haro?"

"Lights. For the pool," he answered in English.

"Lights? Why did you buy lights for the pool when we are so short of money?" My voice was rising.

"Because we need lights. And it was on the list."

"It was *not* on the list!"

Silently he took the dog-eared piece of paper from his uniform pocket and held it out to me.

I looked. "That says 'pots.' Don't you remember Issouf telling you about the pots?"

"I thought it was lights," he said in French. "There are two lights broken by the pool."

"Well, for God's sake! I don't believe it! Issouf!"

Issouf appeared at the door, wiping his hands on his apron.

"Issouf! Look what Haro has brought! Lights! Didn't you tell him about the pots? Didn't you even explain to him where he could get them in the market? And he goes and brings back neon lights! What's the matter with him?"

"Friend, why did you do that?" Issouf asked, bending over Haro, who was squatting over his box of groceries.

No answer. Issouf shrugged his shoulders and hesitantly went back to the kitchen, where Bizo, Boubakar and Francis the barman were craning their necks to see what the problem was.

I sat there fuming. Haro stayed put. He made me uneasy, sulking there over his box. I got up and plunged into the kitchen. Issouf was chopping tomatoes. "Why are you cutting tomatoes? Isn't that Bizo's work? What about the ice cream? Have you made it yet?"

"Not yet, Madame."

"Make it then! In the name of God, what's the matter with you all? This is the reason we are late every Friday!"

I stalked back into the office and flung myself into my chair. Haro was still squatting by his box. I glared at him but he had his head down. "You have ruined everything," I said viciously. "How are we to manage to cook enough rice without those pots?" I slammed open the metal cash drawer and started into a cash count.

The cash seemed to be short. Don't panic. Start again. I started again and as I did a grotesque noise issued from Haro's direction.

"Eeeeeeeeeeeeeeeeeee . . . Eeeeeeeeeeeeeeeeeeee . . ."
One of his horny hands was lifted to his head, covering his forehead, and his lips were drawn back in a grimace. "Eeeeeeeeeeeeeeeeeeeee . . ."

I rose to my feet in horror, still clutching my handful of notes.

"Eeeeeeeeeeeeeeeeeeeee . . . Eeeeeeeeeeeeeeeeeeee . . ."
Great hollow gulping sobs began to come between the keening sound. Dry. Harsh. It didn't sound human.

I felt a sense of dislocation—the sound couldn't be coming from him. I could see the others standing transfixed in the kitchen and I signed to Issouf to come in. I moved back around the big desk, away from Haro.

Issouf came in, cautiously, head to one side. "Friend, what is it?" he asked quietly, fear in his voice.

"Eeeeeeeeeeeeeeeeeee . . . Eeeeeeeeeeeeeeeeeeee . . ."
Tears were now pouring down Haro's face, splashing on his box, his groceries, his neon lights.

"Issouf. Take him out." I was petrified with fear. I just wanted him out of there.

Issouf reached down hesitantly and touched Haro's shoulder. Then he took him by both shoulders, and after a moment Haro rose and, still keening, allowed Issouf to lead him through the kitchen and the mosquito door into the yard outside.

I stayed in the office, listening to Bizo's voice loud and excited in the kitchen. After a few minutes I went through to the mosquito door and looked out. Issouf had taken Haro down the side of the building almost as far as the pool and put some sheets of cardboard—opened-out boxes—on the ground in the shade for him. Now quiet, he lay on his back, an arm thrown across his eyes.

"It's the dog bite," came Bizo's voice almost in my ear. He was staring out over my head, an almost childlike look of excitement and fear on his face.

"Dog bite?"

"Yes, yes, he's crazy, Madame," said the normally unflappable Francis with finality. "You must send him to the hospital. It is very very dangerous, a dog bite."

"*What* dog bite?" A new fear started up.

"He was bitten by a dog," said Bizo. "Last month."

"Didn't he go to the hospital?"

"Yes—he got *many* needles! But, you see, it's still in his blood!"

I went back to the office, staggered by this new development. Dear God, what the fuck should I do? If it were true that he was—rabid? If it were true and I hadn't reported it—what then? We'd all lose our jobs. But if I did report it the Americans would stage a huge panic—about the food, about having eaten here. . . .

Call the Marines.

Hydrophobia. Fear of water, wasn't it? And aggression? Wasn't it? Or was that werewolves? I couldn't sort out the folklore from the facts. Aggression—yes—foaming at the mouth . . . but he wasn't aggressive, so it couldn't be that . . . and yet he was *demented*. . . .

I stood there. The fan was working feebly. The air was humid and heavy. The huge yellow account sheets showed big wet marks where I had rested my hands on them.

Should I phone Harrison? Jesus. I cringed just thinking of

his reaction. And what if he just laughed it off? Put it down to Irish hysteria?

But it had been grotesque, inhuman. Tortured. It *must* be the dog bite. I had never heard any sound like it before. Had I ever even seen a man weep during all the years I had been here? It was their pride to be stoic in the face of hardship. To be gay, even . . . what was it Yeats had said? But Haro's cry—it had such an ugly hideous sound—indescribable, wrenching, torn. . . .

"Madame?"

"Issouf?"

"He's better."

"Tell him to go home and rest."

"He doesn't want to. He wants to go ahead with his work."

"No, he can't! He must go!"

"He says no, Madame. He wants to go ahead with the work."

"Listen. He must go home and stay away for a few days! Bizo told me about the dog bite. If the Americans hear they'll go crazy! They'll turn him away!"

"But, Madame, the dog bite isn't a problem now. That problem has passed."

"How do you know? Are you sure he went to the hospital and got all the needles?"

"Yes. I took him there myself."

"But if that is so, what caused him to cry like that?"

"I asked him. I asked him what was troubling him. . . ."

"So what did he say . . . ?"

"He said it was his two women. You see, his women-of-the-house won't agree to let him bring his bride home. And he's wasting so much money on petrol traveling from one wife to the other that he can't feed his children. . . ."

"*That's* what's troubling him?"

"Yes, Madame. . . ."

"But why can't he *force* his wife to agree?"

"Well . . ." A faint shadow of a smile appeared on his face. "He's afraid of her, Madame."

"*Afraid* of her?"

Issouf's smile was gathering strength. "You know, she's a big strong woman." He ducked his head, with a little laugh. "Sometimes she beats him."

"She *beats* him?"

"Yes. You know, once she even bit him."

I started to laugh. It was so ridiculous. "Issouf—do you honestly know it was a *dog* that bit him last month?"

"Yes," he said, giggling. "That one was a dog all right!"

"So he's healthy? It's his problem at home that made him cry like that?"

"Well, yes, Madame. . . ." He looked at me, poised, gentle, solemn again, faintly ironic. "He has two women giving him trouble and then you started shouting at him . . . you're the third one giving him suffering. . . ."

∾

I never did ask Hadiza.

And so began a vicious tug-of-war that took up three destructive years. I didn't see her in the last stages of our conflict because Sideka had taken her back to her people up north, so that he and I could be together, and her campaign was conducted from way out in the wilds.

She won in the end. I wonder what she lost in the process. I ask this because I sometimes think I lost my soul.

Now they are all distanced—like characters in some particularly vivid movie I've seen. I mightn't think about it at all if it weren't for my dreams.

I dream quite often of Haro, oddly enough. He eventually got his own way and took the girl home, where no doubt his woman-of-the-house exercised her revenge by giving the young bride the hardest of hard times—her right as first wife. Perhaps by now they have formed a united front against wife number three. In my dreams Haro always seems to want to tell me something. Maybe he just wants to ask for a loan.

The Authors

❧

Ivy Bannister is the author of numerous short stories which have been published and anthologized widely and broadcast by RTE and the BBC. Her collection, *Magician,* is published by Poolbeg. She also writes plays for radio and stage. Her awards include a Hennessy Award, the Mobil Ireland Playwriting Award and an Arts Council bursary. She lives in Dublin.

❧

Sheila Barrett was born in Dallas, Texas. A graduate of Vassar College, she came to live in Ireland in 1969. She has written two novels, *Walk in a Lost Landscape,* published in 1994, and *A View to Die For,* published in 1997.

❧

Maeve Binchy has written nine novels, including six number-one best sellers: *Evening Class, The Glass Lake, The Copper Beech, Circle of Friends* and *Firefly Summer.* Several of her books have been adapted for television and cinema, most notably *Circle of Friends*. She is also a prolific short-story writer and has written a number of one-act plays as well as two full-length stage plays, *End of Term* and *Half-Promised Land*. Her television play, *Deeply Regretted By*, won two Jacobs Awards and the Best Script Award at the Prague Film Festival. A native Dubliner, she also writes a regular column and features for *The Irish Times*, and is married to the writer and broadcaster Gordon Snell.

Mary Rose Callaghan is a novelist and biographer. She was educated at University College Dublin and has worked as a teacher and a writer. In 1975 she emigrated to the United States, where she lived for nearly twenty years. She now lives in Bray, County Wicklow, with her husband, Robert Hogan. Her recent novels are published by Poolbeg Press.

Kate Cruise O'Brien was born in Dublin in 1948. She is the author of a short-story collection, *A Gift Horse,* which won the Rodney Prize. "Henry Died," from this collection, also won the Hennessy Award. Her first novel, *The Homesick Garden,* was published in 1991 by Poolbeg. She lives in Dublin with her husband and son.

Ita Daly was born in County Leitrim and moved to Dublin when she was twelve. She worked for many years as a teacher before becoming a full-time writer and has since published five novels and one collection of short stories. She lives in Dublin with her husband and daughter.

∾

Margaret Dolan, a native Dubliner, lives in County Meath and works as a free-lance journalist and playwright. She won the Powers Short Story Competition in 1988 and the Francis MacManus Award in 1992 and 1993. Her first novel, *Nessa*, was published in 1994.

∾

Mary Dorcey is a short-story writer and poet. In 1990 she won the Rooney Prize for Irish Literature for "A Noise from the Woodshed" and was awarded Arts Council bursary for literature in 1990 and 1995. Her poetry has been performed on stage, radio and television and her first collection, *The River That Carries Me,* was published in 1995. She has been widely anthologized and translated in several languages. Her novel *Biography of Desire* was published by Poolbeg in 1997.

∾

Mary Gordon is the Irish American author of the bestselling novels *Final Payments, The Company of Women, Men and Angels,* and *The Other Side,* and, most recently, *The Shadow Man.* She has also published a book of novellas, *The Rest of Life,* a short-story collection, *Temporary Shelter,* and a book of essays, *Good Boys and Dead Girls.* She has received the Lila Acheson Wallace Reader's Digest Writer's Award and a Guggenheim Fellowship. Now working on her sixth novel, *Spending,* she lives in New York and is professor of English at Barnard College.

∽

Katy Hayes was born in Dublin in 1965. Her first collection of short stories, *Forecourt,* was published in 1995, and the title story won the Golden Jubilee Award in the Francis MacManus Short Stories Competition in RTE in 1993. Her stories have been widely anthologized. Her first play, *Playgirl,* was commissioned and produced by the Abbey Theatre on the Peacock stage in 1995, and her first novel, *Curtains,* will be published by Phoenix House in 1997. She also works as a theater director.

∽

Jennifer Johnston is the author of *The Captain and the Kings, The Gates, How Many Miles to Babylon?, Shadows on Our Skin* (short-listed for the Booker Prize in 1977), *The Old Jest* (winner of the 1979 Whitbread Award for Fiction), *The Christmas Tree, The Railway Station Man, Fool's Sanctuary, The Invisible Worm* (short-listed for the *Sunday Express* Book of the Year Award in 1991), and *The Illusionist.*

∽

Marian Keyes was born in Ireland but has lived in London for the past ten years. After graduation from University College Dublin, where she studied law, she changed careers and became an accountant. She began writing short stories in 1993 and has published two novels, *Watermelon* in 1993 and

The Authors

Lucy Sullivan Is Getting Married in 1996, and is now working on a third novel.

∾

Mary Leland is a free-lance journalist who writes for na-
tional newspapers and magazines. She is the author of two
novels, *The Killeen* and *Approaching Priests,* and a collection
of short stories, *The Little Galloway Girls.* Her work has been
broadcast on RTE, BBC Radio Four and BBC Radio Three,
and has appeared in anthologies in Ireland and in the United
Kingdom. She has recently completed a history of the port
of Cork, and work in progress includes a new novel and
second collection of short stories.

∾

Liz McManus is Minister for Housing and Urban Renewal
in the present Irish government. Born in Montreal, Canada,
she lives in County Wicklow and has worked as an architect
and a newspaper columnist as well as a public representative.
As a short-story writer, she won the Hennessy Award in
1981 along with the Irish PEN Short Story Award and Lis-
towel Short Story Award. Her first novel, *Acts of Subversion,*
was nominated for the Aer Lingus/*Irish Times* literature prize
for first books. Her work has been published in a number of
collections and translated into Norwegian. She is married to
Dr. John McManus and has four children.

∾

Mary Maher was born in Chicago and has lived in Ireland
since 1965, when she joined the staff of *The Irish Times.* She

was first women's editor of the paper and a founding member of the Irishwomen's Liberation Movement. Her first novel, *The Devil's Card,* was published in 1992, and she is now working on a novel about the women's movement.

❧

Mary Morrissy was born in Dublin in 1957. She is the author of *A Lazy Eye,* a collection of short stories, and *Mother of Pearl,* a novel. In 1995 she was awarded a U.S. Lannan Award for Literature. *Mother of Pearl* was nominated for the Whitbread Prize. She is currently working on a second novel.

❧

Mary O'Donnell, who was born in Monaghan, is a writer, critic and broadcaster. She was graduated from Maynooth College and after postgraduate studies in Germany translated a number of academic texts, based in Heidelberg. In 1992 she received an Arts Council bursary in literature. Her publications include two collections of poems, one of which was nominated for an *Irish Times* literature prize; a collection of short stories, and two novels, *The Light-Makers* and *Virgin and The Boy.* Her stort stories have been anthologized in Ireland and the United Kingdom, and a third collection of poems was published in 1997. She has also completed a third novel.

❧

Patricia Scanlan is a Dubliner and full-time writer and novelist. She is the author of seven novels published by Poolbeg,

The Authors

City Girl, City Women, Apartment 3B, Foreign Affairs, Finishing Touches, Promises, Promises and *Liar, Liar*.

❧

Gaye Shortland is a native of Cork and has a master's degree in English. She taught Shakespeare at the University of Leeds and T.S. Eliot in Nigeria before turning to restaurant management in Niamey. Returning to Cork with a husband and three children, she won an *Image* magazine short-story award and was short-listed for the Ian St. James Short Story Award. In 1995 she wrote her first novel, *Mind That 'Tis My Brother*, followed by its sequel this year, *Turtles All the Way Down*. She is now working on a novel set in Africa.

❧